THE SINISTER INVASION

By
EDMOND HAMILTON

ARMCHAIR FICTION
PO Box 4369, Medford, Oregon   97501-0168

ENEMY AGENTS FROM THE STARS!

It was strange…how easy it was to step right out of your own life, right out of the familiar Earth you'd always known, and into a cosmic mystery! That's what happened to Ross Birrel, and it all started by opening the door to his own apartment! He soon found himself in the role of a most unlikely undercover agent—an agent with one specific purpose: to uncover an alien spy ring right here on Earth. Only it wasn't that simple, and Birrel soon discovered there was an alien threat far more sinister than anyone on Earth could have imagined. But the key to the mystery depended on whether or not he could trust a female alien—a beautiful woman from beyond the stars who might be a friend to Earth…or its worst enemy.

FOR A COMPLETE SECOND NOVEL, TURN TO PAGE 81

CAST OF CHARACTERS

ROSS BIRREL

He was an ordinary electrical engineer with a steady job—so what could a top-secret security agency want with him?

KARA

She was beautiful, kind, brave, and intelligent. She was also an alien…and she might well hold the key to Earth's destruction.

VANNEVAN

Fissionable materials were what he wanted, not for some government on Earth, but for the war arsenal of another planet!

THILE

This highly skilled star pilot could outmaneuver any spaceship in the galaxy. Well…almost any.

CONNOR

Being the top security man in the government, it was his job to protect his country from all threats—Earthborn and alien alike.

HOLMER

He was Kara's partner in a mission that might well decide the fate of more than one planet.

WOLT

The minister of defense on the far-off planet of Ir. He held command over a vast arsenal of weapons—all totally useless.

CHAPTER ONE

As Birrel walked into his 71st Street apartment, snapping on the light and pocketing his keys, he suddenly stopped, tense with surprise.

A man he had never seen before stood facing him. A commonplace-looking man with a gray hat, gray suit, and a grayish, young-middle-aged face. His voice was mild as he said,

"Ross Birrel?"

"That's right," said Birrel. Then anger swept away his astonishment. "Who are you and how the hell did you get in here?"

"We'll discuss that later," said the gray man. "Right now, I want you to come with me. Official business."

"What kind of official business?"

"We'll discuss that later too."

Birrel started forward, his temper dangerously high. Then he stopped. The gray man's hand was in his coat pocket, and it was gripping something in that pocket. He said,

"Please don't be difficult, Mr. Birrel."

Birrel said, "If you're an official of some sort, let's see your credentials."

"I'm afraid," said the other, "I don't have any."

"I thought so." Birrel began to breathe hard. "Listen, you've made a mistake. I'm not a rich man, or a rival gangster, or anybody you want. I'm an electrical engineer, a bachelor, and I'm stone broke."

"We know that," murmured the gray man. "Now will you come along?"

Birrel suddenly decided that the man was crazy. New

York was full of nuts these days, people flipping their lids and doing daffy things. This was one of them—and there was only one thing to do.

"All right, but you'll regret this," he said. He started to turn his back on the gray man. "When you find out you're wrong—"

Birrel, turning, whirled with sudden speed, his arm snaking out to catch the gray man's neck with the edge of his hand, the old trick they'd taught him in the O. S. S. in wartime.

It didn't work.

The gray man ducked and chopped expertly with his left hand. A numbing pain hit Birrel's extended arm.

For the first time, the gray man smiled. "Sorry. But I was in the O. S. S. too, you see."

Birrel, holding his aching arm, stared. This wasn't a nut after all. But what...?

"Look, Mr. Birrel. I have no sinister designs against you, in any way. We merely have a proposition to put to you. You can accept or refuse it. But unfortunately, I have to do this secretly. That's why I couldn't phone or write or approach you in public."

Birrel thought rapidly. Not a nut, no. But what kind of official business would have to be done *this* secretly? He didn't like it, not at all.

"Shall we go?"

Birrel looked at the hand in the coat pocket. He went.

He came out into the cool dark wetness of 71st Street, the summer shower over and the red and white neon signs toward Broadway reflected cheerily on wet asphalt. A sedan, with a man at its wheel, was waiting.

He heard the mild voice close behind his ear. "Get right in, Mr. Birrel."

The car swept them up the West Side Highway, with the electric glow of Manhattan behind them. Ahead, the strung-out lights of George Washington Bridge arched the black gulf of the river.

Birrel sat in the back seat, with the gray man keeping well away from him at the other end of the seat. He could see nothing of the driver but a thick neck under a crusher hat.

They crossed the Hudson and went on westward, skirting cities and running quietly and fast through a region of small factories and junk-heaps and power plants.

Birrel felt a mounting panic. What the devil had he got mixed up in? He tried to think why anyone would want to grab him like this.

He couldn't think of anything. Since the war he'd completed his education, taken his engineering degree, landed a job in a Long Island electric company, and—that was all. He didn't know any technical secrets; he wasn't doing any top-secret work; he was an utterly undistinguished thirty-year-old engineer and nothing more.

Then why?

"Listen," he said, "I know there's a mistake…"

"No mistake," said the gray man. He added, "We're nearly there."

"There" was a high wire fence with a locked gate and a red sign:

INDUSTRIAL CYANOGEN COMPANY
DANGER—KEEP OUT.

A man came out of a little wooden building inside the gate, and unlocked and opened it. The car went on through.

It stopped after a moment, in front of a big, dark old-fashioned brick factory building with a forlorn, out-of-date look about it. The only light was a dingy bulb over the door in front.

"This is it, Birrel. Come along."

7

Inside, Birrel got a shock of surprise. It wasn't the cavernous, dark interior he expected. There was light, the sound of clicking typewriters and teletypes, the dick of heels on corridor floors.

THE OLD FACTORY building, he saw now was a blind. Behind its dingy walls and masked windows were at least two floors of offices. The doors of them all were closed, but he heard the hum and buzz of earnest activity from behind them.

Gray-face nudged him toward one of the doors. The thick-necked driver went on somewhere.

Birrel looked around a featureless little office with a battered table, some office chairs, and nothing else.

He turned. "What the devil is this place?"

"A government agency," said Gray-face.

Birrel said, "Listen, I'd like to know how long you're going to keep this—"

He stopped, and was aware that his jaw was hanging in foolish surprise. A man had come into the office.

A stocky, iron-haired man of fifty or more, with a heavy, seamed face and eyes not much softer than flint. Birrel had never seen him face to face before, but he knew him.

"Why—"

"Yes," said Gray-face, obviously enjoying himself. "It's Mr. John Connor." He turned and said, "Here he is, Mr. Connor. I believe he thought we were taking him for a ride."

"All right, Paley," said Connor brusquely. "Sit down. Birrel. Sorry to haul you out here, but this is important. Will you take that moronic stare off your face and *sit down?*"

Birrel sat, swallowing hard. This he hadn't expected.

He had been in the O. S. S. more than a year, and he'd never even got within shouting distance of John Connor, the most famous of its directing brains. And now, eleven years later, to meet him this way in a masked factory that was an office—

Birrel said, weakly, "Then this *is* a government agency?"

"It is," said Connor. "The most secret one of all. We don't give out interviews, and have addresses, like the C. I. A. and F. B. I." He nodded toward the gray-faced man. "You'll understand why I sent Paley for you this way, why I couldn't write or phone you."

"But I thought you'd retired, after the war," Birrel said. "The newspapers—"

John Connor said disgustedly, "The hell and all of an O. S. S. man you must have been, if you believe everything you read in newspapers."

Birrel thought he understood now. One of the secret counter-espionage agencies by which America defended itself—so secret that probably few government officials even knew about it. But—

Connor's rough voice answered his thought. "We need a man, Birrel. For a job. And it must be a man we can trust absolutely. That's why we looked through the O. S. S. files— and found you."

"Oh, now, listen," protested Birrel, rising. "My service was years ago. I've got a profession, and this isn't wartime now. You can find better agents than me—"

Connor said brutally, "I could find five hundred agents better than you. I'd rather have anyone of them than you. Unfortunately, you've got something they haven't."

"What?"

"The right face, Birrel."

Birrel didn't get it; he didn't get it at all. But Connor gave him no time to think. He demanded,

"You'd help us if you thought it might mean life or death to your country, wouldn't you?"

Birrel knew he was about to be trapped, but there was

only one way you could answer that. "Sure, but—"

Connor cut him off. "Fine. Now I'm going to show you someone, Birrel. Come along."

They went out of the office, and down a long corridor and then down a flight of concrete steps. Connor said nothing on the way, and neither did Paley.

The cement-walled basement corridor below was chilly. Lights glowed in its ceiling. In front of a closed steel door stood an alert young man with a submachine-gun cradled in his arm.

Connor nodded to him and said, "All right." He produced a key from his pocket and unlocked the door.

Not until they were inside the room, and the door locked behind them, did either Connor or Paley say another word.

Birrel's glance darted around. The room, an ice-cold concrete cubicle, had nothing in it at all but a hospital table on which lay a long something covered by a sheet. From it came a strongly chemical smell.

He felt a wave of relief. So that was why he had been brought here with all the hush-hush—to identify a dead someone? It was the only possible explanation—

"Six weeks ago," Connor was saying, "near one of our most secret atomic depots, a prowler was challenged. He tried to escape. He was shot and instantly killed."

He said then, "All right, Paley. Uncover him."

Paley went to the table. He took hold of the white sheet. His hand trembled a little, and there were sudden beads of sweat on his forehead despite the freezing cold of the room. He looked as though he did not want at all to carry out the order.

Connor's harsh breathing was loud. Birrel wondered why they were so affected. Surely not by the sight of a dead man—they, even more than he, had seen plenty of dead men in the war years.

The sheet was pulled halfway back. A naked man lay on the table, his dark eyes staring sightlessly at the ceiling.

He was fairly young, black-haired, with faintly swarthy skin and a blocky, undistinguished face. He looked vaguely familiar...

With a shock, Birrel realized that the dead man looked not unlike himself. Not a twin-like resemblance, but still, a strong resemblance. He looked up quickly to Connor.

He was amazed by the expression in Connor's heavy face. The lines in it had deepened. His half-narrowed eyes stared almost hauntedly at the dead man.

Paley had moved back from the table, and there was a strain in his gray face as he looked across the body at them.

"He was a spy," Connor said. "There's no doubt about that at all. And a very skillful one, to get into that guarded area."

Birrel asked, "From what country?"

Connor looked at him. He said, "From no country. You see, we ran a post-mortem on him, and—"

He stopped. He looked as though he didn't want to say what he was going to say, as though he had to force himself against a whole lifetime's beliefs and thinking, to say this thing.

"He wasn't an Earthman at all. He was from somewhere else. Some other world."

CHAPTER TWO

BIRREL STILL COULDN'T take it in.

Two hours had passed, and he sat in Connor's office, listening, arguing, still not believing.

Paley was there, hunched as though half-asleep in a chair in the corner. There was another man there, a young man named Garlock, with glittering eyeglasses and teeth and a sharp voice. But Connor did most of the talking.

"I *know* it's fantastic," he said, for the tenth time. "But it's so."

"But he looks human—" Birrel said, again.

"He *is* human. But he's different.

His blood is a type never encountered before. His cells, his nervous system, his bone-and-muscle tissue, they're all different from an Earthman's—unmistakably. I could give you Dr. Blount's report, but it wouldn't mean anything to you. If you'd seen Blount's face, that alone would have convinced you."

"But this is 1956," Birrel argued. "We're still only *talking* about space-flight. And only crackpots believe in ships and people from other worlds."

Connor winced. "Don't... It's like hearing a playback of what I said to Blount. Listen, we had the two most qualified biologists in the country check that body. They agree utterly. It's non-terrestrial."

Birrel opened his mouth to say something and then shut it. He had nothing more to say.

He faced the enormity of an impossible fact, just as these men had had to face it. A man, a visitor, a secret visitor, from another world. In this hard, matter-of-fact office, it seemed impossible, like a story read and thrown away, like a crazy movie you laughed at as you went out. The George Washington Bridge was only a few miles away, and tomorrow the Giants played the Pirates, and Friday was payday, and a man had come from another world.

"But from where?" Birrel whispered, finally. "And *why?*"

Connor sighed heavily. "Now we're getting somewhere. I know how hard it is to take. Every morning I wake up, I think at first it was just a wild dream—" He broke off, then said harshly, "From where? We don't know, haven't an idea. The sky is full of worlds. Take your pick."

A nightmare kaleidoscope of all the stars and planets of the universe rushed through Birrel's head. The sky is full of worlds. Yes. He'd never quite realized it before.

"As to why, there's no doubt at all," Connor was saying. "The man was killed near one of the most heavily guarded atomic weapon depots we have. He was killed trying to escape. He was a spy."

"A spy, for…" Birrel's voice trailed away.

"That's right, Birrel. For someplace else, someplace not on Earth."

Garlock spoke up to Connor, interrupting. "You're giving it to him too fast, John. It took us weeks, and yet you haul him in and hit him in the face with the whole picture. More time—"

"I'm running this, and we haven't *got* more time," Connor said roughly.

Birrel hardly heard them. He felt as though an earthquake had rocked his mind, had shaken up all his preconceived ideas, all the bases of his thinking for a lifetime.

"But," he said slowly to Connor, "a spy from someplace outside, from another world—does that mean danger? A threat…out there?"

Connor spread his big, spatulate hands on the desk. "We don't know. We don't know what it means. But this agency has top responsibility for the country's safety against secret enemies. Whether they're Earthmen or not! We have to assume it *does* mean a threat."

"Yet it could be just accidental, his being near the atomic depot?" A thought sprang into Birrel's mind. "A visitor from outside, coming secretly, wanting to learn about our science."

Connor smiled grimly. "I wish I could think so. But we know it isn't so. Show him what we found, Jay."

Garlock went to a safe and unlocked it and took out a small object and came back. He said to Birrel,

13

"We found two things beside the man himself. A quarter-mile from him we found a queer burned place in the ground, a charred gouge. We don't understand it at all. The other thing we found was in his pocket. This."

He put the little object on the desk. To Birrel, it looked rather like a black plastic film-viewer of the type used for looking at colored slides. He said so, and Garlock nodded.

"That's just what it is. Only it's the someplace-else type of viewer. I'll turn it on. Then you look into it."

His nerves taut, Birrel put the lenses to his eyes. Would he look at the incredible vistas of another planet, at—

But no. He was looking at a colored picture of a big laboratory's interior, and it was definitely an Earth lab of the present day. He could name many of the gadgets in the room. It looked like an atomic experimenter's workshop on a big scale.

Birrel got that one glimpse and then started violently and tore the viewer away from his eyes.

A MAN'S VOICE HAD SPOKEN, close to his ear—small in volume but rapid, authoritative, precise in diction.

The language it spoke was one he had never heard.

"What?" he cried, startled. Connor and Garlock nodded. "The voice," said the latter, "is on the film."

"And that," Connor said flatly, "was a picture of the most secret atomic laboratory at Los Alamos." He reached out and took the viewer into his own hand. "There are fifty-six pictures in this thing, each with a detailed vocal commentary like that you heard. They're pictures—*detailed* pictures—of top secret atomic depots, storehouses and arsenals."

"But how could they—" Birrel began. Connor cut him off.

"We haven't the faintest idea how. They've obviously got instruments that we don't have, for looking into places.

'Why' and 'who' are what we want to know. Especially, 'who'."

He got up and walked back and forth in a little pattern. With a shock of surprise, Birrel realized that it was not yet midnight. It seemed that an eternity must have passed, not just a few hours.

Connor stopped and turned toward him. "That's where you come in, Birrel."

It wrenched Birrel suddenly back from his chaotic imaginings of faraway worlds and stars, of a cosmic plot and an unsuspecting Earth.

"Me?"

"You're going to help us find this ring of Someplace-else agents."

"But you said yourself you had better agents than me?"

Connor nodded. "But, as I told you, you have the right face. We went through photos of several thousand former agents to find your face, Birrel." He paused, then went on, "Our only concrete lead to this bunch of whoever-they-are, is that dead man. He was one of them. If he were alive, he could be trailed back to the others. But he isn't alive. So, to find that trail, we have to use a ringer."

Birrel was numb with amazement, but he was not a fool, and he got Connor's implication instantly.

It was one of the oldest tricks in the book of counter-espionage. You had one of your own men pose as an enemy spy, so that a contact would be made that could lead you to the others. An old trick, and a risky one—even in ordinary circumstances. But in this case, it was fantastic.

"Oh, no," said Birrel. "It wouldn't work, there isn't a chance. I don't look that much like him—"

"You have the necessary basic feature," Connor said. "The skull shape, the ears, the things that can't be disguised. Our makeup experts can do the rest."

"But how can I pose for a minute as that man, when I don't know his language? The first moment any of the others spoke to me, I'd be through."

"We can teach you a fair bit of the language," Connor said. "Enough so that you won't be instantly recognized as a fake. You'd soon be found out—but by then we'd be jumping on them."

Birrel stared, wondering if the strain of this hadn't been too much for the man. "*You* can teach me some of that other-world language?"

Connor said, "Grossman can. He is, in case you don't know, one of the world's greatest philologists. He was called in on this weeks ago. Using that spoken commentary on the film-viewer, that voice that each time described a specific pictured scene, he worked away relating words and pictures until he built up the whole language. It's rough yet—but he's got a vocabulary of a couple thousand words, a set of grammar rules, and—above all—an accurate reproduction of accent and pronunciation, in that recorded voice. Enough, with luck, to get you by for a little time with the others. That should be time enough for us."

Garlock interrupted, saying heatedly to Connor, "Look at his face! I tell you, you're giving this to him too fast, you can't throw it at him like this."

Connor ignored the protest. He sat down again at the desk, and his bleak eyes held on Birrel's face.

"This is how it stands. Where they came from, what that place is like, we haven't a glimmering. How many of them there are on Earth, we don't know either. But one man couldn't come alone. So there are others. All right."

He bent forward, his harsh voice beating at Birrel. "We make you look like that dead man. We have Grossman cram you with that language till you can get by. Then we stick you in jail. We announce that an unidentified spy was caught near an atomic installation, weeks ago, and that we're still holding him for questioning. We let that out in the newspapers."

"And then?"

Connor said, "The others—they'll be wondering what happened to their boy. He was alone on that job, we're sure of that. When they hear he's in prison, they'll surely try to contact him—you."

"What makes you so sure they will?"

"Because," Connor said slowly, "they have to. This is a secret operation. They must prevent our finding out who our prisoner is, finding out that he's from outside Earth."

His voice became raw-edged. "They're a threat, Birrel. Wherever they came from, they're danger. Perhaps the worst danger that ever threatened us. We have to find them. You have to help."

He did not ask for that help, he commanded it. And with a feeling of unreality, Birrel knew that he could not disobey that command.

Connor rose. "You'll stay here, while we set this up. It'll take weeks, working every minute, to get you ready."

Weeks later, wearing another man's face, Birrel sat solitary in an isolated cell of a New York prison. He sat there unbelievingly waiting for the impossible, for the secret ones from the wider cosmos.

He did not have to wait long.

CHAPTER THREE

THEY CAME AT TEN minutes before midnight.

Birrel had been sitting in this cell for some twenty hours. The cell was deep in a jail in downtown Manhattan. It was a solitary cell, for a solitary and important prisoner.

He had a different face now, a dead man's face. The clothing he wore had belonged to that man. He could speak that man's language, to a certain extent. He was not Ross Birrel; he was a man from Someplace-else.

"What's my name, on that other world?" Birrel wondered. *"I'm impersonating somebody and don't know who, or what, he was—"*

Except that the man he impersonated had been a spy. Secret agent of an unguessable, distant world...ferreting out Earth's defense secrets.

A wave of cold disbelief swept Birrel. It was still too fantastic, too incredible. The scientists were wrong about that body, they must be wrong. Connor was wrong.

But Connor remained grimly convinced. Before his men took Birrel to the prison, he had said,

"They've lost an agent, those people from outside. A valuable man with valuable information. They'll contact you, somehow when our newspaper story appears."

"In a locked cell in prison?" Birrel had said, incredulously. "How can they?"

"I've an idea," Connor had said, "that they can do quite a lot of things we can't. But we'll be ready for them. The prison guards aren't in on our set-up, of course. But we'll be in the building, watching."

He had added, "You may not fool them long. But try. Remember, the important thing is to get them to lead you to the others, to the center of this thing, to their base, wherever it is. We'll follow."

That had been twenty hours ago. And now Birrel sat in the cold, stone-walled little cell, and stared at the blank steel door, and told himself that he was a fool, and that Connor was mad.

No one could reach him here, even if anybody tried.

Birrel suddenly looked up. Something had happened to the light, the single bulb that illuminated his cell.

A greenish tinge had come into the light. It deepened, and there was a buzzing in his ears, and—

Birrel pitched to the floor, unconscious.

He came out of blackness, later, with a vague consciousness of someone touching him and the sound of a voice in his ears.

It was a woman's voice, low and hurried and husky with strain. He didn't know what it was saying; the words didn't make sense.

Suddenly, Birrel's heart pounded. Some of those words, those strange-sounding syllables, *did* make sense. They were words he had learned in the weeks of preparation—words that Grossman, the philologist, had beaten into him by endless repetitions.

The words—the language—of the secret ones from Someplace-else.

He wrenched his eyes open. He looked into the dark, handsome face of a young woman. Her eyes were brilliant with excitement, and her hands were shaking Birrel by the shoulders. She spoke swiftly to him again, and now his clearing mind could translate the words.

"Rett, there's little time! Please!"

"Rett?" That was a word he didn't know. But of course— that would be his name. Or, rather, the name of the man he impersonated. Rett—

Birrel was too foggy yet to try to answer in that alien language. He was dazed, off balance, and dared not make a slip.

She helped him to his feet. His legs were like strings. He felt as though a pile driver had hit him. What had happened?

Hanging to the edge of the bunk for support, Birrel stared groggily. He saw now that the girl wore an ordinary tan suit, with no covering on her shoulder-length black hair. Beyond her, the steel door now gaped wide open. How had it been opened? And what had struck him senseless? There had been a sudden greenishness in the light—

The light was *still* green, a baleful emerald tinge. He didn't understand. He looked down at himself, and found that around his neck now hung a chain from which depended an egg of silvery metal. The egg hummed.

Birrel reached numb fingers toward the thing, but the girl caught away his hand. Again in that alien tongue, she said quickly,

"No, Rett—don't touch your shield! We have to get out fast—Holmer can't blank this building forever. Please try to walk!"

His shield? Shield against what?

He saw now that she too wore a humming metal egg around her neck.

Birrel's brain was beginning to clear. But he purposely kept his bewildered expression. Acting dazed would give him a little more time.

"Holmer?" he said.

"He's outside," the girl said. "Holding the—(and here she used a word Birrel did not know at all)—on the whole building. But we must hurry!"

Birrel began to understand. They had come indeed, the secret ones from beyond the world. One of them, outside, had hit the whole prison with some stunning force, some super-encephalographic vibration. That was what had knocked him out. But the greenish glow was still there, the force still on. How was it he was conscious now?

Was the "shield" a shield against the stunning force? The girl had put it on him and he had revived. And she was wearing one herself—

IT SUDDENLY RUSHED over Birrel, the full, overwhelming realization that he was face to face with someone not of Earth. He stared into her dark, smooth face, into her wide, worried black eyes, and he felt the short hairs on his neck bristle.

She seemed utterly human and Earthly, and she was not. The eyes meeting his had looked on unguessable vistas across the cosmic abyss. The strong hands that steadied him were alien hands.

Woman not of this world...

He shivered involuntarily and the girl misunderstood that. She said urgently,

"I know you're shaken up but you must walk! We must get out of here—come—"

She tugged him toward the open door of the cell. Birrel stumbled through it, with her. His feet would not coordinate; they kept scuffling and tripping as he went down the corridor and up the stair.

There was a guard office at the top of the stair. Two jail guards in uniform sprawled—one in a chair, the other on the floor. They were not dead, for he could see the rise and fall of their chests. But they were gripped by an insensibility like death.

Birrel began to get it. "Holmer can only hold the building blanked for a little longer!" The one outside, the confederate of the girl, had stricken everyone in the prison into a coma. Protected by a shield-device, she had walked right in, unchallenged.

The thought appalled Birrel. Connor and Paley and their men were in this building, waiting to follow Birrel and whoever contacted him. And Connor and Paley and the others must right now be as unconscious as these guards. Their whole plan was shattered.

"Hurry, Rett!" She was urging him almost fiercely forward, out of the office and into a main hall.

They came to a barred door, now swinging open. How had she opened the doors, Birrel wondered? But a science that could throw this deathlike trance on a building full of men would make short work of locks.

The girl quickened her pace, urging him along faster. In a moment they came out into the darkness of the summer night, in a parking-court with a half-dozen official cars in it. The high gate to the street was closed. Just inside it was a long sedan whose motor purred softly. She ran toward it, her strong fingers clutching Birrel's wrist.

As she opened the rear door of the sedan, the flashing-on of the roof-light disclosed a man sitting at the wheel.

He was older than the girl was, dark like her but with a craggy lined face, and eyes that might have been humorous if they were not so alert and alarmed. He too wore around his neck a silver egg that hummed.

"Kara, you took too long!" he said. "Any minute—"

"It took time to find him," she said. "I'll open the gate. No, Rett—you get in, quick!"

As Birrel climbed unsteadily into the rear seat, the girl—so her name was Kara?—ran and swung open the street-gate, then ran back to the car.

Birrel's mind was clearing but things were happening too fast. He heard a continuous thin, whining sound that was coming from the front seat. It came from a square black box that rested on the seat beside the driver.

The girl Kara leaped into the back with Birrel and said, "Turn it off now, Holmer—and *go!*"

The man at the wheel reached and touched the box, and the whining sound ceased. Then, instantly, he flicked on the headlights, and sent the car leaping out through the open gate into the alley.

Within two minutes, they were out in the glittering stream of Fourth Avenue's night traffic, heading north.

Only then did the girl turn to Birrel. She said, almost passionately,

"Rett, where have you *been?* All these weeks, Holmer and I almost going crazy—"

Birrel had an answer for that all prepared. "They caught me. They questioned me, time after time. Finally, when they couldn't get anything out of me, they were going to hold me for trial."

Kara nodded swiftly. "We guessed that, when we finally saw the newspaper mention of an unidentified spy being held. They didn't suspect who you really are?"

He had his answer ready for that too. "No. They still don't dream of such a thing. They thought I was from another country here."

"But the Irrian?" Kara pressed. "What became of *him?*"

It took Birrel completely by surprise. "Irrian?" It was only a meaningless name to him. He had no answer for this, at all.

He said, floundering, "What do you mean—"

"Vannevan's man," she said, impatiently. "The Irrian you were trailing. Rett, try to clear your mind. Did the Earthmen catch the Irrian too?"

IT MADE NO SENSE at all to Birrel. All he could gather was that the dead spy, Rett, had, when killed near that atomic depot, been trailing someone. Someone called "the Irrian" and "Vannevan's man." Who was Vannevan?

He had to take a chance. He said, slowly, "I was the only one they captured."

She said again, "But what about the Irrian? Did you have to blast him?"

Birrel, his mind racing like a trapped animal seeking escape, suddenly remembered something. The word "blast" made him remember. It was the thing that had puzzled Connor's agents, the charred gouge in the ground that they had found near the dead spy.

Again, he had to gamble. Aware that it was a complete leap in the dark he said, "Yes. I had to blast him."

Her small, strong hands clenched together. "If only you

could have taken him, as you planned. If we could have taken him back, it would be complete proof of what Vannevan's doing here."

Birrel couldn't get this at all. He was bewildered, all his previous assumptions and those of Connor completely upset.

They had had it figured out, they thought. The dead man was a spy from another world. He would have colleagues—a group who had come here to search out Earth's most potent defense secrets, with some deadly purpose surely. Birrel's job, his imposture, was to lead to the others.

But—it seemed now that these secret ones, this Kara and Holmer, themselves had enemies. The dead man, Rett, had been trailing one. An Irrian. Who were the Irrians? Who was Vannevan, and what was *he* up to?

A sense of nightmare unreality suddenly swept Birrel. Their car was crossing lower Times Square. The blaze of lights, the after-show crowds, the winking signs—all were so utterly normal. And here, in the midst of it, he rode with a man and woman of a far world, speaking their language, talking tensely of things he didn't even understand.

Birrel felt a frantic desire to rip the door open and plunge out of the car, to run and lose himself in the cheerful crowds.

He couldn't. He'd taken the job and he had to go through with it—to find out where their base was, to find out what threat they represented.

"But I have to play it alone," he thought, with sinking heart.

Connor and Paley and the rest, who had planned so carefully to follow them, had never foreseen the stunning force that had struck.

Birrel became aware that they had crossed town and were running through the Lincoln Tunnel. In a few minutes they were on a main highway, heading north.

How long could he keep up this imposture? How long

until he made some slip, some blunder?

Holmer, his voice quiet but with a sudden edge to it, said, "There's a car following us. I wasn't sure till we got through the Tunnel."

With sudden reaction, Birrel's hopes leaped. Then Connor and the others had come to in time to follow? Yet it hardly seemed possible…

"*Vannevan!*" Kara's exclamation was so fierce that it startled him.

"It can't be anybody else," Holmer grimly agreed. "That newspaper story about the captured spy—it drew *him* to the prison too, it seems."

Whoever Vannevan might be, Birrel thought, it was evident that these two hated and feared him like the devil.

Holmer gripped the wheel tighter, and the car suddenly lunged faster. He said, without turning, "You know what it means. The Irrians know now that we followed them to Earth. Hold on, we have to lose them!"

As by a lightning flash, the shocking truth was abruptly revealed to Birrel. *Two* groups of secret agents, bitterly hostile to each other, playing a vast and deadly game against each other, were on the unsuspecting Earth!

CHAPTER FOUR

BIRREL FELT THE imminence of onrushing danger. Danger, not just to himself, but to all his world. For in him lay the only chance to find out about the threat to Earth before it materialized.

Who their pursuers were, who the Irrians and Vannevan might be, and why they had come to Earth, he could not guess. But about Kara and Holmer, he was sure. Their colleague, the dead Rett, had had those pictures of Earth's most secret weapons and defenses on him. They, therefore, were the danger—and he must not lose them.

"Turn at the next side road!" he said to Holmer. "We can give them the slip in the back roads."

Holmer nodded. Birrel looked back. A pair of headlights swung steadily along a quarter-mile behind them.

"They're closer," said Kara.

Birrel looked ahead, saw the sign that marked a crossroad, and said, "Turn there!"

Next moment, he thought they were all three done for. For Holmer turned into the dark side road without slowing down at all, and the sedan careened on screaming tires and threatened to go over.

Birrel, slammed into a corner of the back seat, felt Kara bump against him. He held her with one arm and groped frantically for something to hold onto when they rolled over.

They didn't roll over. By scared reaction, Holmer spun the wheel at the right second. The sedan tottered, then thumped back onto all four wheels, its motor stalled.

Out on the main highway, a car flashed by fast.

"These cursed Earth vehicles!" said Holmer, in a shaky voice. "No gyroscopic controls, no built-in stability factor at all!"

Birrel felt like yelling, "What the devil made you think you could turn a right angle at full speed?" But he didn't. It would give him away, as Rett he mustn't know too much more about automobiles than the others did.

But for the sake of survival he had to get Holmer away from the wheel.

He said, "Let me drive it—since I saw you last I've learned to handle them pretty well."

Holmer crowded over in the front seat, holding the black box in his lap. Birrel climbed over fast, and took the wheel.

"They went past, but now they're coming back!" cried Kara. "I can hear—"

Birrel kicked the starter and then the gas-pedal. The sedan shot up the dark asphalt country road like a frightened rabbit.

Kara was looking back, and her voice came clear over the rising whine of the motor.

"They're back there. Gaining on us…"

Birrel glanced up at the mirror and the headlights coming up fast behind. He jammed the gas-pedal down, sending the sedan hurtling past the lighted windows of houses, the black masses of trees. The headlights came no closer.

Kara cried to Holmer, "Use the—" Again, the word that Birrel did not know.

He knew what it meant. The square box in Holmer's lap, the thing that had stricken all in the prison unconscious by its potent vibrations.

Holmer fiddled with the box. Over the roar of the motor, Birrel could not hear it come on. But he looked up hopefully at the mirror.

The headlights stayed right with them.

"No use," said Holmer. "They've got their shields on. They must have known how we did it at the prison."

He turned the thing off. Birrel realized, with a certain desperation, that it was up to him.

He had one advantage, he thought. If those pursuing were from another world, they would not be able to drive an Earth automobile as expertly as he could.

Kara said, "They could cut us down with the—(another totally incomprehensible word)—but they won't dare use *that* here. It would let everyone in this part of Earth know they're here!"

What weapon it was that the pursuers, the Irrians, had but might not dare to use, Birrel could not guess. But the fear in Kara's voice was enough to make him conjure up nightmare visions of awful agencies and powers that might be loosed on them.

It decided Birrel. Better to take the risk of cracking up than let that car hang onto them. He would use his one advantage.

"Hold tight," he said, and turned sharply at the next side road.

BIRREL BEGAN A CRAZY twisting and turning on the network of back roads. He had always been a good driver. Tonight, with desperate purpose urging him, he forgot all about road-risks.

He forgot about everything except the ribbon of road under his headlights, the sharp curves that he skidded around in racing turns, the instinctive feel of what grade, what dip, what crossroads, came next. It was late and the farmhouses were dark now, sleeping people in them not dreaming of what screamed past them in the night, what flight and pursuit of folk from far worlds.

The rhythm of the racing motor got into Birrel's mind as his tension rose higher. There was nothing but the headlights and the road and the dread of what came behind them. He was sharply startled when Kara's voice broke the spell, speaking close to his ear.

"We lost them, long ago!" she was saying. "Rett, slow this thing before you wreck us."

Birrel eased the gas-pedal. Beside him, Holmer looked scared.

"These clumsy Earth cars. I'll never get into one again!" he said, with feeling.

They were running up a hillside, with scrub woods on either side of the road.

"Stop on the crest, and we'll listen," said Kara.

He stopped, cutting the motor and lights. They got out and looked back. In the soft summer night, the little woods-sounds, the monotonous song of peepers, were somehow shocking in their ordinariness, to Birrel. Impossible that it was just another July night in New Jersey, when beside him stood a man and woman not of Earth.

He looked up at the summer sky, decked with chains and hives of stars. From which dot in the sky had these two come? From where had those others come, those who pursued, the Irrians? *"The sky is full of worlds,"* Connor had said. And the sky was full of mystery and menace...

"Yes," said Holmer. "We've lost them. But we'd better not linger here."

They got back into the car, and Birrel drove on again. Holmer said, "We'll go back to the house. We've got to decide fast, what to do—now that Vannevan knows we're on Earth. We can stay here, and keep watching them. Or we can go home, with what we already know."

With a queer icy feeling, Birrel realized that "home" meant the world from which they had come somewhere across the abyss of space. There must be a ship, hidden somewhere, waiting for these people. If he could keep up his imposture till he reached that ship, and then get word to Connor...

"Rett, you're going wrong, the other road is the way to the house!" Kara said suddenly.

They had just passed a crossroads. Birrel braked the car, and with dismay realized that he had not the faintest notion where "the house" was. Yet that was something that, as Rett, he obviously should know.

He said, "I'm sorry, it's been so many weeks. You had better call out the turns for me."

Neither Kara nor Holmer seemed to find it surprising that he should not clearly remember. But as he drove on, with the girl warning him of each turn on these far-back-in country roads, Birrel wondered how long he could maintain this impossible imposture. He had never been supposed to maintain it for long, the plan had been that Connor and his agents would be following quick and close, but that plan had been irretrievably ruined and he had to ram ahead alone and do what he could, find out what he could.

He was driving down a dark, bumpy road between untilled fields when he became aware that now Holmer and the girl were both peering more intently ahead. Birrel made out the dark loom of an unlighted farmhouse.

Was this "the house"? He dared not ask them that—as Rett, he might have forgotten the network of roads but he certainly wouldn't have forgotten this. But if he turned in, and it was the wrong place...

Birrel thought of a stratagem. As they approached the dark house, he slowed down as though to turn in. If they protested, he could explain that he only wanted to stop and listen again.

But they didn't protest, it must be the place. Birrel turned the car right into the rutted drive, with the headlights striking past an old lilac bush to the front of a ramshackle barn.

"Cut off the lights," said Holmer, worriedly. Birrel did so, his hand shaking a little. He couldn't gamble like this forever without slipping.

THEY WENT INTO the dark house, Kara first going through the rooms and pulling down the blinds, and then carefully lighting a kerosene lamp. They had, Birrel thought, picked a hideout far off the main roads indeed, to be without power.

The place was cold, musty, with some battered old furniture that looked as though it had been there for a long time. There was no evidence at all of how many people had been living within it, and there was no evidence that its occupants were aliens from a far world. It was just an old house in the country, silent and lonely.

Birrel sat down and he was glad to do so, for his feeling of desperation was increasing. So far, he'd found out little. This house was obviously only a temporary headquarters. The real base of these people was somewhere else—but where? That was what he had to find out for Connor.

He gambled once more. He said, "Haven't any of the others been here with you?"

The others. The ones who had come with them to Earth, who *must* have come with Kara and Holmer and Rett to Earth, and who must be found!

Holmer, setting down his square black box on the floor, said uneasily, "Thile was down last week. He's afraid of the ship being discovered. He kept urging us to leave. I told him we couldn't, without you."

Kara came and sat down in front of Birrel. She said, "I know you've been through a lot, Rett. But we have to decide fast. Have you enough proof of what Vannevan's doing on Earth to take home?"

And this was it, Birrel thought. He had got by in the rush of their flight, but he could not possibly bull it out in a conference where his ignorance must betray him.

Holmer said worriedly, "I say, go! Now that the Irrians know that Ruun has taken a hand in this, that we've followed them to Earth, they'll never rest until they hunt down us *and* the ship. You know what Vannevan is like! I say, go with what we've found—right now."

"It all depends," the girl said quickly, "on what Rett has learned. Rett—"

She never finished. At that moment, quite without warning, something like an enormous hand struck Birrel and knocked him in perfect silence to the floor.

He did not lose consciousness. He was able to see the others fall too, stricken by that same silent power. Only he could see from their horrified eyes that they knew what the power was, while he did not. He tried with desperate urgency to move but every nerve was paralyzed, and he could only lie there and watch.

The door of the room opened. Two men came in, moving fast, dark ordinary men in ordinary clothes. Each one carried in his hand a thick, fluted metal cylinder. The cylinders must generate the paralyzing force, which had worked effectively from outside the house, Birrel thought.

A third man followed them.

He was no taller than the others, but he was wider in the shoulders, a powerful easy-moving man. His face was the face of a man born to command, dedicated to it, living for and by it—a man to whom life without personal and immediate power over everything in sight would be intolerable. Just now he had it, and he was happy.

Holmer spoke, but his stiff lips could make only a terrible whisper.

"Irrians—*Vannevan!*"

CHAPTER FIVE

THERE WERE SIX PEOPLE in the living room of the old New Jersey farmhouse, and only one of them was an Earthman.

It seemed a madly impossible thing, to Birrel. The year was 1957 and it was twenty-five minutes to midnight on the eighth of July, and this couldn't be happening but it was.

"You were easy, easy," Vannevan was saying. "Did you think I *wanted* to overtake you out there on the road? All I wanted was to get close enough to pop a tracer on the back of your vehicle, and then follow you."

He was a very happy man, Vannevan. He had outwitted and beaten his enemies, and he was enjoying that part of it more than the actual capture.

He strode up and down on the old, faded carpet, but he

was careful not to get in front of Birrel and Kara and Holmer.

The three sat in chairs and across the room stood Vannevan's two men. Each of them held one of the fluted metal cylinders, and each cylinder was pointing toward the three prisoners, reminding them how quickly they could be paralyzed again, or killed.

The incongruity of it gave Birrel a crazy desire to laugh. The musty old farmhouse, the smoky kerosene lamp, the ticking cuckoo clock on the wall—and five strangers from the stars.

He wondered what a "tracer" was. He supposed it was some sort of tiny gadget that could be shot to stick onto a moving car, and broadcast a signal that could be read and followed. He doubted if he'd live long enough to find out if that was right.

Vannevan said to Birrel, "You killed Jull, didn't you?"

There was no amusement in his hard face now. It was cut out of cold iron, and Birrel had the feeling that Vannevan was every bit as tough as he thought he was.

"Who," said Birrel, "is Jull?"

"A man of Ir," said Vannevan. "My man. The man you trailed and killed. We found the blaster-scar in the ground."

Birrel began to understand a little. He shrugged. "If you know, why ask me?"

Vannevan came closer and his eyes had a yellow glow in their dark depths.

"You wouldn't just blast him outright. You'd shock him and search him first. Just as we're doing to you. Where are the—(he used another unfamiliar word)—you found on him?"

Birrel said, "I found nothing. I just blasted."

Something exploded in his face. He reeled in the chair, putting up his hands blindly, half-stunned. Then he saw Vannevan's clenched fist drawing back. Vannevan, keeping carefully to one side, let the fist go again in Birrel's face.

"You're lying," he said. "You wouldn't come all the way here from Ruun, spying on us, and trail Jull all that way, and then just blast him. Did you pass them on to Holmer before the Earthmen caught you?"

Birrel felt blood running down his face, and he felt a hate and rage that he had never suspected he could experience. He started to get up, and the Irrians with the weapons across the room pointed their cylinders at him. He didn't want to die, any sooner than he had to. He sat down again.

"The men of Ruun are brave," said Vannevan, mockingly. "Now will you tell me—"

He stopped suddenly. An expression of interest and amazement crossed his face. He reached out his hand, toward Birrel's eyes.

Birrel recoiled—but Vannevan's hand swiped across his forehead, across his eyebrows. Then Vannevan uttered an incredulous exclamation.

"This isn't a man of Ruun at all. He's an *Earthman!*"

BIRREL REALIZED what had happened. The blow, the blood streaming down his face, had effectively ruined the careful work of Connor's makeup experts.

Before he could resist, Vannevan rubbed a handkerchief across his face. Birrel, a little dazed and half-blinded by the blood in his eyes, struck out savagely but hit nothing.

Kara's voice reached him. "Rett, you can't be..." Her voice trailed away, and then it came on a different note. "But you're not Rett. He's right, you're an Earthman. Where's Rett?"

Birrel got his eyes open, and now he could see her face, and Holmer's, and the pallor of shocked surprise on both.

He felt a queer guilt. There was no reason for it, they were spies and he was a counter-spy defending his country, defending Earth, but he couldn't rid himself of the feeling.

"Yes," said Vannevan fiercely, "where is Rett? Where's the man you've been impersonating?"

Birrel looked at him and said nothing.

One of the Irrians came to Vannevan's side and spoke so rapidly that Birrel could not follow it.

Vannevan said somberly to him, "Your people—the Earth people—have this Rett, don't they? They captured him, didn't they?"

That was so obvious that there was no use denying it. "They did," said Birrel.

"And they disguised you as Rett, and published that report of a captured spy, to draw the others," Vannevan said, "Of course. Which means—they know there are strangers on their world."

Holmer said, with a taunt in his voice, "You don't like it, do you, Vannevan? It spoils the plans of Ir, doesn't it?"

Vannevan looked at him. "No. There will be no check at all in the plans of Ir. And when we've got what we need from Earth, our plans for *your* world will go right ahead. Be sure of that."

Birrel's mind vainly tried to grapple with the hint in that by-play. Then this was not merely a personal enmity, or a factional one? Then the world of Ir and the world of Ruun— wherever those far worlds might be—were enemies? Then the Irrians, at least, had come to Earth secretly for something they needed for conquest?

It didn't make sense! These star-strangers had already used weapons far subtler and more complex than any weapon of Earth. Why would they need to filch the arms of a less scientifically advanced planet?

"*You* can wait," said Vannevan to Birrel, with a certain contempt. He turned and looked at Holmer and Kara. "But you two are important. No word is going back to Ruun of our plans! Where is your ship hidden?"

"Where is the ship of Ir hidden?" countered Holmer.

Vannevan smiled grimly. "Where you couldn't find it. And you've tried long enough, haven't you? This planet has a lot of wild places. Which one is your ship hidden in?"

Holmer merely laughed.

"You'll tell, one of you," promised Vannevan. He spoke to the Irrian beside him. "The man, first. Take him upstairs. He'll talk more freely and readily if she can't hear him."

The other man pointed his weapon at Holmer. Holmer, without a look at Kara or Birrel, started up the old stairway in the hall, with the Irrian close behind him.

Vannevan followed them.

Birrel looked at Kara. Her face was a stony mask. He looked at the Irrian across the room. In the yellow light of the lamp, the man's face was wrong. It was wrong because it was just a dark, average face. It didn't belong to an enemy from the stars. But the cylinder in his hand pointed levelly at Birrel and the girl.

The dusty cuckoo clock ticked toward midnight. Strange, that it was running, Birrel thought. One of them—Kara or Holmer—must have started it out of curiosity.

He knew he was only thinking these thoughts so that his brain wouldn't crack from the insane unreality of the situation.

Birrel suddenly felt sweat on his forehead. Sounds were coming from upstairs, not loud sounds, but thumping, gasping noises. There was a voice, and then more of the gasping sounds.

Kara started to get to her feet and the man with the fluted metal cylinder said, "Sit down."

Birrel looked at the clock. Two minutes to midnight. A cuckoo clock and a spy from the stars. Unreal. But a wild notion began to grow in his mind...

A SHRIEK, A FADING, choking death-cry, came down the stairs. And then Vannevan's voice came down, loud with anger.

"Damn him, he's dead."

"*Sit down*," said the armed Irrian, again.

A half-minute to midnight. He'd have to try it, there'd never be another chance, not after Vannevan came down those stairs for another of them, for Kara first, and then for Birrel—

The cuckoo clock said, "*Cuckoo.*"

At the sharp sound, at the little flirt of movement by the out-popping bird, the Irrian with the weapon looked up, startled.

Birrel had thought he would.

He thought it unlikely that they had cuckoo clocks out in the stars. He had waited for the moment, and as the Irrian's head turned, he sprang.

He didn't try to reach the Irrian himself. He was too far off. He went for the table with the kerosene lamp on it, which was quite near. He hooked his fingers under the edge of the table and heaved it over as hard as he could. The lamp went flying. It hit the floor, splashing hot oil and flame, and the Irrian screamed. The carpet was suddenly burning around his feet and little flames blossomed like magic where the oil spattered his clothes. There was no need for Birrel to tackle him. He fled screaming into the hall, tearing off his coat and beating in panic at his legs.

The room was in darkness now except for the splashes of fire that ran over the floor and up the window curtains and in erratic streaks on the wallpaper. Birrel grabbed Kara's hand and lunged for the outer door.

"Holmer!" she cried frantically, dragging back.

"He's dead, you heard—come *on!*" He pulled her, with

rough determination.

They banged out over the sagging porch-floor into darkness, and he ran, not toward the car but toward the brush beyond the house, the black thickets that promised protection.

He looked over his shoulder and saw the leaping red glow spreading fast inside the grimy windows. The screams of the Irrian had sunk to a kind of groaning, and Birrel could hear Vannevan's fierce voice over it.

He kept tight hold of Kara's wrist, and now they were in the thicket, moving through saplings and brush. Then Birrel stopped.

Back there, three dark figures had come out of the house. Two of them were twined together, as though one half carried the other. The third was alone and in the lead. They stood silhouetted against the glowing windows, looking this way and that.

Birrel whispered to Kara, "Quiet. If we try to get any farther, he'll hear us."

"They will search until they find us," she whispered.

He shook his head. "That house is beginning to burn nicely. I don't think they'll stay here long."

He felt her gesture of negation. "I don't understand."

"We have a thing on Earth called a Fire Department. In the country every man is his brother's fire warden. Pretty soon the place will be swarming with trucks and volunteer firemen. Stand still and wait."

They waited.

Vannevan and the men spoke together. Finally they left the hurt one to groan and crawl in the grass, and the two of them began to move back and forth in the brush, circling out.

A great plume of flame shot up through some airshaft in the house and stood out gloriously above the roof.

Vannevan and his man had vanished now in the brush.

Birrel held Kara's hand and sweated, and prayed for a sound.

It came. The hoarse, harsh wailing of a country siren, designed to waken every sleeping volunteer in the township.

It rose and fell on the night air, ominous and loud. Vannevan and his man hastily reappeared in the shaking red light. They picked up the hurt man and took him limping away between them. They went down the dark road. Presently, in the distance, Birrel heard a car start.

When he could not hear it any more he said, "All right, let's go."

And he took Kara away across the dark brushy fields running, stumbling, toward a future whose incredible outlines he was beginning vaguely and against his will to see.

CHAPTER SIX

THEY SAT TOGETHER in a brushy hollow by a stream.

Frogs chorused in the marshy spots. The stars swung overhead, above the dark trees. Close by in the warm night an owl sang a weird fluttering song to his love, and there were crickets.

Birrel and Kara spoke of things so strange and far away that they were doubly unbelievable in this setting.

Birrel was stubborn. "I've got to take you back to Connor." He had explained to her who Connor was. "He'll study the facts and decide what to do, After all, you've got to remember that Earth is our world. It's more important to us than any other."

Kara was stubborn, too. "The threat is not against your Earth! It's against Ruun, my world. I told you—"

"But your man Rett, the real Rett—he had that probe-ray record of our most secret atomic installations on him."

"Of course he did," she said angrily. Birrel gathered that she had liked Rett, not romantically but as a good comradein-arms. She had taken the news of his death rather hard. "Why do you think he was there at all? He took that record from the Irrian. It was the proof we needed of the Irrians' activities here, so that our government back home will act before it's too late. If your people hadn't shot him, everything would have been arranged by now. As it is, it's worse than ever."

"Look," said Birrel. "I want to believe you, Kara. I do believe you. But it's just too big a responsibility for me to take on my own shoulders. Connor—"

"Connor!" she said contemptuously. "You're afraid."

"Yes," he said. "I'd be a fool if I wasn't."

She put her head between her hands and said in a very patient voice, "I am trying to remember your side of it. Now listen to me once again. There is a star—you call it Wolf 359. It has several planets, of which five are inhabited. We, the people of Ruun—"

"Control four of the five planets," Birrel said, with a faint edge of skepticism for the story he had already heard from her.

"Peaceably," she said. "The other three worlds allied themselves with us voluntarily. They are completely autonomous. But they are less favorably situated than Ruun and they can't support large populations, so they're relatively weak. And they wanted a strong friend, rather than a strong master—like Ir. Would *you* enjoy living under Vannevan?"

He had to admit he would not. "But are the Irrians all like him?"

"Of course not," said Kara. "But Ir, the fifth world, is ruled by oligarchs, of whom Vannevan is one. The people of Ir may not like it—indeed, we've heard some of them don't—but they're pretty well held down."

But still, Birrel thought, both parties to this interstellar quarrel were strangers to him. And anyway, the decision was not his to make.

He said so, and she said, "But it *is* yours to make. Nobody else can make it. There isn't time."

She plunged on desperately, trying to make him understand. "For centuries we've fought the Irrian oligarchs to keep them from dominating the whole system. The only time we had any peace was when the oligarchs took to fighting among themselves for power at home. Because of that struggle, many years ago they finally exhausted every bit of fissionable matter on Ir. We were able to prevent them from getting any more from our federated planets, and so for a long time there has been peace. You see? We had atomic weapons, they did not. They were no longer any danger. And of course we didn't need our strong military forces anymore. All we've had for decades is just enough to act as an interplanetary police force. And now—"

"And now the Irrians have stolen a march on you," Birrel said. Kara had explained the significance of that probe-ray record, and he had to admit that it seemed to make sense. "They've decided to steal fissionable material from Earth. So they sent Vannevan and his men here to spy out our installations preparatory to raiding them. And if that doesn't constitute a threat to Earth I don't know what does."

"But the weapons they make won't be used against you!" she cried. "They'll be used against us, and unless we can mobilize in time we won't have a chance."

"Look," said Birrel. "Connor will see to it that our installations are so heavily guarded that no one can raid them. Then there's no threat to either of our worlds."

SHE GROANED, as though in despair at trying to deal with an idiot. "Your prison was strong and carefully guarded. Did we have trouble breaking into it? Would we have trouble breaking in anywhere? Guards consist of men and electronic devices. We can blank them both, in many different ways. So can the Irrians. Your defenses wouldn't hold."

And Birrel realized with a sinking heart that that was true.

"But we've got to fight. We've got to do what we can."

"Yes. Of course you do. And there is only one way." Her voice was eager now, forceful, hammering home her points with relentless logic.

"Come back with us to Ruun. Tell the authorities what you know, what you have actually seen. That will be enough to make them believe and mobilize. Vannevan and his men are only the forerunners here. A small fleet must come from Ir for the actual raid. Ruun can stop them, you cannot. You understand? Your defense is out there!"

And she pointed at the glittering sky above the trees.

Birrel followed her gesture and thought, *Oh Lord, I can't! I'm scared. How far is Wolf 359? I never even heard of it.*

And then he thought: *But she's right. Connor, all our armed forces—we'd be like babies against a fleet from Ir. We have atomic weapons but we'd never have the chance to use them. It would be just as it was at the prison—*

He listened to the owl and the crickets and the gurgle of running water, and smelled the cool sweetness of the summer night and dug his fingers into the grass because he wanted to hold on to Earth and all that was familiar.

But overhead the stars glittered and shone, and there was a decision to be made.

"If you want to fight for your world and your people," said Kara softly, "you must have courage to do what you know is right, even if it is against orders."

Yes, thought Birrel. Yes, indeed. Have courage.

Well, the whole thing had gone wrong from the start. He couldn't see that he would make it any better by delivering Kara to Connor. The chances were she couldn't be made to tell anyway where the ship from Ruun was hidden, and it would undoubtedly take off at the first hint of danger. And in any case, it seemed that the Irrians were the threat to Earth, and she didn't know where their ship was. If Kara was telling the truth, the resultant delay might be fatal to both their causes. He thought she was telling the truth.

Very quickly, before he could change his mind, he said, "It seems I have to go with you to Ruun."

"Good," she said fiercely. "Good! Then we have a chance." She jumped to her feet and tugged at him impatiently. "We've wasted too much time already. Let's go."

"Now hold on," he said. "We'll make better time if we plan ahead. Where is your ship?"

"North. In a wild place beyond a big body of water—I think it's called the Hudson's Bay."

Well, if you wanted to hide a spaceship, Birrel thought, that would be as good a place as any. But it was the devil of a long way off.

"How did you get down here?" Birrel asked.

"By hopper."

"By *what?*"

"Hopper. A small flier for planetary hops. It's hidden right here in the woods. We made a shelter for it as soon as we got the farmhouse and flew it in by night. Before that it was in some mountains where we first landed. Come on."

And there was no problem. No problem at all. You found the camouflaged shelter in the summer woods and you got into the neat impossible craft that was in it and watched a girl in a tan suit manipulate a couple of controls with the casual ease of a teenager using a record player. Some quiet force—compressed air, Birrel thought, remembering experimental aerodyne models he had seen—lifted the hopper high and took it away, and the last red coals of a smoldering farmhouse winked in the black countryside and were gone.

By dawn they were far north and rifling with incredible speed through the sky, at a fantastic altitude. Any radarman who chanced to catch them on his screen would lose them so fast he would never believe he had seen anything. And Birrel now knew a lot more about Kara and her people than before.

Kara's father had been a high officer in Ruun's intelligence service in the days when, according to her, the existence of four peaceful planets hung on its efficiency. She herself, as a kind of proud inheritance, also belonged to the intelligence service, which in these later times had dwindled to a small and neglected group of people dedicated to not trusting the Irrians.

IT WAS THESE intelligence people who had discovered the departure of the Irrian ship for Earth and deduced the reason for its going. But official Ruun had refused to be hustled into a panic. They were not going to put four planets on a full war footing, with all that implied, merely because a ship had made the voyage to another Solar System. Rather, they thought, this star voyage might well be the beginning of a new era in peaceful expansion, with the Irrians finally taking a place in a civilized community of worlds. They had allowed a shipload of agents from Ruun to follow and check on the Irrians, but no more. And any future action would be determined by what documented information they brought back.

Kara's people had been forced to lose a little time while they learned the language and customs of the part of planet Earth in which they had business. They had done this—as presumably the Irrians had too—by adapting their televisors to receive terrestrial broadcasts, which they could pull in from amazing distances, and then staring at them for hours at a time with the help of a philologist and a social scientist.

Then, when they came south after the Irrians, they had been able to slip quite easily into the polyglot life of New York, which is accustomed to accents and odd ways.

"There's the ship," said Kara suddenly.

She had brought the hopper down in an express elevator plunge and was pointing at a wedge-shaped piece of barren land between two rocky arms at the base of a mountain. The light of the rising sun made a sort of dazzle in the air, but apart from that there was nothing.

"I don't see any ship," he said. "Where?"

"I forgot, you don't have the refraction-type camouflage. When you're used to it you can spot it without a scope, if you know where to look. Here..." She made rapid adjustments in a small gadget like a camera viewfinder. "This is tuned to our chosen vibration rate. Makes it harder for an enemy to find us."

Birrel looked into the scope and saw a slim silver spire standing on the flat land, its nose pointed toward the sky.

He looked out the port again and saw nothing.

"Light rays bent in a magnetic field around the ship," she said. "They'll drop it now. Watch."

She depressed a switch, activating some automatic signal system. The dazzle of sunlight vanished and the silver ship was there. She landed beside it.

She stepped out and waited for Birrel to follow. He hesitated, looking at the ship. A hatch opened and a magnetic grapple dropped down toward the hopper. Below, a much smaller hatch appeared and extruded a ladder. Once he climbed that ladder, Birrel knew, he was trapped. The ship would take off and...

"There's nothing to be afraid of," Kara said, smiling.

He set his jaw and went with her to the ladder and climbed it and passed into the ship.

It smelled like a submarine, of oil and metal and canned

air. There was a man in an odd-looking coverall who stared at him and spoke to Kara. He heard Kara explaining, and in the meanwhile the lock door behind him was grinding shut and locking itself with relentless precision.

Kara said, "This is Thile. He commands the ship."

Birrel shook hands with him. He was a small lean man with very keen eyes and a hard competent jaw.

"So Holmer and Rett are both dead," he said, with grim regret. "Well, we'll make Vannevan pay for them. Help him strap in, Kara. We're taking off at once." He looked at Birrel. "If we can get back to Ruun without delay, you may be able to convince our sheep-like leaders in time. I hope so."

He hurried away somewhere forward—or up. Kara took Birrel into a small cabin where there were several padded couches, and helped him secure himself with broad webbing straps.

"Scared?"

"Not a bit."

"Liar. Don't worry about it. The first take-off is always the worst." She leaned over impulsively and kissed him, ludicrously like a mother tucking a fretful child into bed. The ship suddenly gave a great roar and a quiver, and a raucous horn began to sound. She scrambled into the couch next to his.

Birrel's heart pounded wildly and the blood in his veins turned cold and thin as water.

There was noise. A stunning, deafening crescendo of it. Then there was a feeling of motion. He lay on the top of a rising piston that pressed him slowly and relentlessly against air compressed into a smaller and smaller space. He opened his mouth and yelled in panic fear, seeing himself crushed into a flattened pulp. The cry was lost in the bursting roar that enveloped the ship. Ages seemed to pass. And then miraculously the pressure eased and finally was gone.

Thile's voice came suddenly from a speaker in the wall. "Trouble, Kara. Radar says another ship has taken off from Earth, right behind us."

Birrel heard her quick, fierce exclamation. "So Vannevan was watching his radar for our takeoff, I knew he'd never let us get back to Ruun if he could help it…"

CHAPTER SEVEN

THEY WERE ALL in the ship's bridge now. Thile and Kara and a young man named Vray were conferring tensely with the radarman and checking a bristling array of instruments.

Birrel was looking at space.

The ports on one side were shielded against the sun, so he couldn't see it. Earth was behind, or below them, so he couldn't see that either. All he could see was nothing, an infinity of it, without top or bottom, front or back, beginning or end. The stars floated in it, by the millions and billions, like shoals of fiery fish gleaming red and gold and blue and green, white and violet, orange and dull crimson. They were not crowded. There was plenty of room between them. The eye was drawn farther and farther into those distances and the body unconsciously tried to follow, until the mind recoiled from the edge of some psychic calamity and screamed for solidity. Birrel spun away from the port and grabbed hold of a stanchion and stood with his eyes shut, sweating and shaking as though he had just run a race.

Kara said, "It gets you, doesn't it?"

He indicated that it did, beyond words. She nodded.

"It's no different with us. We look up at our summer skies just as you have, and dream about what it's like. We read books and we see pictures. But you can't know until you actually get out into space and see it for yourself. And I don't think you ever get over being awed. I never have."

Birrel opened his eyes again, but kept them firmly fixed on the inside of the bridge. Thile and Vray were still hanging over their instruments, looking grim.

"That ship," said Birrel. "It'll try and catch us, I suppose. Stop us from getting word to Ruun."

"I can't imagine Vannevan letting us go without a fight." Her voice was not exactly frightened, but it had a sort of clipped tightness about it that was far from carefree.

"Can he? Catch us, I mean?"

"The Irrians are good spacemen, and their ships are about as fast as ours. But Thile is a wizard. He can out-fly anything in space."

Thile heard her and looked up. He said sourly, "Thanks. But you might as well tell him the truth. Vannevan is not going to rely on speed and skill alone, but on weapons. And we're not carrying any atomic armaments. The government brains didn't think it was wise, considering that we were trespassing on a strange world and might conceivably have an accident, such as falling into a city. They're thoughtful that way."

"As an Earthman, I appreciate it," said Birrel. "You have conventional weapons, don't you? That's at least an equal footing."

"We're not used to them," Thile said. "They are. But we'll do our best. Believe me."

He glanced at Vray and nodded.

"Stand by for translation."

Birrel looked at Kara.

"That only means," she said, "that we're going faster."

"How much faster?"

"Well, just at first," she said, "about double the speed of light."

Birrel stopped trying to go along intelligently with any of it. He just let it happen.

The lights inside the ship dimmed and burned blue. There was a screeching whine that rose up and out of hearing, clawing at the nerves as it went, and then there was a moment of awful vertigo when the ship and everything in it seemed to slip and fall sideways in an insane fashion.

The open ports slid shut automatically. Just before they closed Birrel caught a glimpse through them of the stars he had been looking at only a few moments before. They shifted, streamed like burning rain, and vanished, to be replaced by squiggling lines of lights.

Then the ports were shut and there was nothing except the personal sense of disorientation to show that anything had happened.

Complacently, like one who knows he is dreaming and that therefore these strange things are not really happening and so need not be taken seriously, Birrel listened to the voices of the men, speaking technical words of no meaning to him as they went through what was apparently a routine check.

Then the radarman said, "They're right with us."

Thile grunted. "Full acceleration," he said. "Build up as fast as you can. Maybe their generators aren't as good as ours."

THE WHINING BEGAN again but on a different note. Birrel pictured himself inside an iron egg flying through space (what kind of space?) at double, triple, quadruple the speed of light. He erased the thought from his mind as quickly as he could. He said to Kara,

"Why haven't people done more star-travelling? You obviously have a workable drive."

"We haven't had the time until recently," Kara said. "The

Irrians kept us too busy. Then the few exploratory trips we did make to neighboring systems were discouraging. In most cases the planets were uninhabitable, and the ones that did have life forms were pretty awful. Our government hasn't encouraged star flight. I think they're afraid of what might come flying back our way."

The ship quivered and trembled. Birrel thought he could almost feel the atoms crawling in the metal under his hand.

"Do you ever hit things?" he asked. "Like stars, I mean."

"Not very often. But I believe the results are quite spectacular. You become a nova almost at once."

He laughed. He did not ask any more questions.

The whining leveled off at last, refusing to go any higher. A collection of needles steadied on the main control board.

Vray said, "That's it."

The radarman shook his head and said, "They're still with us."

The lines deepened in Thile's face, turning it grim and hard.

"Action stations. We'll try and get them before they get us."

Birrel said, "What do you want me to do?"

"Back in your bunk and strap in. This is liable to be rough."

He shook his head. "There must be something I can do."

"You'd only be in the way," Kara said. She was already removing a protective panel from a control board ominously marked in red. She smiled, to take the sting out of the words. "You'll need a vac-suit. Here, Rett's will fit you."

She took a baggy-looking suit and a plastic helmet out of a locker and handed it to him. The others were putting on similar suits, leaving the helmets open. Birrel said, "Why?"

"In case we're hulled. If you hear the warning-horn, clap your helmet shut. *Fast.*"

She showed him how and then practically pushed him out of the bridge. He shuffled back to the cabin and lay down on the bunk, feeling worse than he had at any time since the beginning of this hare-brained venture. He was scared, and he didn't mind admitting it. If he had been able to do something, anything at all, it wouldn't have been so bad. But just to lie here alone in this completely incredible ship, thinking of the completely incredible but perfectly real destruction that faced him—that was something no man ought to be asked to do.

He did it.

He was able to sense the "feel" of the ship, and from that to gauge the variations—the slight recoil and shudder as missiles presumably were launched, the greater perturbations of what could only be the near-miss blasts of the enemy weapons. It occurred to him that what these star folk meant by "conventional weapons" were probably not at all the simple explosive types referred to by that name on Earth. The technical problems involved in launching any kind of missile at all at light-plus speeds were so far beyond him that he didn't even try to figure them. But there was no doubt that it was being done. Every leap and jar of the ship told him that unmistakably.

Even so, Birrel was not prepared for the suddenness and violence of what happened.

There was a crash. He felt it physically and heard it, too, this time, transmitted by the ship's air. He fell upward against the straps as the gravitational axis of the ship was brutally reversed. The lights dimmed to an eerie blue and there was a horrible tortured howling of overtaxed generators. The ship rammed through into normal space with much the same effort as of a speeding car hitting a stone wall, only greatly magnified. Birrel heard the warning horn start. He clapped his helmet shut, and then inertia flung him into the recoil couch as into a slab of granite and the joints of the ship began to spring around him. Then everything was dead, generators, horn, everything. The ship was silent except for one sound, the hiss of escaping air.

STUNNED BUT STILL, incredibly, alive, Birrel unfastened the straps and floated out of the couch.

The ship was still moving, but there was no longer any gravity field to speak of. Birrel was in free fall. He floated like a great clumsy balloon out of the cabin and toward the bridge, clawing his way while the ship bent and wavered and wobbled around him, its rigid frame gone limp. As limp as his own body felt. Currents of escaping air whirled papers, garments, pieces of equipment, bits of wreckage wildly around in the interior. He was in a panic lest his helmet be cracked or his suit torn.

The bridge was a shambles of buckled steel and shattered glass. The radarman was crumpled among the remains of his equipment, which had toppled and crushed him. Thile, strapped into the pilot's chair, was stirring feebly. Birrel looked frantically around for Kara.

She was strapped into a recoil chair in front of the fire-control panel. He thought at first she was dead, but when he looked closer he could see that she was breathing. There was nothing he could do for her at the moment and she was safer where she was, so he left her and went to help Thile. There was no sign of Vray at all, except for a few small red icicles formed on the edge of a jagged rift in the hull through which everything movable in the bridge had already been sucked.

Thile's voice came faintly through the helmet audio. "I told you they were better shots."

"Are you hurt?"

"Are you?"

"I don't know yet. Haven't had time."

"Nor me," said Thile. "I can stand up, so I guess I'll live." Blood was trickling from his helmet. He snuffled at it and made futile pawing motions at his helmet. "Well, that does it. Vannevan's won hands down." He swore, a dejected and bitter man. "Four good men dead, and all for nothing. It wasn't even a good try."

He pointed through the riven wall, to the black peaceful gulf beyond with the far stars shining in it.

"See there?"

There was a ship, matching its pace to the slow drift of the derelict. From its slim belly a much smaller craft dropped and jetted fire.

"They'll be aboard us in a few minutes."

Remembering how Vannevan had done his questioning at the farmhouse, Birrel could see little hope. If he and Thile and Kara were going to be at Vannevan's mercy, they might better have gone the way of Vray and the radarman.

Unless...

"Listen," said Birrel suddenly. "Listen, there's one thing we might do." He went over to Kara and shook her until she opened her eyes. "There isn't much time, you've both got to play along with me or it won't work. It might give us an edge, to use against Vannevan. Listen—"

He spoke rapidly, forcefully, and they listened, while the lifeboat of the Irrian ship came closer, riding its fiery jet across the black gulf outside.

Thile said, "It might work—"

"It'll be dangerous," whispered Kara. "If he finds out—"

"I don't figure I have much to lose anyway," said Birrel dryly. "Hurry up!"

When Vannevan and his men came into the broken ship they found Thile and Kara clinging quietly together, apart from the Earthman Birrel, who was strapped into a recoil chair with his hands bound tightly behind him.

CHAPTER EIGHT

THERE WERE SIX of the Irrians, counting Vannevan. They wore vac-suits and they were all armed. Two of them went immediately to Thile and Kara and searched them for weapons, but they had none. The time for resistance was past.

Another man, on Vannevan's instructions, began to tear open the lockers that were still intact, looking for papers. The others stood guard. They handled themselves easily, experts at null gravity.

Birrel looked at Vannevan and said sourly, "Out of the frying pan into the fire. I don't know which of you is worse."

Vannevan's eyes were bright, cruel, competent and happy. Very happy. He had wiped out, and with interest, the defeat he had suffered at the farmhouse. He had crushed the Ruunites completely. For him it was a good day.

He smiled at Birrel. "You see what happens to meddlers."

"I wouldn't call it meddling," Birrel said. "We caught a spy. It was natural to want to know who he was working for, and why."

"When you found out," Vannevan said, "why didn't you report back to your superiors? You were free. I remember distinctly that you were free."

Birrel indicated Kara with a savage movement of his chin. "She talked me out of it, damn her. With a gun."

"So," said Vannevan, and smiled, and shook his head. "But she had no weapon. I myself had seen to that."

"She had one," Birrel said bitterly. "In the hopper. She told me there was another car hidden there for emergencies, and like a fool, I believed her. Instead there was that flying thing, and she pulled a weapon from inside it. The next thing I knew I was aboard this ship, a prisoner. They were going to take me back to Ruun whether I wanted to go or not."

Kara spoke sullenly. "His people killed Rett. It was the least we could do."

"Listen," said Birrel, struggling angrily against the straps that held him. "I don't give a curse what quarrel you have between you. I don't care if you blow each other's worlds out of the sky. I'm an Earthman. I don't belong here. I—"

He looked around at the broken ship, at space gaping monstrously beyond the riven hull. It was not difficult for Birrel to let an expression of fear come into his face.

"I want to go back," he said.

Vannevan looked at him. "How badly?"

Birrel would not meet his eyes. He muttered, "Bad enough."

"Well," said Vannevan. "We'll see." He motioned to one of his men. "Cut him loose. Did you find anything?"

The Irrian who had been searching shook his head, and Thile said, "I could have told you. We don't keep written records."

Vannevan shrugged and said, "Let's go."

They floated gracefully through the ship, with Birrel lumbering and floundering in their midst. They passed through the airless lock and into the life-craft. In a short time they were being taken up into the belly-pod of the Irrian ship, and a little while after that Birrel found himself a prisoner with Thile and Kara in a locked cabin.

The ship paused only long enough to finish the destruction of the derelict. Then it went into overdrive, on its way to Ir.

During the rest of the voyage, knowing full well that they were being watched, the three kept up their pretense of hostility. But Birrel came more and more to admire Thile and

Kara. They were personally defeated and in a desperate situation. Their mission was a failure. Their world and way of life, which had hung on that mission, were threatened with destruction. But they clung quietly to their hope and courage and never whined—in striking contrast to Birrel himself, whose part called for constant complaint.

Birrel thought he was establishing himself sufficiently well as a frightened man who might be talked into doing almost anything for the right reward. He hoped so. Because not only his own life but the lives of Thile and Kara depended upon that, not to speak of the safety of several worlds, including his own. He was a little upset to discover that Kara's safety loomed larger in importance than anything else. He decided then that he was in love with her.

There came finally a time when the warning rang, and the lights burned blue and the ship shuddered, and then the port unmasked.

"We're out of overdrive," said Thile. "We're there."

AN AWE FELL on Birrel as he looked out the port with them. The ship, in normal space again, was sweeping in a curved pattern toward a sun whose diamond incandescence eclipsed the stars.

Almost lost in that overpowering glare, three points of light swung far on the other side of this system. It was toward the biggest of the three that Thile and Kara were gazing.

"Ruun," whispered Kara. "If they only knew, if we could only get a message to them…"

Thile said bitterly, "What good would it do even if we could send a warning? Our cautious government would merely say, as they did before, 'You have no proof that the Irrians mean war, and without proof we cannot act'."

The ship swung on in its landing pattern and now, below,

Birrel saw a planet coming up toward them.

It was a scarred world of black-and-green. He thought at first that these were land-and-water divisions, but as they went lower he saw that they were not—that the greens were fertile plains but that the ominous black areas were utterly lifeless lands, black and blasted and barren.

"That's what the oligarchs of Ir have made of their world," said Kara. "Those burned-out regions are the scars of their wars between themselves. And now, with no fissionable matter left, they must go to space for the means of destruction!"

The ship went down toward one of the wide green areas. There was a city here—a far-stretching grimness of gray, massive buildings, with a movement of hoppers and ground-cars over and through it. A spaceport lay outside the city, with the silver towers of many ships there flashing back the diamond sun.

They felt the landing. Then there was silence. They waited for Vannevan to come, but he did not. Instead, armed Irrian guards came and marched them out of the ship onto a blackened concrete apron. They stood there for a few minutes, in a chill wind.

Birrel thought, shivering, *Not Earth, this world I stand on. Not my own world—*

The diamond blaze of sunlight was wrong, the color of the sky was wrong, the too-light feeling of his body was strange. The silver ship behind them, the great gray city ahead, all wrong, queer...

"Remember your plan," whispered Kara.

Birrel steadied. He had a part to play, and upon how he carried it through might depend their last slender chance. He played that part now.

He gave a vivid imitation of a man who was in a panic. He looked up at the sun and cried out and shut his eyes, and then opened them again and looked wildly around him. Then, crying out in a voice edged with hysteria, he broke back toward the spaceship.

The guards grabbed him and hauled him back. He told them shrilly, "I can't stay here, I won't stay—I want to go back—"

The Irrian guards laughed at him. When a covered vehicle not unlike a light truck came speeding up, they shoved him and Kara and Thile into it and got in after them, still laughing.

As the truck sped into the city, Birrel shivered, and looked at everything in a numb, scared way.

THE CITY WAS AS GRIM as it had looked from afar. The gray, utilitarian cement building-material used universally did not make for beauty. The men and women in the streets were mostly in a drab sort of coverall garment that was not beautiful either. Birrel saw them looking at the truck and guards as they passed, and he thought there was a sullenness in some of the watching faces. He remembered what Kara had said, that many of the Irrian people were discontented with their oligarchs' rule but were held down tightly. He thought they looked it.

The truck turned finally into a courtyard and stopped. Heavy gates were locked behind it. Birrel and the others were ordered out. He managed to get close to Kara and give her hand a reassuring touch. Then they were taken inside a building made of greenish stone, instead of cement, with ominous-looking horizontal slits in the walls in place of windows.

Inside, without a word of explanation, they were separated. Thile and Kara were marched away up a stairway while Birrel's guards took him on down a main hallway. The hall was painted a utilitarian gray and it had guards stationed at regular intervals. About halfway down there was a door with a double guard in front of it. Birrel's armed escort stopped him here, spoke to the guard, who spoke to someone inside by means of an intercom with a small video screen. Presently the door opened and Birrel was ushered inside.

Vannevan sat at one side of a big square table. A second man, older than Vannevan and that much more experienced in the ways of those who wage war out of choice and not necessity, sat behind it. His face was a mask, his curiously opaque eyes watching Birrel narrowly as the guards were sent away.

Vannevan said, "This is our Earthman." And to Birrel he said, "This is Wolt, our Minister of Defense."

Birrel refrained from making the obvious comment. From here on he was on his own and had to be careful. Any hope of advantage he might gain by making the Irrians think he was their not unwilling tool could be lost by a single incautious word.

"I understand," said Wolt, "that the Ruunites kidnapped you and brought you into space by force."

"They did."

"A serious act. And I understand that you are quite anxious to return to your world."

Birrel said eagerly, "Can I, is there any way? I can't take this, space and stars and a world I never saw. I've got to get back—"

He saw Wolt and Vannevan watching him keenly as he babbled in pretended hysteria, and he thought they looked satisfied by what they saw.

Wolt said, "Some of our ships will be going back to Earth on a mission. You could go back with them, if—"

"If?" prompted Birrel eagerly.

Vannevan answered. "You're a secret agent of a great Earth power. You could assist our mission."

Now Birrel's face became apprehensive, cautious. "Just

how do you mean that, Vannevan? Listen, I want to go back, sure. But I'm not going to betray any secrets or help you steal plutonium or—"

Wolt's hard voice cut in. "Let's consider the situation realistically. The loss of some fissionable material will make very little difference to Earth, with its enormous resources. Isn't that so?"

Cautiously, grudgingly, Birrel said that he couldn't see that it would make much difference, no.

"Now you must accept one fact. No matter what you as an individual may or may not do, we are going to take those materials. The very life of our planet depends on it. You understand that?"

"Yes."

"Very well. Now the decision that faces you is this. Will you be doing your world a greater service by denying us the information we want and thereby forcing us to take possible violent measures in carrying out our mission—or by helping us do it quietly and thus saving a great number of lives?"

"Think of the weapons we have," Vannevan said. "Think how your Earthmen are armed. You know how much chance they have of fighting us off."

Birrel thought they would have a very good chance, but he didn't say so. He frowned, and looked uneasily at the floor.

"What would you want me to do?"

"Vannevan tells me that your people are in possession of a certain probe-ray record that was taken from our man. We'd want that back."

"That's impossible," Birrel said. "The President himself couldn't get at it."

Wolt shrugged. "In that case, you would have to supply us with similar information."

There was a long silence. Then Birrel said, with just the right lack of conviction,

"No, I can't do it."

Vannevan stood up. "I think we'd better show him the cavern, Wolt. I don't believe he understands yet just how much the safety of Earth depends on him."

Wolt nodded. He rose, too, and walked to the wall. It appeared perfectly blank and solid, but under the pressure of his hand a segment of it swung in, revealing a tiny lift. The three men got in, the door closed, and the lift plunged down.

Birrel tried to keep his excitement well hidden. His act was already paying off—apparently they were about to show him something that even the Ruunites didn't know about.

Just how he might use that knowledge to help himself and his two friends he could not figure yet. But his stretch in the O. S. S. had taught him well. Keep your mind alert and flexible, play it by ear, and wait for the break that may come in a hundred ways and from the most unexpected sources.

The lift let them out onto a narrow platform beside a car that ran from a track through a tunnel hollowed roughly out of bedrock underneath the city. They got into it and the car shot through stale darkness relieved by a few dim lights. It went fast.

BIRREL STOLE A GLANCE at the other two men, and decided against any precipitate action. Vannevan had something hidden in his hand, and it would be something small and nastily potent as a weapon, he was sure. He'd wait, play it along—

There was light again, sudden and bright. The car burst into it, into vast and unexpected space. For a second Birrel thought they had come back to the surface again. Then he saw the rocky vault high overhead and the walls going away on either side and he knew it was a mammoth cavern.

The car stopped. They stepped out onto a platform.

"This way," said Wolt. "I want you to see it all."

They moved off the platform and onto a railed shelf cut out of the rocky wall. And Birrel stared in amazement.

The end of the tunnel and the shelf on which they stood were about halfway up the cavern wall. Below, and stretching away as far as he could see, rank upon rank of great metal shapes stood, some painted in dour red or gray, others naked, gleaming steel or copper. There was no one in the cavern, no sound, no movement—nothing but the brooding silence and the loom of the endless rows of enigmatic mechanisms.

Wolt and Vannevan looked down on them, with the faces of men who see a beautiful and splendid vision. And Wolt said,

"Do you know what those are?"

Birrel said, "No."

"And how should you? Your world is still in the nursery. Those are weapons—or they will be, when they are mounted in ships. Mighty weapons, which lack just one thing—the fissionable matter that must power them. The matter that our world doesn't have. Perhaps you understand now why we must raid your atomic stockpiles?"

"But," said Birrel, staring wide-eyed at the terrifying array of giants below him, "where are your ships? You'd need hundreds—"

"We have them," Vannevan said. "All we need to put at end to the domination of Ruun forever."

He turned to Birrel with an expression of serious and friendly candor that might have fooled him if he not known Vannevan so well.

"We have no interest whatsoever in Earth as a conquest. But don't overlook the fact that now the Ruunites know how rich your planet is. They might decide to take it over, just as they've taken over every world in this system but Ir. So in helping us break Ruun's power, you're actually protecting your own world. Now what do you say?"

Birrel looked out over the silent cavern with the endless ranks of deadly machines. He pretended to be miserable, torn between doubt and longing. Finally he said,

"I've got to think it over. Give me time—"

Wolt started to speak, but Vannevan shot him a look and said easily, "Of course, take all the time you want. There will be several days before the ships are ready."

"Ships?"

"Going to Earth. I'll be going with them, of course, to lead the raid. Or I should say, ahead of them. They'll wait in space until they get my signal. You could come back with me, if you decide to help."

Again, on a note of desperation, Birrel said, "I've got to think."

They took him back to the car and through the tunnel and into the building again. There guards took him upstairs and placed him in a small square room without even slits in the wall, furnished with a bed, a table, and a chair. They locked the door and left him alone there, with nothing to do and nothing to see, and nothing even to hear but the soft blowing of air through an iron-barred duct in the ceiling.

Maximum security, and no distractions. In this place a man couldn't do anything but think.

Food was brought. The guard who brought it admitted it was now night outside, but he refused to say anything about Kara and Thile, where they were or if they were still alive.

Birrel ate a little and after that the lights went off. He groped his way to the bed and lay down, trying to see a way out, a way to help Thile and Kara and stop the evil that was about to be done, and seeing only darkness.

Eventually, without meaning to, he fell asleep.

He was wakened by a sound. It was a very slight sound, and it took him a minute to identify it as the clink and creak of an iron grating being moved. By that time it was too late.

Somebody was already in the dark room, and before Birrel could call out a man's body was on top of him and strong hands were fastening on his throat.

CHAPTER NINE

BIRREL HAD BEEN CLOSE to death before, but never closer. Those hands clamped down, shutting off voice and breath, and the weight of a powerful body bore on him, holding him. He heard quick harsh breathing, and then the booming of his own blood in his ears drowned it out. He clawed at the wrists that would not be moved, and felt the first cold edge of darkness sliding over him.

Then memory circuits clicked over—circuits long unused, but needing only the right stimulus to activate them.

Birrel put his two clenched fists together and rammed them upward with the desperate strength of an animal that knows it has to shake itself loose or die. The fists hit something and there was a noise in the dark above him. The hands on his throat loosened a little and he thrashed his arms up and back at the same time he got what position he could with his feet and heaved.

The hands let go. The body floundered on him, not wanting to be thrown off. He pounded at it, wildly, viciously, gasping air into his lungs. He felt hair under his fingers. He grabbed a fistful of it and hauled it sideways. Someone whimpered and cursed, not making much noise about it. He hauled and heaved and the body rolled off him and thumped onto the floor. Instantly, Birrel threw himself on top of it.

And now it was his turn.

He dug his knee into a yielding belly and heard the breath go out. Fists flailed at his face but he kept his head pulled in between his hunched-up shoulders. He pawed in the dark and found an ear, and then another one, and he held onto them like handles and beat the skull between them up and down on the floor.

"Who is it?" he snarled. "Vannevan? No, he doesn't like his odds this even. But he sent you, didn't he?"

A hoarse, half-articulate "No!" came from the man pinned beneath him.

Birrel paused. "The devil he didn't."

"The devil he did. I'd kill that murdering bastard too, if I could get my hands on him." The man squirmed and sobbed for breath. "Anyway, why would Vannevan want to kill you? You're going to help him."

"How do you know?" asked Birrel, his eyes narrowing in the dark.

"The whole underground knows it. You're helping him get fissionables from your world. Why do you think I'm here? To keep you from doing it!"

He erupted into sudden action, catching Birrel off guard as he grappled with this new concept of an Irrian underground opposed to Vannevan. It wasn't too surprising, remembering those sullen faces in the streets... But then they were rolling over, clawing and pounding at each other. Now, though, Birrel's movements were chiefly defensive.

"Hold it," he panted. "Hold it! I've got an idea that we're on the same side."

The man laughed hoarsely and went on hunting for his throat.

"All right," said Birrel. "We'll play it your way."

He gave the man a slashing blow with the edge of his hand, guessing at the distance. It hit a little low on the shoulder, but it jarred him enough to slow him down. Birrel moved quickly. In a second he had his forearm under the man's chin, in a stranglehold. He applied pressure, and the man became quiet.

He let up. "Now will you listen?"

The man whispered, "Yes."

"There's an underground movement here, against Vannevan and Wolt and the other oligarchs?"

"Against war. We're sick of it. You must have seen what it's done to our world. So we organized ourselves when this plan to steal fissionables from another solar system came up." He struggled against Birrel's grip. "Today we heard Vannevan had brought back an Earthman who was going to help—"

"Relax," said Birrel. "I'm not going to help Vannevan do anything." He explained rapidly. "I was stalling for time, waiting for a chance to make a break. Get me out of here, and I'll prove it."

The man remained unconvinced.

IMPATIENTLY, Birrel hauled him to his feet. "Two friends of mine, Ruunites, are somewhere in this building. If you could get to me, you can get to them. I want them freed. And I want to talk to the leaders of your underground. Between us I think we might have a chance to stop Vannevan and his party for good. Anyway, what have you got to lose? If your people have me, I can't help Vannevan."

The man said, grudgingly, "Well, all right. I can get to your friends if you really want them freed. I helped build this place." He stepped away from Birrel, rubbing his throat. "Take off your shoes and any metal you have on you."

Birrel did as he was told.

"Now reach up toward the grating. You'll find a knotted rope. Be as quiet as you can."

Birrel climbed the rope, to a place where the duct became level enough to crawl in. He heard the man replace the grating behind them. Then he joined him, and they began a slow mole-like journey through the maze of air ducts that supplied these inner cells of the Ministry's private prison.

The man found his way quite easily. At every intersection of the ducts luminous code numbers glowed. "To help us when we make repairs," the man whispered, and laughed. "We use the ducts all the time for spying. I suppose tonight will finish their usefulness, but we'll find some other way."

The underground had known where Thile and Kara were imprisoned almost as soon as they had been put there. Twice the knotted rope was let down and twice gratings were removed and then replaced. Birrel went down after Kara himself and took a second or two to hold her in his arms before he lifted her into the duct.

Some time later—he had no idea how long—they had worked their way down below the level of the building and into a dry conduit that their guide said was left over from an earlier day, before the city was rebuilt. The conduit took them for some distance, and then they climbed a flight of wooden stairs into a cellar, and from there went up into the main room of a modest house, where half a dozen active and hard-faced men sat waiting.

They sprang up when Birrel and the others came in, two or three of them pulling weapons. There was a period of heated conversation, and then one of the men shouted for order and got it.

"Now then," he said, "let's hear about it. You first."

He listened, and the others listened, and all the time they watched Birrel with hatred and distrust.

Impatiently, before the man was through telling why he had not killed the Earthman, Birrel broke in on him to speak to Thile and Kara.

"They showed me something today," he said. "Vannevan and Wolt. A cavern full of armaments—enough to blow Ruun out of the sky as soon as they get the fissionable material they need."

Thile said, "We had an idea there was such a place." He

looked grimly at Kara and Birrel. "Can you imagine it? Once these weapons are armed, their ships would fill the skies over Ruun. They would blast down our buildings, our cities, our culture, anything that moved. Try to imagine the peaceful people of our planet looking up at such a sight. Try to imagine the total terror they would feel." He shook his head. "It's unthinkable. Yes...we've often suspected that such a weapons stockpile existed, but we could never pin it down."

"Neither could we," said the man who seemed to be the leader of the group. He looked hard at Birrel. "It's a mighty well-kept secret."

"There's a direct way into it from Wolt's office," Birrel said, and described it. "Now listen. If we can get away, get word to Ruun—"

"If you're thinking of ships, it's impossible. They're too well guarded on the ground, and the batteries would blow you apart before you could clear the atmosphere."

"Well, then," said Birrel, "is there any way to send a message? Can you communicate from world to world?"

"Quite easily," said Thile. "But there it comes down to the same old thing. Proof."

"For God's sake," said Birrel, "how much proof do they need?"

"Quite a bit, to get them to act in time. I assume that's what you have in mind, isn't it? Blast the cavern and destroy the armaments?"

"I want to stop that fleet from taking off for Earth. If he hasn't any way to use fissionable matter, Vannevan may not be in such a rush to get it."

The other men were listening now with intense interest. They seemed to have forgotten a lot of their distrust in the excitement of learning about the cavern. The leader, who said his name was Shannock, said fiercely,

"Those armaments have taken years of work and a fortune

in money, taxed out of our pockets. They've kept us poor, when we might have been building up trade and business on a peaceful world. If they were wiped out, the war party would go with them."

Thile said wistfully, "It's a beautiful thought. But by the time our cautious leaders on Ruun have assured themselves that they're not making a mistake, it'll be far too late."

"There must be some way," Birrel said, striding around in an agony of frustration. "Some way. Some—listen, can you transmit visually, from world to world? Could you send a picture to Ruun?"

"Of course," said Shannock, rather shocked at his ignorance. "The interplanetary automatic-relay system has been working ever since we learned how to build spaceships."

Then a queer look came over his face.

"You mean to transmit right from the cavern?"

"That would be proof enough, wouldn't it?" Birrel demanded. "If we showed them the actual cavern, down to the actual armaments?"

LOOKING A LITTLE stunned, Thile said it ought to, be proof enough for anyone. "There's just one question. How are you going to do it?"

"Technically, can it really be done?"

"With a special type of transmitter, yes."

Birrel looked at the men of the underground. "If you'll help, we ought to be able to make a pretty good try. How many men can you muster in a hurry—armed?"

"About twenty," Shannock said. "Besides us."

"And can you get portable equipment?"

"Easy. We can get into the Ministry building, too, by a way we know. But from then on we'll have to fight. Likely some of us won't make it."

"Likely," Birrel admitted, thinking privately that probably

none of them would make it all the way. "But since we're all due for the gallows one way or another, this looks like our only chance to make Wolt and Vannevan sweat. Want to try it?"

"Give me half an hour," said Shannock. His eyes blazed with a feral light.

Birrel waited. It was a little less than a half hour and it seemed like no time at all because he spent it all talking to Kara, and the things he wanted to say to her would have taken hours. Perhaps years. When finally, armed now and accompanied by twenty-seven determined men of the underground, he and Thile started back through the conduit, Kara went with them. There was no safe place to leave her, and in any case Kara was a soldier, share and share alike. She carried a weapon and walked beside Birrel, and after a while it didn't seem strange to him that she should do so, but rather as it should be.

This time they did not enter the duct system. They came through a drainage pit into an unused cellar and from there directly into the main hall of the Ministry.

It was past midnight and the building was quiet. The guards stood at their posts, but the eruption of armed men into the hall came so suddenly that they had only time for a few scattered shots before they were dropped. Shouts and sounds of alarm and running feet came from other parts of the building. Leaving one man on the floor of the hall, the attacking party rushed into Wolt's office and barred the door.

"Hold it," Birrel panted, "while I find the right stone."

He pawed frantically at the wall, trying to remember exactly where Walt had placed his hand. Outside there was a tramping of feet and a growing clamor of voices. "Can't you find it?" Thile said.

Shannock ordered his men back from the door. They grouped themselves behind Birrel with the men who carried the portable transmitter in their center. "You better find it," Shannock said, "or—"

His words were drowned in a roaring crash as the door was blown in. Weapons began to hiss and whine. "Hold them, hold them," Birrel begged. "Here it is—"

The stone shifted under his fingers. The concealed door swung open. Birrel pushed Kara through it and then the men with the transmitter. They packed into the small lift and shot down, still firing as the automatic door slammed shut. They had lost four more in the office.

"There's no guard in the cavern itself; they didn't want too many knowing about it," Birrel said. "But they'll soon be after us from this end."

They wrecked the lift door as well as they could, hoping to cripple it, and then loaded themselves into the car and raced away down the dark tunnel.

"They'll come after us, yes, but it'll take them a little time to walk," said Shannock.

THE CAR RUSHED OUT of the dark and into the cavern, stopping by the lighted platform. And in this great space of looming, silent, ugly metal shapes, their voices and the noises they made seemed loud.

Shannock rattled out orders. "Set up your transmitter on the shelf here. Wreck that car. Then we'd better split our forces. Half here to hold the tunnel, half down below in case they come in by some other way."

Thile and Kara stayed with the technicians. They were going to have to do the talking. Birrel stayed at the tunnel mouth, with Shannock's lieutenant and half the men. Shannock and the rest of the men climbed down a spiral steel stair that dropped dizzily from the shelf to the cavern floor.

They had collected extra weapons from their own fallen and from guards they had killed in the building, and with these they crouched down behind the barrier of the wrecked car.

Birrel watched the technicians out on the shelf. He had gathered that they had ways of surmounting what would have been insurmountable difficulties on Earth, using types of impulses and rectifiers and carrier-beams unknown there. The equipment did not particularly resemble television equipment as he knew it. Anyway, the technicians seemed to know what they were doing. He hoped they did. It would be a pity to go to all this trouble for nothing.

He saw Thile, and then Kara, making animated gestures as they talked into the transmitter. They were, apparently, going to have time at least to get the message on its way. Then, with terrifying unexpectedness, the voice of God seemed to speak from the air, deafening them.

"Lay down your arms!" it said. "Surrender—you are surrounded on all sides—"

"Amplifiers," said Birrel. "They must have needed them to order things done, in a place this size. Look out, now. They'll rush us any minute…"

And they did, coming out of the dark tunnel in a fury of flashing beams from their weapons.

From behind the wrecked car someone threw an energy-grenade and then another. The results were a little too good. The whole roof of the tunnel fell in, effectively blocking it to the enemy, but also sealing off any possibility of fighting their way back out through it.

Birrel looked around. Thile and Kara and the technicians were still sticking to their task. Down below, on the cavern floor, Shannock had driven back an attack, but from up here Birrel could see the men hiding among the looming machines and knew how badly Shannock was outnumbered.

He flung himself down the spiral stair, and the others followed. The loudspeakers roared monotonously overhead, ordering them to surrender. Birrel took up a position behind a huge looming metal bulk and then looked up at the shelf. Thile, Kara and the technicians had disappeared. A second later he saw them coming at breakneck speed down the stair, and in almost the same second something exploded with a blinding flash on the shelf and the transmitter vanished.

"Surrender," said the amplifiers. "We will grant you a fair trial if you do, but if you do not you will be killed to the last one. Surrender—"

Thile and Kara joined Birrel behind his metal bulwark, panting.

"Did you get through?" he cried.

"We don't know. There wasn't time to receive acknowledgement."

"Here they come!" yelled Shannock.

AND THEY CAME, slipping among the looming shapes of potential destruction, firing, killing, being killed, being for the second time driven back.

And now for a moment the amplifiers fell silent and another voice spoke close at hand. Vannevan's voice.

"Count your dead. You can't replace them, but we can. How long can you hold out?"

"As long as there's one of us left!" Shannock shouted back.

"That won't be long, will it? Don't be a fool, man. Surrender."

Birrel answered him. "You'll be the one to surrender, when the ships come from Ruun."

Vannevan laughed. "The Earthman. You still think the Ruunites will fight, eh? They won't."

They attacked again, and were again fought off—or rather, Birrel thought, they withdrew, content to hack away at their opponents' numbers without exposing themselves any more than they had to.

The amplifiers spoke again. But suddenly the voice had a different tone, and it did not talk about surrender.

"A message has just been received from Ruun. Ruunite ships will position over this target in one hour and destroy it. All persons are warned to get clear of the area at once. I report that message. Ruunite ships will position—"

Pandemonium broke out in the rebel ranks.

"You hear that, Vannevan?" Birrel shouted. "You're through."

Vannevan did not answer.

The amplifiers fell silent. Birrel looked at Thile, and then at Shannock, who said,

"They're not going away."

"Vannevan," said the amplifiers, "this is Wolt. I am leaving as of now and I advise you to do so. There's no virtue like knowing when it's time to run."

Still there was no sound or sign from Vannevan.

The amplifiers were silent. In the distance were noises made by people going away.

One of the men, impatient, sprang up and into the open aisle between the machines. "Hell," he said, "they must have gone. We'd better..."

He died between words, and suddenly from where they had crept close seven or eight men sprang out and rushed, firing. Vannevan led them. There would be no peace, no surrender, no flight for Vannevan.

He saw Birrel with Thile and Kara and he smiled and flung his weapon up, and Birrel shot him just before his finger touched the firing-stud.

Those of the seven or eight who were still alive threw their weapons down.

Shannock said, "I guess we can go now."

They followed the captive soldiers to the far entrance of

the cavern, leaving Vannevan where he had fallen among the machines.

An hour later, Birrel stood with the others in the forefront of a close-packed crowd outside the city, and watched the great Ruunite ships position over a particular spot. Mighty lightnings crashed downward from their bellies. Smoke and dust and shattered rock rose in a vast cloud, and settled again, and there was a huge gaping hole in the ground, and still the lightnings pounded at it until there was nothing left of the cavern or anything it had contained.

Shannock and his men cheered mightily. The bulk of the Irrian crowd watched silently, not used yet to the idea of peace.

Birrel, oddly enough, was not thinking of Ruun or Ir, but of Earth.

CHAPTER TEN

THE SHIP SWEPT IN toward the night side of Earth in a great curve, and first of all Earthmen that had ever lived, Birrel felt the sharp, nostalgic emotion of coming back to the world that would always be "the" world.

He was in the bridge with Thile arid Kara. Kara was very silent, looking at the shadowed planet-face ahead, not looking at Birrel at all. But Thile was busy, and vocal about it.

"It's hard enough to make a landing on a strange planet," he said. "But to have to do it secretly, without being seen—well, I'm glad this will be the last time."

The last time, Birrel thought. The last ship that would come from the stars to Earth—at least, for a long, long time. He didn't like that thought. He had argued against it, back there at the other system, at Ruun.

The men who governed Ruun were wise and well-meaning men—but obstinate. They had welcomed Birrel. They had been grateful to him. They had agreed to return him to his own world. But on one thing, they were adamant. There would be no sudden opening up of the starways, no open contact between Ruun and Earth.

Birrel, his head full of visions of a sudden leap into the stars by the men of Earth, had pleaded. But in vain.

"Your world Earth is not ready," had said the leader of the Council of Ruun. "It is not even one world, yet. When it has become one—when it has forgotten the folly of wars and weapons—then we will not need to come to you. You will come to us."

He had softened that final refusal by an offer. "But you, who have done much for us, can stay here at Ruun if you wish."

"I can't," Birrel had said heavily. "I'm an agent, with a mission. If I didn't go back, those who sent me would never know what happened—they'd live in perpetual apprehension of attack from outside. I have to return with my report."

"Then you will be taken. And after that, no more of our ships will go there."

And now this last ship from outside was quietly coming down toward the nighted face of Earth, and Kara still was silent, and there was a sickness in Birrel's heart.

Thile, by the control panel, told the helmsman, "Now softly, softly...are you trying to wake the whole damned continent? Softly...*ahhh!*"

They had landed.

Thile and Kara went down the ladder in the darkness, with Birrel. They stood with him by the loom of the ship.

The tall trees around them were black and vague, but the smell of pine was on the keen air, and the smells, the sounds, the feel of everything was subtly right again.

"We landed a lot farther south than last time, so you can soon find a road and people," said Thile. "Well, lad—"

He shook hands with Birrel, and then he turned and shook hands with Kara, and kissed her, and said, "You're a bloody fool but I'd do the same thing," and turned and started back up the ladder.

Birrel said, finally, "Kara—"

"Yes," she said. "I'm staying."

He took her in his arms and could only speak her name again, and then she said, "We have to stand clear, before the ship takes off."

"I can't let you do this!" he cried. "It's why I wouldn't ask you to do it. No ship will come again, and you'll weary of it here, and—"

"Yes, yes," she said, as one might quiet a troubled child. "I know all that. But right now, we must get clear of the ship."

Minutes later, from a ridge a thousand yards away, they heard a boom of thunder and saw a quickly-muffled blast of flame, and then glimpsed the great silver bulk riding skyward, vanishing almost at once.

Birrel, holding Kara, looked up with her into the starry sky and saw the flying shadow against the stars, that was there for an instant and then was not there at all.

He wondered if, in the years ahead, she would look more and more with memory and longing at that starry sky. He hoped, he prayed, that she would not.

THE END

If you've enjoyed this book, you will not want to miss these terrific titles...

ARMCHAIR SCI-FI & HORROR DOUBLE NOVELS, $12.95 each

D-71 **THE DEEP END** by Gregory Luce
TO WATCH BY NIGHT by Robert Moore Williams

D-72 **SWORDSMAN OF LOST TERRA** by Poul Anderson
PLANET OF GHOSTS by David V. Reed

D-73 **MOON OF BATTLE** by J. J. Allerton
THE MUTANT WEAPON by Murray Leinster

D-74 **OLD SPACEMEN NEVER DIE!** John Jakes
RETURN TO EARTH by Bryan Berry

D-75 **THE THING FROM UNDERNEATH** by Milton Lesser
OPERATION INTERSTELLAR by George O. Smith

D-76 **THE BURNING WORLD** by Algis Budrys
FOREVER IS TOO LONG by Chester S. Geier

D-77 **THE COSMIC JUNKMAN** by Rog Phillips
THE ULTIMATE WEAPON by John W. Campbell

D-78 **THE TIES OF EARTH** by James H. Schmitz
CUE FOR QUIET by Thomas L. Sherred

D-79 **SECRET OF THE MARTIANS** by Paul W. Fairman
THE VARIABLE MAN by Philip K. Dick

D-80 **THE GREEN GIRL** by Jack Williamson
THE ROBOT PERIL by Don Wilcox

ARMCHAIR SCIENCE FICTION CLASSICS, $12.95 each

C-25 **THE STAR KINGS**
by Edmond Hamilton

C-26 **NOT IN SOLITUDE**
by Kenneth Gantz

C-32 **PROMETHEUS II**
by S. J. Byrne

ARMCHAIR SCIENCE FICTION & HORROR GEMS SERIES, $12.95 each

G-7 **SCIENCE FICTION GEMS, Vol. Four**
Jack Sharkey and others

G-8 **HORROR GEMS, Vol. Four**
Seabury Quinn and others

If you've enjoyed this book, you will not want to miss these terrific titles…

ARMCHAIR SCI-FI, FANTASY, & HORROR DOUBLE NOVELS, $12.95 each

D-81   **THE LAST PLEA** by Robert Bloch
          THE STATUS CIVILIZATION by Robert Sheckley

D-82   **WOMAN FROM ANOTHER PLANET** by Frank Belknap Long
          HOMECALLING by Judith Merril

D-83   **WHEN TWO WORLDS MEET** by Robert Moore Williams
          THE MAN WHO HAD NO BRAINS by Jeff Sutton

D-84   **THE SPECTRE OF SUICIDE SWAMP** by E. K. Jarvis
          IT'S MAGIC, YOU DOPE! by Jack Sharkey

D-85   **THE STARSHIP FROM SIRIUS** by Rog Phillips
          FINAL WEAPON by Everett Cole

D-86   **TREASURE ON THUNDER MOON** by Edmond Hamilton
          TRAIL OF THE ASTROGAR by Henry Haase

D-87   **THE VENUS ENIGMA** by Joe Gibson
          THE WOMAN IN SKIN 13 by Paul W. Fairman

D-88   **THE MAD ROBOT** by William P. McGivern
          THE RUNNING MAN by J. Holly Hunter

D-89   **VENGEANCE OF KYVOR** by Randall Garrett
          AT THE EARTH'S CORE by Edgar Rice Burroughs

D-90   **DWELLERS OF THE DEEP** by Don Wilcox
          NIGHT OF THE LONG KNIVES by Fritz Leiber

ARMCHAIR SCIENCE FICTION CLASSICS, $12.95 each

C-28   **THE MAN FROM TOMORROW**
          by Stanton A. Cobllentz

C-29   **THE GREEN MAN OF GRAYPEC**
          by Festus Pragnell

C-30   **THE SHAVER MYSTERY, Book Four**
          by Richard S. Shaver

ARMCHAIR MASTERS OF SCIENCE FICTION SERIES, $16.95 each

MS-7   **MASTERS OF SCIENCE FICTION AND FANTASY, Vol. Seven**
          Lester del Rey, "The Band Played On" and other tales

MS-8   **MASTERS OF SCIENCE FICTION, Vol. Eight**
          Milton Lesser, "'A' is for Android" and other tales

If you've enjoyed this book, you will not want to miss these terrific titles...

ARMCHAIR SCI-FI & HORROR DOUBLE NOVELS, $12.95 each

D-91   **THE TIME TRAP** by Henry Kuttner
THE LUNAR LICHEN by Hal Clement

D-92   **SARGASSO OF LOST STARSHIPS** by Poul Anderson
THE ICE QUEEN by Don Wilcox

D-93   **THE PRINCE OF SPACE** by Jack Williamson
POWER by Harl Vincent

D-94   **PLANET OF NO RETURN** by Howard Browne
THE ANNIHILATOR COMES by Ed Earl Repp

D-95   **THE SINISTER INVASION** by Edmond Hamilton
OPERATION TERROR by Murray Leinster

D-96   **THE WORLD-MOVER** by George O. Smith
TRANSIENT by Ward Moore

D-97   **FORTY DAYS HAS SEPTEMBER** by Milton Lesser
THE DEVIL'S PLANET by David Wright O'Brien

D-98   **THE CYBERENE** by Rog Phillips
BADGE OF INFAMY by Lester del Rey

D-99   **THE VENGEANCE OF MARTIN BRAND** by Raymond A. Palmer
THE JUSTICE OF MARTIN BRAND by Raymond A. Palmer

D-100 **WIDE-OPEN PLANET** by L. Sprague de Camp
ULLR UPRISING by H. Beam Piper

ARMCHAIR SCIENCE FICTION CLASSICS, $12.95 each

C-31   **THE GOLDEN GUARDSMEN**
by S. J. Byrne

C-32   **ONE AGAINST THE MOON**
by Donald A. Wollheim

C-33   **HIDDEN CITY**
by Chester S. Geier

ARMCHAIR SCIENCE FICTION & HORROR GEMS SERIES, $12.95 each

G-9   **SCIENCE FICTION GEMS, Vol. Five**
Clifford D. Simak and others

G-10   **HORROR GEMS, Vol. Five**
E. Hoffman Price and others

THE COMING OF ALIENS TO EARTH

The radar complex had picked up the strange object in space just as it neared the Earth's surface. It was described as "an object of considerable size." The impact of its landing at Boulder Lake Park, Colorado was felt on every seismograph around the world. Then, the first reports began to trick in: there were "creatures" on board—creatures who soon left their ship and began exploring the area…

Where was the ship from, and what was the quest of the strange visitors— these visitors who were armed with a terrifying paralysis ray that blinded its victims, filling their nostrils with a reptilian odor of the jungle? Only one man in the area could hope to solve the mystery of these aliens—aliens who had come to call Earth "theirs."

ABOUT MURRAY LEINSTER

Murray Leinster...

...was born William F. Jenkins on June 16th, 1896 in Norfolk, Va. His writing career began in 1916 with the publishing of his first story, "The Foreigner" in *The Smart Set* magazine. Although he is considered one of the great writers of the science fiction genre, in his early years Leinster wrote many tales in other genres: jungle, mystery, horror, and western. Leinster broke into the science fiction field with his story, "The Runaway Skyscraper," which appeared in a 1919 issue of *Argosy* magazine. During the '30s, '40s, '50s, and '60s Leinster was a regular contributor to well-known pulp and digest magazines such as *Astounding Stories, Amazing Stories,* and *Weird Tales*. Leinster is considered the father of "parallel universe" stories with the publication of his 1934 story, "Sidewise in Time." During his long career Leinster was nominated for many writing awards, including the coveted Hugo Award, which he won in 1956 for his novelette, "Exploration Team." During his science fiction career, Leinster published over 30 novels and over 170 short stories. He passed away on June 8th, 1975.

OPERATION TERROR

By
MURRAY LEINSTER

ARMCHAIR FICTION
PO Box 4369, Medford, Oregon   97501-0168

*For more information about Armchair Books and products, visit our
website at…*

www.armchairfiction.com

Or email us at…

armchairfiction@yahoo.com

CHAPTER ONE

On the morning the radar reported something odd out in space, Lockley awoke at about twenty minutes to eight. That was usual. He'd slept in a sleeping bag on a mountain-flank with other mountains all around. That was not unprecedented. He was there to make a base line measurement for a detailed map of the Boulder Lake National Park, whose facilities were now being built. Measuring a base line, even with the newest of electronic apparatus, was more or less a commonplace job for Lockley.

This morning, though, he woke and realized gloomily that he'd dreamed about Jill Holmes again, which was becoming a habit he ought to break. He'd only met her four times and she was going to marry somebody else. He had to stop.

He stirred, preparatory to getting up. At the same moment, certain things were happening in places far away from him. As yet, no unusual object in space had been observed. That would come later. But far away up at the Alaskan radar complex a man on duty watch was relieved by another. The relief man took over the monitoring of the giant, football-field-sized radar antenna that recorded its detections on magnetic tape. It happened that on this particular morning only one other radar watched the skies along a long stretch of the Pacific Coast. There was the Alaskan installation, and the other was in Oregon. It was extremely unusual for only those two to be operating. The people who knew about it, or most of them, thought that official orders had somehow gone astray. Where the orders were issued, nothing out of the ordinary appeared. All was normal, for example, in the Military Information Center in Denver. The Survey saw nothing unusual in Lockley's being at his post, and other men at places corresponding to his in the area which was to become Boulder Lake National Park. It also seemed perfectly natural that there should be bulldozer operators, surveyors, steelworkers, concrete men and so on, all comfortably at breakfast in the construction camp for the project. Everything seemed normal everywhere.

Up to the time the Alaskan installation reported something strange in space, the state of things generally was neither alarming nor consoling. But at 8:02 a.m. Pacific time, the situation changed. At that time Alaska reported an unscheduled celestial object of considerable size, high out of atmosphere and moving with surprising slowness for a body in space. Its course was parabolic and it would probably land somewhere in South Dakota. It might be a bolide—a large, slow-moving meteorite. It wasn't likely, but the entire report was improbable.

The message reached the Military Information Center in Denver at 8:05 a.m. By 8:06 it had been relayed to Washington and every plane on the Pacific Coast was ordered aloft. The Oregon radar unit reported the same object at 8:07 a.m. It said the object was seven hundred fifty miles high, four hundred miles out at sea, and was headed toward the Oregon coastline, moving northwest to southeast. There was no major city in its line of travel. The impact point computed by the Oregon station was nowhere near South Dakota. As other computations followed other observations, a second place of fall was calculated, then a third. Then the Oregon radar unbelievably reported that the object was decelerating. Allowing for deceleration, three successive predictions of its landing point agreed. The object, said these calculations, would come to earth somewhere near Boulder Lake, Colorado, in what was to become a national park. Impact time should be approximately 8:14 a.m.

These events followed Lockley's awakening in the wilds, but he knew nothing of any of them. He himself wasn't near the lake, which was to be the center of a vacation facility for people who liked the outdoors. The lake was almost circular and was a deep, rich blue. It occupied what had been the crater of a volcano millions of years ago. Already bulldozers had ploughed out roads to it through the forest. Men worked with graders and concrete mixers on highways and on bridges across small rushing streams. There was a camp for them. A lakeside hotel had been designed and stakes were driven in the ground where its foundation would eventually be poured. There were infant big-mouthed bass in the lake and fingerling trout in many of the streams. A huge Wild Life Control trailer-truck went grumbling about such trails as were practical, attending to these matters. Yesterday Lockley had seen it gleaming in bright sunshine as it moved toward Boulder Lake on the highway nearest to his station.

But that was yesterday. This morning he awoke under a pale gray sky. There was complete cloud cover overhead. He smelled conifers and woods-mould and mountain stone in the morning. He heard the faint sound of tree branches moving in the wind. He noted the cloud cover. The clouds were high, though. The air at ground level was perfectly transparent. He turned his head and saw a prospect that made being in the wilderness seem entirely reasonable and satisfying.

Mountains reared up in every direction. A valley lay some thousands of feet below him, and beyond it other valleys, and somewhere a stream rushed white water to an unknown destination. Not many wake to such a scene.

Lockley regarded it, but without full attention. He was preoccupied with thoughts of Jill Holmes, and unfortunately she was engaged to marry Vale, who was also working in the park some thirty miles to the northeast, near Boulder Lake itself. Lockley didn't know him well since he was new in the Survey. He was up there to the northeast with an electronic survey instrument like Lockley's and on the same job. Jill had an assignment from some magazine or other to write an article on how national parks are born, and she was staying at the construction camp to gather material. She'd learned something from Vale and much from the engineers while Lockley had tried to think of interesting facts himself. He'd failed. When he thought about her, he thought about the fact that she was engaged to Vale. That was an unhappy thought. Then he tried to stop thinking about her altogether. But his mind somehow lingered on the subject.

At ten minutes to eight Lockley began to dress, wilderness fashion. He began by putting on his hat. It had lain on the pile of garments by his bed. Then he donned the rest of his garments in the exact reverse of the order in which he'd removed them.

At 8:00 he had a small fire going. He had no premonition that anything out of the ordinary was going to happen that day. This was still before the first Alaskan report. At 8:10 he had bacon sizzling and a small coffeepot almost enveloped by the flames. Events occurred and he knew nothing at all about them. For example, the Military Information Center had been warned of what was later privately called Operation Terror while Lockley was still tranquilly cooking breakfast and thinking—frowning a little—about Jill.

Naturally he knew nothing of emergency orders sending all planes aloft. He wasn't informed about something reported in space and apparently headed for an impact point at Boulder Lake. As the computed impact time arrived, Lockley obliviously dumped coffee into his tin coffeepot and put it back on the flames.

At 8:13 instead of 8:14—this information is from the tape records—there was an extremely small earth shock recorded by the Berkeley, California, seismograph. It was a very minor shock, about the intensity of the explosion of a hundred tons of high explosive a very long distance away and barely strong enough to record its location, which was Boulder Lake. The cause of that explosion or shock was not observed visually. There'd been no time to alert observers, and in any case the object should have been out of atmosphere until the last few seconds of its fall, and where it was reported to fall the cloud cover was unbroken. So nobody reported seeing it. Not at once, anyhow, and then only one man.

Lockley did not feel the impact. He was drinking a cup of coffee and thinking about his own problems. But a delicately balanced rock a hundred yards below his camp site toppled over and slid downhill. It started a miniature avalanche of stones and rocks. The loose stuff did not travel far, but the original balanced rock bounced and rolled for some distance before it came to rest.

Echoes rolled between the hillsides, but they were not very loud and they soon ended. Lockley guessed automatically at half a dozen possible causes for the small rock-slide, but he did not think at all of an unperceived temblor from a shock like high explosives going off thirty miles away.

Eight minutes later he heard a deep-toned roaring noise to the northeast. It was unbelievably low-pitched. It rolled and reverberated beyond the horizon. The detonation of a hundred tons of high explosives or an equivalent impact can be heard for thirty miles, but at that distance it doesn't sound much like an explosion.

He finished his breakfast without enjoyment. By that time well over three-quarters of the Air Force on the Pacific Coast was airborne and more planes shot skyward instant after instant. Inevitably the multiplied air traffic was noted by civilians. Reporters began to telephone airbases to ask whether a practice alert was on, or something more serious.

Such questions were natural, these days. All the world had the jitters. To the ordinary observer, the prospects looked bad for everything but disaster. There was a crisis in the United Nations, which had been reorganized once and might need to be shuffled again. There was a dispute between the United States and Russia over satellites recently placed in orbit. They were suspected of carrying fusion bombs ready to dive at selected targets on signal. The Russians accused the Americans, and the Americans accused the Russians, and both may have been right.

The world had been so edgy for so long that there were fallout shelters from Chillicothe, Ohio, to Singapore, Malaya, and back again. There were permanent trouble spots at various places where practically anything was likely to happen at any instant. The people of every nation were jumpy. There was constant pressure on governments and on political parties so that all governments looked shaky and all parties helpless. Nobody could look forward to a peaceful old age, and most hardly hoped to reach middle age. The arrival of an object from outer space was nicely calculated to blow the emotional fuses of whole populations.

But Lockley ate his breakfast without premonitions. Breezes blew and from every airbase along the coast fighting planes shot into the air and into formations designed to intercept anything that flew on wings or to launch atom-headed rockets at anything their radars could detect that didn't.

At eight-twenty, Lockley went to the electronic base line instrument which he was to use this morning. It was a modification of the devices used to clock artificial satellites in their orbits and measure their distance within inches from hundreds of miles away. The purpose was to make a really accurate map of the park. There were other instruments in other line-of-sight positions, very far away. Lockley's schedule called for them to measure their distances from each other some time this morning. Two were carefully placed on bench marks of the continental grid. In twenty minutes or so of cooperation, the distances of six such instruments could be measured with astonishing precision and tied in to the bench marks already scattered over the continent. Presently photographing planes would fly overhead, taking overlapping pictures from thirty thousand feet. They would show the survey points and the measurements between them would be exact, the photos could be used as stereo-pairs to take off contour lines, and in a few days there would be a map—a veritable cartographer's dream for accuracy and detail.

That was the intention. But though Lockley hadn't heard of it yet, something was reported to have landed from space, and a shock like an impact was recorded, and all conditions would shortly be changed. It would be noted from the beginning, however, that an impact equal to a hundred-ton explosion was a very small shock for the landing of a bolide. It would add to the plausibility of reported deceleration, though, and would arouse acute suspicion. Justly so.

At 8:20, Lockley called Sattell who was southeast of him. The measuring instruments used microwaves and gave readings of distance by counting cycles and reading phase differences. As a matter of convenience the microwaves could be modulated by a microphone, so the same instrument could be used for communication while measurements went on. But the microwaves were directed in a very tight beam. The device had to be aimed exactly right and a suitable reception instrument had to be at the target if it was to be used at all. Also, there was no signal to call a man to listen. He had to be listening beforehand, and with his instrument aimed right, too.

So Lockley flipped the modulator switch and turned on the instrument. He said patiently, "Calling Sattell. Calling Sattell. Lockley calling Sattell."

He repeated it some dozens of times. He was about to give it up and call Vale instead when Sattell answered. He'd slept a little later than Lockley. It was now close to nine o'clock. But Sattell had expected the call. They checked the functioning of their instruments against each other.

"Right!" said Lockley at last. "I'll check with Vale and on out of the park, and then we'll put it all together and wrap it up and take it home."

Sattell agreed. Lockley, rather absurdly, felt uncomfortable because he was going to have to talk to Vale. He had nothing against the man, but Vale was, in a way, his rival although Jill didn't know of his folly and Vale could hardly guess it.

He signed off to Sattell and swung the base line instrument to make a similar check with Vale. It was now ten minutes after nine. He aligned the instrument accurately, flipped the switch, and began to say as patiently as before, "Calling Vale. Calling Vale. Lockley calling Vale. Over."

He turned the control for reception. Vale's voice came instantly, scratchy and hoarse and frantic.

"Lockley! Listen to me! There's no time to tell me anything. I've got to tell you. Something came down out of the sky here nearly an hour ago. It landed in Boulder Lake, and at the last instant there was a terrific explosion and a monstrous wave swept up the shores of the lake. The thing that came down vanished under water. I saw it, Lockley!"

Lockley blinked. "Wha-a-at?"

"A thing came down out of the sky!" panted Vale. *"It landed in the lake with a terrific explosion. It went under. Then it came up to the surface minutes later. It floated. It stuck things up and out of itself, pipes or wires. Then it moved around the lake and came in to the shore. A thing like a hatch opened and…creatures got out of it. Not men!"*

Lockley blinked again. "Look here—"

"Dammit, listen!" said Vale shrilly, *"I'm telling you what I've seen. Things out of the sky. Creatures that aren't men. They landed and set up something on the shore. I don't know what it is. Do you understand? The thing is down there in the lake now. Floating. I can see it!"*

Lockley swallowed. He couldn't believe this immediately. He knew nothing of radar reports or the seismograph record. He'd seen a barely balanced rock roll down the mountainside below him, and he'd heard a growling bass rumble behind the horizon, but things like that didn't add up to a conclusion like this! His first conviction was that Vale was out of his head.

"Listen," said Lockley carefully. "There's a short wave set over at the construction camp. They use it all the time for orders and reports and so on. You go there and report officially what you've seen. To the Park Service first, and then try to get a connection through to the Army."

Vale's voice came through again, at once raging and despairing, *"They won't believe me. They'll think I'm a crackpot. You get the news to somebody who'll investigate. I see the thing, Lockley. I can see it now. At this instant. And Jill's over at the construction camp—"*

Lockley was unreasonably relieved. If Jill was at the camp, at least she wasn't alone with a man gone out of his mind. The reaction was normal. Lockley had seen nothing out of the ordinary, so Vale's report seemed insane.

"*Listen here!*" panted Vale again. "*The thing came down. There was a terrific explosion. It vanished. Nothing happened for a while. Then it came up and found a place where it could come to shore. Things came out of it. I can't describe them. They're motes even in my binoculars. But they aren't human! A lot of them came out. They began to land things. Equipment. They set it up. I don't know what it is. Some of them went exploring. I saw a puff of steam where something moved. Lockley?*"

"I'm listening," said Lockley. "Go on!"

"*Report this!*" ordered Vale feverishly. "*Get it to Military Information in Denver, or somewhere! The party of creatures that went off exploring hasn't come back. I'm watching. I'll report whatever I see. Get this to the government. This is real. I can't believe it, but I see it. Report it, quick!*"

His voice stopped. Lockley painfully realigned the instrument again for Sattell, thirty miles to the southeast.

Sattell surprisingly answered the first call. He said in an astonished voice, "*Hello! I just got a call from Survey. It seems that the Army knew there was a Survey team in here, and they called to say that radars had spotted something coming down from space, right after eight o'clock. They wanted to know if any of us supposedly sane observers noticed anything peculiar about that time.*"

Lockley's scalp crawled suddenly. Vale's report had disturbed him, but more for the man's sanity than anything else. But it could be true! And instantly he remembered that Jill was very near the place where frighteningly impossible things were happening.

"Vale just told me," said Lockley, his voice unsteady, "that he saw something come down. His story was so wild I didn't believe it. But you pass it on and say that Vale's watching it. He's waiting for instructions. He'll report everything he sees. I'm thirty miles from him, but he can see the thing that came down. Maybe the creatures in it can see him. Listen!"

He repeated just what Vale had told him. Somehow, telling it to someone else, it seemed at once even less real but more horrifying as a possible danger to Jill. It didn't strike him forcibly that other people were endangered, too.

When Sattell signed off to forward the report, Lockley found himself sweating a little. Something had come down out of space. The fact seemed to him dangerous and appalling. His mind revolted at the idea of non-human creatures who could build ships and travel through space, but radars had reported the arrival of a ship, and there were official inquiries that nearly matched Vale's account, which was therefore not a mere crackpot claim to have seen the incredible. Something had happened and more was likely to, and Jill was in the middle of it.

He swung the instrument back to Vale's position. His hands shook, though a part of his mind insisted obstinately that alarms were commonplace these days, and in common sense one had to treat them as false cries of "Wolf!" But one knew that some day the wolf might really come. Perhaps it had...

Lockley found it difficult to align the carrier beam to Vale's exact location. He assured himself that he was a fool to be afraid; that if disaster were to come it would be by the imbecilities of men rather than through creatures from beyond the stars. And therefore...

But there were other men at other places who felt less skepticism. The report from Vale went to the Military Information Center and thence to the Pentagon. Meanwhile the Information Center ordered a photo-reconnaissance plane to photograph Boulder Lake from aloft. In the Pentagon, hastily alerted staff officers began to draft orders to be issued if the report of two radars and one eye-witness should be further substantiated. There were such-and-such trucks available here, and such-and-such troops available there. Complicated paper work was involved in the organization of any movement of troops, but especially to carry out a plan not at all usual in the United States.

Everything, though, depended on what the reconnaissance plane photographs might show.

Lockley did not see the plane nor consciously hear it. There was the faintest of murmuring noises in the sky. It moved swiftly toward the north, tending eastward. The plane that made the noise was invisible. It flew above the cloud cover which still blotted out nearly all the blue overhead. It went on and on and presently died out beyond the mountains toward Boulder Lake.

Lockley tried to get Vale back, to tell him that radars had verified his report and that it would be acted on by the military. But though he called and called, there was no answer.

An agonizingly long time later the faint and disregarded sound of the plane swept back across the heavens. Lockley still did not notice it. He was too busy with his attempts to reach Vale again, and with grisly imaginings of what might be done by aliens from another world when they found the workmen near the lake—and Jill among them. He pictured alien monsters committing atrocities in what they might consider scientific examination of terrestrial fauna. But somehow even that was less horrible than the images that followed an assumption that the occupants of the spaceship might be men.

"Calling Vale…Vale, come in!" He fiercely repeated the call into the instrument's microphone. "Lockley calling Vale! Come in, man! Come in!"

He flipped the switch and listened. And Vale's voice came.

"*I'm here.*" The voice shook. "*I've been trying to find where that exploring party went.*"

Lockley threw the speech switch and said sharply, "The Army asked Survey if any of us had seen anything come down from the sky. I gave Sattell your report to be forwarded. It's gone to the Pentagon now. Two radars reported tracking the thing down to a landing near you. Now listen! You go to the construction camp. Most likely they'll get orders to clear out, by short wave. But you go there! Make sure Jill's all right. See her to safety."

The switch once more. Vale's voice was desperate.

"A…while ago a party of the creatures started away from the lake. An exploring party, I think. Once I saw a puff of steam as if they'd used a weapon. I'm afraid they may find the construction camp, and Jill…"

Lockley ground his teeth. Vale said unsteadily, *"I…can't find where they went… A little while ago their ship backed out into the lake and sank. Deliberately! I don't know why. But there's a party of those…creatures out exploring! I don't know what they'll do…"*

Lockley said savagely, "Get to the camp and look after Jill! The workmen may have panicked. The Army'll know by this time what's happened. They'll send copters to get you out. They'll send help of some sort, somehow. But you look after Jill!"

Vale's voice changed.

"Wait. I heard something. Wait!"

Silence. Around Lockley there were the usual sounds of the wilderness. Insects made chirping noises. Birds called. There were those small whispering and rustling and high-pitched sounds which in the wild constitute stillness.

A scraping sound from the speaker. Vale's voice, frantic.

"That…exploring party. It's here! They must have picked up our beams. They're looking for me. They've sighted me! They're coming…"

There was a crashing sound as if Vale had dropped the communicator. There were pantings, and the sound of blows, and gasped profanity—horror-filled profanity—in Vale's voice. Then something roared.

Lockley listened, his hands clenched in fury at his own helplessness. He thought he heard movements. Once he was sure he heard a sound like the unshod hoof of an animal on bare stone. Then, quite distinctly, he heard squeakings. He knew that someone or something had picked up Vale's communicator. More squeakings, somehow querulous. Then something pounded the communicator on the ground. There was a crash. Then silence.

Almost calmly Lockley swung his instrument around and lined it up for Sattell's post. He called in a steady voice until

Sattell answered. He reported with meticulous care just what Vale had said, and what he'd heard after Vale stopped speaking—the roaring, the sound of blows and gasps, then the squeakings and the destruction of the instrument intended for the measurement of base lines for an accurate map of the Park.

Sattell grew agitated. At Lockley's insistence, he wrote down every word. Then he said nervously that orders had come from Survey. The Army wanted everybody out of the Boulder Lake area. Vale was to have been ordered out. The workmen were ordered out. Lockley was to get out of the area as soon as possible.

When Sattell signed off, Lockley switched off the communicator. He put it where it would be relatively safe from the weather. He abandoned his camping equipment. A mile downhill and four miles west there was a highway leading to Boulder Lake. When the Park was opened to the public it would be well used, but the last traffic he'd seen was the big trailer-truck of the Wild Life Control service. That huge vehicle had gone up to Boulder Lake the day before.

He made his way to the highway, following a footpath to the spot where he'd left his own car parked. He got into it and started the motor. He moved with a certain dogged deliberation. He knew, of course, that what he was going to do was useless. It was hopeless. It was possibly suicidal. But he went ahead.

He headed northward, pushing the little car to its top speed. This was not following his instructions. He wasn't leaving the Park area. He was heading for Boulder Lake. Jill was there and he would feel ashamed for all time if he acted like a sensible man and got to safety as he was ordered.

Miles along the highway, something occurred to him. The base line instrument had to be aimed exactly right for Vale or Sattell to pick up his voice as carried by its beam. Vale's or Sattell's instruments had to be aimed as accurately to convey their voices to him. Yet after the struggle he'd overheard, and after Vale had been either subdued or killed, someone or something seemed to have picked up the communicator, and Lockley had heard squeakings, and then he had heard the instrument smashed.

It was not easy to understand how the beam had been kept perfectly aligned while it was picked up and squeaked at. Still less was it understandable that it remained aimed just right so he could hear when it was flung down and crushed.

But somehow this oddity did not change his feelings. Jill could be in danger from creatures Vale said were not human. Lockley didn't wholly accept that non-human angle, but something was happening there and Jill was in the middle of it. So he went to see about it for the sake of his self-respect. And Jill. It was not reasonable behavior. It was emotional. He didn't stop to question what was believable and what wasn't. Lockley didn't even give any attention to the problem of how a microwave beam could stay pointed exactly right while the instrument that sent it was picked up, and squeaked at, and smashed. He gave that particular matter no thought at all.

He jammed down the accelerator of the car and headed for Boulder Lake.

CHAPTER TWO

The car was ordinary enough; it was one of those scaled-down vehicles which burn less fuel and offer less comfort than the so-called standard models. For fuel economy too, its speed had been lowered. But Lockley sent it up the brand-new highway as fast as it would go.

Now the highway followed a broad valley with a meadow-like floor. Now it seemed to pick its way between cliffs, and on occasion it ran over a concrete bridge spanning some swiftly flowing stream. At least once it went through a cut which might as well have been a tunnel, and the crackling noise of its motor echoed back from stony walls on either side.

He did not see another vehicle for a long way. Deer, he saw twice. Over and over again coveys of small birds rocketed up from beside the road and dived to cover after he had passed. Once he saw movement out of the corner of his eye and looked automatically to see what it was, but saw nothing. Which meant that it was probably a mountain lion, blending perfectly with its background as it watched the car. At the end of five miles he saw a motor truck, empty, trundling away from Boulder Lake and the construction camp toward the outer world.

The two vehicles passed, combining to make a momentary roaring noise at their nearest. The truck was not in a hurry. It simply lumbered along with loose objects in its cargo space rattling and bumping loudly. Its driver and his helper plainly knew nothing of untoward events behind them. They'd probably stopped somewhere to have a leisurely morning snack, with the truck waiting for them at the roadside.

Lockley went on ten miles more. He begrudged the distances added by curves in the road. He tended to fume when his underpowered car noticeably slowed up on grades, and especially the long ones. He saw a bear halfway up a hillside pause in its exploitation of a berry patch to watch the car go by below it. He saw more deer. Once a smaller animal, probably a coyote, dived into a patch of brushwood and stayed hidden as long as the car remained in sight.

More miles of empty highway. And then a long, straight stretch of road, and he suddenly saw vehicles coming around the curve at the end of it. They were not in line, singlelane, as traffic usually is on a curve. Both lanes were filled. The road was blocked by motor-driven traffic heading away from the lake, and not at a steady pace, but in headlong flight.

It roared on toward Lockley. Big trucks and little ones; passenger cars in between them; a few motorcyclists catching up from the rear by riding on the road's shoulders. They were closely packed, as if by some freak the lead had been taken by great trucks incapable of the road speed of those behind them, yet with the frantic rearmost cars unable to pass. There was a humming and roaring of motors that filled the air. They plunged toward Lockley's miniature roadster. Truck horns blared.

Lockley got off the highway and onto the right-hand shoulder. He stopped. The crowded mass of rushing vehicles roared up to him and went past. They were more remarkable than he'd believed. There were dirt mover trucks. There were truck-and-trailer combinations. There were sedans and dump trucks and even a convertible or two, and then more trucks— even tank trucks—and more sedans and half-tonners—a complete and motley collection of every kind of gasoline-driven vehicle that could be driven on a highway and used on a construction project.

And every one was crowded with men. Trailer-trucks had their body doors open, and they were packed with the workmen of the construction camp near Boulder Lake. The sedans were jammed with passengers. Dirt mover trucks had men holding fast to handholds, and there were men in the backs of the dump trucks. The racing traffic filled the highway from edge to edge. It rushed past, giving off a deafening roar and clouds of gasoline fumes.

They were gone, the solid mass of them at any rate. But now there came older cars, no less crowded, and then more spacious cars, not crowded so much and less frantically pushing at those ahead. But even these cars passed each other recklessly. There seemed to be an almost hysterical fear of being last.

One car swung off to its left. There were five men in it. It braked and stopped on the shoulder close to Lockley's car. The driver shouted above the din of passing motors, "You don't want to go up there. Everybody's ordered out. Everybody get away from Boulder Lake! When you get the chance, turn around and get the hell away."

He watched for a chance to get back on the road, having delivered his warning. Lockley got out of his car and went over, "You're talking about the thing that came down from the sky," he said grimly. "There was a girl up at the camp. Jill Holmes.

Writing a piece about building a national park. Getting information about the job. Did anybody get her away?"

The man who'd warned him continued to watch for a reasonable gap in the flood of racing cars. They weren't crowded now as they had been, but it was still impossible to start in low and get back in the stream of vehicles without an almost certain crash. Then he turned his head back, staring at Lockley.

"Hell! Somebody told me to check on her. I was routing men out and loading 'em on whatever came by. I forgot!"

A man in the back of the sedan said, "She hadn't left when we did. I saw her. But I thought she had a ride all set."

The man at the wheel said furiously, "She hasn't passed us! Unless she's in one of these…"

Lockley set his teeth. He watched each oncoming car intently. A girl among these fugitives would have been put with the driver in the cab of a truck, and he'd have seen a woman in any of the private cars.

"If I don't see her go by," he said grimly, "I'll go up to the camp and see if she's still there."

The man in the driver's seat looked relieved.

"If she's left behind, it's her fault. If you hunt for her, make it fast and be plenty careful. Keep to the camp and stay away from the lake. There was a hell of an explosion over there this morning. Three men went to see what'd happened. They didn't come back. Two more went after 'em, and something hit them on the way. They smelled something worse than skunk. Then they were paralyzed, like they had hold of a high-tension line. They saw crazy colors and heard crazy sounds and they couldn't move a finger. Their car ditched. In a while they came out of it and they came back—fast! They'd just got back when we got short wave orders for everybody to get out. If you look for that girl, be careful. If she's still there, you get her out quick!" Then he said sharply, "Here's a chance for us to get going. Move out of the way!"

There was a gap in the now diminishing spate of cars. The driver of the stopped car drove furiously onto the highway. He shifted gears and accelerated at the top of his car's power. Another car behind him braked and barely avoided a crash while blowing its horn furiously. Then the traffic went on. But it was lessening now. It was mostly private cars, owned by the workmen.

Suddenly there were no cars coming down the long straight stretch of road. Lockley got back on the highway and resumed his rush toward the spot the others fled from. He heard behind him the diminishing rumble and roar of the fugitive motors. He jammed his own accelerator down to the floor and plunged on.

There'd been an explosion by the lake, the man who'd warned him said. That checked. Three men went to see what had happened. That was reasonable. They didn't come back. Considering what Vale had reported, it was almost inevitable. Then two other men went to find out what happened to the first three and—that was news! A smell that was worse than skunk. Paralysis in a moving car, which ditched. Remaining paralyzed while seeing crazy colors and hearing crazy sounds... Lockley could not even guess at an explanation. But the men had remained paralyzed for some time, and then the sensations lifted. They had fled back to the construction camp, evidently fearing that the paralysis might return. Their narrative must have been hair-raising, because when orders had come for the evacuation of the camp, they had been obeyed with a promptitude suggesting panic. But apparently nothing else had happened.

The first three men were still missing—or at least there'd been no mention of their return. They'd either been killed or taken captive, judging by Vale's account and obvious experience. He was either killed or captured, too, but it still seemed strange that Lockley had heard so much of that struggle via a tight beam microwave transmitter that needed to be accurately aimed. Vale had been captured or killed. The three other men missing probably had undergone the same fate. The two others had been made helpless but not murdered or taken prisoner. They'd simply been held until when they were released they'd flee.

The car went over a bridge and rounded a curve. Here a deep cut had been made and the road ran through it. It came out upon undulating ground where many curves were necessary.

Another car came, plunging after the others. In the next ten miles there were, perhaps a dozen more. They'd been hard to start, perhaps, and so left later than the rest. Jill wasn't in any of them. There was one car traveling slowly, making thumping noises. Its driver made the best time he could, following the others.

Sober common sense pointed out that Vale's account was fully verified. There'd been a landing of non-human creatures in a ship from outer space. The killing or capture of the first three men to investigate a gigantic explosion was natural enough—the alien occupants of a space ship would want to study the inhabitants of the world they'd landed on. The mere paralysis and release of two others could be explained on the theory that the creatures who'd come to earth were satisfied with three specimens of the local intelligent race to study. They had Vale, too. They weren't trying to conceal their arrival, though it would have been impossible anyhow. But it was plausible enough that they'd take measures to become informed about the world they'd landed on, and when they considered that they knew enough, they'd take the action they felt was desirable.

All of which was perfectly rational, but there was another possibility. The other possible explanation was—considering everything—more probable. And it seemed to offer even more appalling prospects.

He drove on. Jill Holmes. He'd seen her four times; she was engaged to Vale. It seemed extremely likely that she hadn't left the camp with the workmen. If Lockley hadn't been obsessed with her, he'd have tried to make sure she was left behind before he tried to find her. If she was still at the camp, she was in a dangerous situation.

There'd been no other car from the camp for a long way now. But there came a sharp curve ahead. Lockley drove into it. There was a roar, and a car came from the opposite direction, veering away from the road's edge. It sideswiped the little car Lockley drove. The smaller car bucked violently and spun crazily around. It went crashing into a clump of saplings and came to a stop with a smashed windshield and crumpled fenders, but the motor was still running. Lockley had braked by instinct.

The other car raced away without pausing.

Lockley sat still for a moment, stunned by the suddenness of the mishap. Then he raged. He got out of the car. Because of its small size, he thought he might be able to get it back on the road with saplings for levers. But the job would take hours, and he was irrationally convinced that Jill had been left behind in the construction camp.

He was perhaps five miles from Boulder Lake itself and about the same distance from the camp. It would take less time to go to the camp on foot than to try to get the car on the road. Time was of the essence, and whoever or whatever the occupants of the landed ship might be, they'd know what a road was for. They'd sight an intruder in a car on a road long before they'd detect a man on foot who was not on a highway and was taking some pains to pass unseen.

He started out, unarmed and on foot. He was headed for the near neighborhood of the thing Vale had described as coming from the sky. He was driven by fear for Jill. It seemed to him that his best pace was only a crawl and he desperately needed all the speed he could muster.

He headed directly across country for the camp. All the world seemed unaware that anything out of the ordinary was in progress. Birds sang and insects chirruped and breezes blew and foliage waved languidly. Now and again a rabbit popped out of sight of the moving figure of the man. But there were no sounds, or sights or indications of anything untoward where Lockley moved. He reflected that he was on his way to search for a girl he barely knew, and whom he couldn't be sure needed his help anyway.

Outside in the world, there were places where things were not so tranquil. By this time there were already troops in motion in long trains of personnel-carrying trucks. There were mobile guided missile detachments moving at top speed across state lines and along the express highway systems. Every military plane in the coastal area was aloft, kept fueled by tanker planes to be ready for any sort of offensive or defensive action that might be called for. The short wave instructions to the construction camp had become known, and all the world knew that Boulder Lake National Park had been evacuated to avoid contact with non-human aliens. The aliens were reported to have hunted men down and killed them for sport. They were reported to have paralysis beams, death beams and poison gas. They were described as indescribable, and described in "artist's conceptions" on television and in the newspapers. They appeared—according to circumstances—to resemble lizards or slugs. They were portrayed as carnivorous birds and octopods. The artists took full advantage of their temporarily greater importance than cameramen. They pictured these diverse aliens in their one known aggressive action of trailing Vale down and carrying him away. This was said to be for vivisection. None of the artists' ideas were even faintly plausible, biologically. The creatures were even portrayed as turning heat rays upon humans, who dramatically burst into steam as the beams struck them. Obviously, there were also artist's conceptions of women being seized by the creatures from outer space. There was only one woman known to be in the construction camp, but that inconvenient fact didn't bother the artists.

The United States went into a mild panic. But most people stayed on their jobs, and followed their normal routine, and the trains ran on time.

The public in the United States had become used to newspaper and broadcast scares. They were unconsciously relegated to the same category as horror movies, which some day might come true, but not yet. This particular news story seemed more frightening than most, but still it was taken more or less as shuddery entertainment. So most of the United States shivered with a certain amount of relish as ever new and ever more imaginative accounts appeared describing the landing of intelligent monsters, and waited to see if it was really true. The truth was that most of America didn't actually believe it. It was like a Russian threat. It could happen and it might happen, but it hadn't happened so far to the United States.

An official announcement helped to guide public opinion in this safe channel. The Defense Department released a bulletin: An object had fallen from space into Boulder Lake, Colorado. It was apparently a large meteorite. When reported by radar before its landing, defense authorities had seized the opportunity to use it for a test of emergency response to a grave alarm. They had used it to trigger a training program and test of defensive measures made ready against other possible enemies. After the meteorite landed, the defense measures were continued as a more complete test of the nation's fighting forces' responsive ability. The object and its landing, however, were being investigated.

Lockley tramped up hillsides and scrambled down steep slopes with many boulders scattered here and there. He moved through a landscape in which nothing seemed to depart from the normal. The sun shone. The cloud cover, broken some time since, was dissipating and now a good two-thirds of the sky was wholly clear. The sounds of the wilderness went on all around him.

But presently he came to a partly-graded new road, cutting across his way. A bulldozer stood abandoned on it, brand-new and in perfect order, with the smell of gasoline and oil about it. He followed the gash in the forest it had begun. It led toward the camp. He came to a place where blasting had been in progress. The equipment for blasting remained. But there was nobody in sight.

Half a mile from this spot, Lockley looked down upon the camp. There were Quonset huts and prefabricated structures. There were streets of clay and wires from one building to another. There was a long, low, open shed with long tables under its roof. A mess shed. Next to it metal pipes pierced another roof, and wavering columns of heated air rose from those pipes. There was a building which would be a commissary. There was every kind of structure needed for a small city, though all were temporary. And there was no movement, no sound, no sign of life except the hot air rising from the mess kitchen stovepipes.

Lockley went down into the camp. All was silence. All was lifeless. He looked unhappily about him. There would be no point, of course, in looking into the dormitories, but he made his way to the mess shed. Some heavy earthenware plates and coffee cups, soiled, remained on the table. There were a few flies. Not many. In the mess kitchen there was grayish smoke and the reek of scorched and ruined food. The stoves still burned. Lockley saw the blue flame of bottled gas. He went on. The door of the commissary was open. Everything men might want to buy in such a place waited for purchasers, but there was no one to buy or sell.

The stillness and desolation of the place resulted from less than an hour's abandonment. But somehow it was impossible to call out loudly for Jill. Lockley was appalled by the feeling of emptiness in such bright sunshine. It was shocking. Men hadn't moved out of the camp. They'd simply left it, with every article of use dropped and abandoned; nothing at all had been removed. And there was no sign of Jill. It occurred to Lockley that she'd have waited for Vale at the camp, because assuredly his first thought should have been for her safety. Yes. She'd have waited for Vale to rescue her. But Vale was either dead or a captive of the creatures that had been in the object from the sky. He wouldn't be looking after Jill.

Lockley found himself straining his eyes at the mountain from whose flank Vale had been prepared to measure the base line between his post and Lockley's. That vantage point could not be seen from here, but Lockley looked for a small figure that might be Jill, climbing valiantly to warn Vale of the events he'd known before anybody else.

Then Lockley heard a very small sound. It was faint, with an irregular rhythm in it. It had the cadence of speech. His pulse leaped suddenly. There was the mast for the short wave set by which the camp had kept in touch with the outer world. Lockley sprinted for the building under it. His footsteps sounded loudly in the silent camp, and they drowned out the sound he was heading for.

He stopped at the open door. He heard Jill's voice saying anxiously, "But I'm sure he'd have come to make certain I was safe!" A pause. "There's no one else left, and I want…" Another pause. "But he was up on the mountainside! At least a helicopter could—"

Lockley called, "Jill!"

He heard a gasp. Then she said unsteadily, "Someone just called. Wait a moment."

She came to the door. At sight of Lockley her face fell.

"I came to make sure you were all right," he said awkwardly. "Are you talking to outside?"

"Yes. Do you know anything about—"

"I'm afraid I do," said Lockley. "Right now the important thing is to get you out of here. I'll tell them we're starting. All right?"

She stood aside. He went up to the short wave set which looked much like an ordinary telephone, but was connected to a box with dials and switches. There was a miniature pocket radio—a transistor radio—on top of the short wave cabinet. Lockley picked up the short wave microphone. He identified himself. He said he'd come to make sure of Jill's safety, and that he'd been passed by the rushing mass of cars and trucks that had evacuated everybody else. Then he said, "I've got a car about four miles away. It's in a ditch, but I can probably get it out. It'll be a lot safer for Miss Holmes if you send a helicopter there to pick her up."

The reply was somehow military in tone. It sounded like a civilian being authoritative about something he knew nothing about. Lockley said, "Over" in a dry tone and put down the microphone. He picked up the pocket radio and put it in his pocket. It might be useful.

"They say to try to make it out in my car," he told Jill wryly. "As civilians, I suppose they haven't any helicopters they can give orders to. But it probably makes sense. If there are some queer creatures around, there's no point in stirring them up with a flying contraption banging around near their landing place. Not before we're ready to take real action. Come along. I've got to get you away from here."

"But I'm waiting…" She looked distressed. "He wanted me to leave yesterday. We almost quarrelled about it. He'll surely come to make sure I'm safe…"

"I'm afraid I have bad news," said Lockley. Then he described, as gently as he could, his last talk with Vale. It was the one which ended with squeaks and strugglings transmitted by the communicator, and then the smashing of the communicator itself. He didn't mention the puzzling fact that the communicator had stayed perfectly aimed while it was picked up and squeaked at and destroyed. He had no explanation for it. What he did have to tell was bad enough. She went deathly pale, searching his face as he told her.

"But—but—" She swallowed. "He might have been hurt and—not killed. He might be alive and in need of help. If there are creatures from somewhere else, they might not realize that he could be unconscious and not dead! He'd make sure about me! I—I'll go up and make sure about him…"

Lockley hesitated. "It's not likely," he said carefully, "that he was left there injured. But if you feel that somebody has to make sure, I'll do it. For one thing, I can climb faster. My car is ditched back yonder. You go and wait by it. At least it's farther from the lake and you should be safer there. I'll make sure about Vale."

He explained in detail how she could find the car. Up this hillside to a slash through the forest for a highway. Due south from an abandoned bulldozer. Keep out of sight. Never show against a skyline.

She swallowed again. Then she said, "If he needs help, you could—do more than I can. But I'll wait there where the woods begin. I can hide if I need to, and I—might be of some use."

He realized that she deluded herself with the hope that he, Lockley, might bring an injured Vale down the mountainside and that she could be useful then. He let her. He went through the camp with her to put her on the right track. He gave her the pocket radio, so she could listen for news. When she went on out of sight in brushwood, he turned back toward the mountain on which Vale had occupied an observation post. It was actually a million-year-old crater wall that he climbed presently. And he took a considerable chance. As he climbed, for some time he moved in plain view. If the crew of the ship in Boulder Lake were watching, they'd see him rather than Jill. If they took action, it would be against him and not Jill. Somehow he felt better equipped to defend himself than Jill would be.

He climbed. Again the world was completely normal, commonplace. There were mountain peaks on every hand. Some had been volcanoes originally, some had not. With each five hundred feet of climbing, he could see still more mountains. The sky was cloudless now. He climbed a thousand feet. Two. Three. He could see between peaks for a full thirty miles to the spot where he'd been at daybreak. But he was making his ascent on the back flank of this particular mountain. He could not see Boulder Lake from there. On the other hand, no creature at Boulder Lake should be able to see him. Only an exploring party which might otherwise sight Jill would be apt to detect him, a slowly moving speck against a mountainside.

He reached the level at which Vale's post had been assigned. He moved carefully and cautiously around intervening masses of stone. The wind blew past him, making humming noises in his ears. Once he dislodged a small stone and it went bouncing and clattering down the slope he'd climbed.

He saw where Vale could have been as he watched something come down from the sky. He found Vale's sleeping bag, and the ashes of his campfire. Here too was the communicator. It had been smashed by a huge stone lifted and dropped upon it, but before that it had been moved. It was not in place on the bench mark from which it could measure inches in a distance of scores of miles.

There was no other sign of what had apparently happened here. The ashes of the fire were undisturbed. Vale's sleeping bag looked as if it had not been slept in, as if it had only been spread out for the night before. Lockley went over the rock shelf inch by inch. No red stains which might be blood. Nothing...

No. In a patch of soft earth between two stones there was a hoofprint. It was not a footprint. A hoof had made it, but not a horse's hoof, nor a burro's. It wasn't a mountain sheep track. It was not the track of any animal known on earth. But it was here. Lockley found himself wondering absurdly if the creature that had made it would squeak, or if it would roar. They seemed equally unlikely.

He looked cautiously down at the lake which was almost half a mile below him. The water was utterly blue. It reflected only the crater wall and the landscape beyond the area where the volcanic cliffs had fallen. Nothing moved. There was no visible apparatus set up on the shore, as Vale had said. But something had happened down in the lake. Trees by the water's edge were bent and broken. Masses of brushwood had been crushed and torn away. Limbs were broken down tens of yards from the water, and there were gullies to be seen wherever there was soft earth. An enormous wave had flung itself against the nearly circular boundary of the lake. It had struck like a tidal wave dozens of feet high in an inland body of water. It was extremely convincing evidence that something huge and heavy had hurtled down from the sky.

But Lockley saw no movement nor any other novelty in this wilderness. He heard nothing that was not an entirely normal sound.

But then he smelled something.

It was a horrible, somehow reptilian odor. It was the stench of jungle, dead and rotting. It was much, much worse than the smell of a skunk.

He moved to fling himself into flight. Then light blinded him. Closing his eyelids did not shut it out. There were all colors, intolerably vivid, and they flashed in revolving combinations and forms which succeeded each other in fractions of seconds. He could see nothing but this light. Then there came sound. It was raucous. It was cacophonic. It was an utterly unorganized tumult in which musical notes and discords and bellowings and shriekings were combined so as to be unbearable. And then came pure horror as he found that he could not move. Every inch of his body had turned rigid as it became filled with anguish. He felt, all over, as if he were holding a charged wire.

He knew that he fell stiffly where he stood. He was blinded by light and deafened by sound and his nostrils were filled with the nauseating fetor of jungle and decay. These sensations lasted for what seemed years.

Then all the sensations ended abruptly. But he still could not see; his eyes were still dazzled by the lights that closing his eyelids had not changed. He still could not hear. He'd been deafened by the sounds that had dazed and numbed him. He moved, and he knew it, but he could not feel anything. His hands and body felt numb.

Then he sensed that the positions of his arms and legs were changed. He struggled, blind and deaf and without feeling anywhere. He knew that he was confined. His arms were fastened somehow so that he could not move them.

And then gradually—very gradually—his senses returned. He heard squeakings. At first they were faint as the exhausted nerve ends in his ears only began to regain their function. He began to regain the sense of touch, though he felt only furriness everywhere.

He was raised up. It seemed to him that claws rather than fingers grasped him. He stood erect, swaying. His sense of balance had been lost without his realizing it. It came back, very slowly. But he saw nothing. Clawlike hands—or handlike claws—pulled at him. He felt himself turned and pushed. He staggered. He took steps out of the need to stay erect. The pushings and pullings continued. He found himself urged somewhere. He realized that his arms were useless because they were wrapped with something like cord or rope.

Stumbling, he responded to the urging. There was nothing else to do. He found himself descending. He was being led somewhere which could only be downward. He was guided, not gently, but not brutally either.

He waited for sight to return to him. It did not come.

It was then he realized that he could not see because he was blindfolded.

There were whistling squeaks very near him. He began helplessly to descend the mountain, surrounded and guided and sometimes pulled by unseen creatures.

CHAPTER THREE

It was a long descent, made longer by the blindfold and clumsier by his inability to move his arms. More than once Lockley stumbled. Twice he fell. The clawlike hands or handlike claws lifted him and thrust him on the way that was being chosen for him. There were whistling squeaks. Presently he realized that some of them were directed at him. A squeak or whistle in a warning tone told him that he must be especially careful just here.

He came to accept the warnings. It occurred to him that the squeaks sounded very much like those button-shaped hollow whistles that children put in their mouths to make strident sounds of varying pitch. Gradually, all his senses returned to normal. Even his eyes under the blindfold ceased to report only glare blindness, and he saw those peculiar, dissolving grayish patterns that human eyes transmit from darkness.

More squeakings. A long time later he moved over nearly level grassy ground. He was led for possibly half a mile. He had not tried to speak during all his descent. It would have been useless. If he was to be killed, he would be killed. But trouble had been taken to bring him down alive from a remaining bit of crumbling crater wall. His captors had evidently some use for him in mind.

They abruptly held him still for a long time—perhaps as much as an hour. It seemed that either instructions were hard to come by, or some preparation was being made. Then the sound of something or someone approaching. Squeaks.

He was led another long distance. Then claws or hands lifted him. Metal clanked. Those who held him dropped him. He fell three or four feet onto soft sand. There was a clanging of metal above his head.

Then a human voice said sardonically, "Welcome to our city! Where'd they catch you?"

Lockley said, "Up on a mountainside, trying to see what they were doing. Will you get me loose, please?"

Hands worked on the cord that bound his arms close to his body. They loosened. He removed the blindfold.

He was in a metal-walled and metal-ceilinged vault, perhaps eight feet wide and the same in height, and perhaps twelve feet long. It had a floor of sand. Some small amount of light came in through the circular hole he'd been dropped through, despite a cover on it. There were three men already in confinement here. They wore clothing appropriate to workmen from the construction camp. There was a tall lean man, and a broad man with a moustache, and a chunky man. The chunky man had spoken.

"Did you see any of 'em?" he demanded now.

Lockley shook his head. The three looked at each other and nodded. Lockley saw that they hadn't been imprisoned long. The sand floor was marked but not wholly formed into footprints, as it would have been had they moved restlessly about. Mostly, it appeared, they'd simply sat on the sand floor.

"We didn't see 'em either," said the chunky man. "There was a hell of a explosion over at the lake this mornin'. We piled in a car—my car—and came over to see what'd happened. Then something hit us. All of us. Lights. Noise. A godawful stink. A feeling all over like an electric shock that paralyzed us. We came to blindfolded and tied. They brought us here. That's our story so far. What's happened to you—and what really happened to us?"

"I'm not sure," said Lockley.

He hesitated. Then he told them about Vale, and what he'd reported. They'd had no explanation at all of what had happened to them. They seemed relieved to be informed, though the information was hardly heartening.

"Critters from Mars, eh?" said the moustached man. "I guess we'd act the same way if we was to get to Mars. They got to figure out some way to talk to who lives here. I guess that makes us it—unless we can figure out something better."

Lockley, by temperament, tended to anticipate worse things in the future than had come in the past. The suggestion that the occupants of the spaceship had captured men to learn how to communicate with them seemed highly optimistic. He realized that he didn't believe it. It seemed extremely unlikely that the invaders from space were entirely ignorant of humanity. The choice of Boulder Lake as a landing place, for example, could not have been made from space. If there was need for deep water to land in—which seemed highly probable—then it would have been simple good sense to descend in the ocean. The ship could submerge, and it could move about in the lake. Vale had said so. Such a ship would almost inevitably choose deep water in the ocean for a landing place. To land in a crater lake—one of possibly two or three on an entire continent suitable for their use—indicated that they had information in advance. Detailed information. It practically shouted of a knowledge of at least one human language, by which information about Crater Lake could have been obtained. Whoever or whatever made use of the lake was no stranger to earth!

Yes... They'd needed a deep-water landing and they knew that Boulder Lake would do. They probably knew very much more. But if they didn't know that Jill waited for him where the trail toward his ditched car began, then there was no reason to let them overhear the information.

"I was part of a team making some base line measurements," said Lockley, "when this business started. I began to check my instruments with a man named Vale."

He told exactly, for the second time, what Vale said about the thing from the sky and the creatures who came out of it. Then he told what he'd done. But he omitted all reference to Jill. His coming to the lake he ascribed to incredulity. Also, he did not mention meeting the fleeing population of the construction camp. When his story was finished he sounded like a man who'd done a very foolhardy thing, but he didn't sound like a man with a girl on his mind.

The broad man with the moustache asked a question or two. The tall man asked others. Lockley asked many.

The answers were frustrating. They hadn't seen their captors at all. They'd heard squeaks when they were being brought to this place, and the squeaks were obviously language, but no human one. They'd been bound as well as blindfolded. They hadn't been offered food since their capture, nor water. It seemed as if they'd been seized and put into this metal compartment to wait for some use of them by their captors.

"Maybe they want to teach us to talk," said the moustached man, "or maybe they're goin' to carve us up to see what makes

116

us tick. Or maybe," he grimaced, "maybe they want to know if we're good to eat."

The chunky man said, "Why'd they blindfold us?"

Lockley had begun to have a very grim suspicion about this. It came out of the realization of how remarkable it was that a ship designed to be navigable in deep water should have landed in a deep crater lake. He said, "Vale said at first that they weren't human, though they were only specks in his binoculars. Later, when he saw them close, he didn't say what they look like."

"Must be pretty weird," said the tall man.

"Maybe," said the man with the moustache, attempting humor, "maybe they didn't want us to see them because we'd be scared. Or maybe they didn't mean to blindfold us, but just to cover us up. Maybe they wouldn't mind us seeing them, but it hurts for them to look at us!"

Lockley said abruptly, "This box we're in. It's made by humans."

The moustached man said quickly, "We figured that. It's the shell of a compost pit for the hotel that's goin' to be built around here. They'll sink it in the ground and dump garbage in it, and it'll rot, and then it'll be fertilizer. These critters from space are just using it to hold us. But what are they gonna do with us?"

There were faint squeakings. The cover to the round opening lifted. Three rabbits dropped down. The cover closed with a clang. The rabbits shivered and crouched, terrified, in one corner.

"Is this how they're gonna feed us?" demanded the chunky man.

"Hell, no!" said the tall man, in evident disgust. "They're dumped in here like we were. They're animals. So are we. This is a temporary cage. It's got a sand floor that we can bury things in. It won't be any trouble to clean out. The rabbits and us, we stay caged until they're ready to do whatever they're goin' to do with us."

"Which is what?" demanded the chunky man.

There was no answer. They would either be killed, or they would not. There was nothing to be done. Meanwhile Lockley evaluated his three fellow captives as probably rather good men to have on one's side, and bad ones to have against one. But there was no action which was practical now. A single guard outside, able to paralyze them by whatever means it was accomplished, made any idea of escape in daylight foolish.

"What kind of critters are they?" demanded the chunky man. "Maybe we could figure out what they'll do if we know what kind of thing they are!"

"They've got eyes like ours," said Lockley.

The three men looked at him.

"They landed by daylight," said Lockley. "Early daylight. They could certainly have picked the time for their landing. They picked early morning so they could have a good long period of daylight in which to get settled before night. If they'd been night moving creatures, they'd have landed in the dark."

The tall man said, "Sounds reasonable. I didn't think of that."

"They saw me at a distance," said Lockley, "and I didn't see them. They've got good eyes. They beat me up to the top of the mountain and hid to see what I'd do. When they saw me looking the lake over after checking up on Vale, they paralyzed me and brought me here. So they've got eyes like ours."

"This guy Vale," said the chunky man. "What happened to him?"

Lockley said, "Probably what'll happen to us."

"Which is what?" asked the chunky man.

Lockley did not answer. He thought of Jill, waiting anxiously at the edge of the woods not far from the camp. She'd surely have watched him climbing. She might have followed his climb all the way to where he went around to Vale's post. But she wouldn't have seen his capture and she might be waiting for him now. It wasn't likely, though, that she'd climb into the trap that had taken Vale and then himself. She must realize that that spot was one to be avoided.

She'd probably try to make her way to his ditched car. She'd heard him ask on short wave for a helicopter to come to that place to pick her up. It hadn't been promised; in fact it had been refused. But if she remained missing, surely someone would risk a low-level flight to find out if she were waiting desperately for rescue. A light plane could land on the highway if a helicopter wasn't to be risked. Somehow Jill must find a way to safety. She was in danger because she'd waited loyally for Vale to come to her at the camp. Now…

Time passed. Hot sunshine on their prison heated the metal. It became unbearably hot inside. There came squeakings. The cover of the compost pit shell lifted. Half a dozen wild birds were thrust into the opening. The cover closed again. Lockley listened closely. It was latched from the outside. There would naturally be a fastening on the cover of a compost pit to keep bears from getting at the garbage it was built to contain.

The heat grew savage. Thirst was a problem. Once and only once they heard a noise from the world beyond their prison. It was a droning hum which, even through a metal wall, could be nothing but the sound of a helicopter. It droned and droned, very gradually becoming louder. Then, abruptly, it cut off. That was all. And that was all that the four in the metal tank knew about events outside of their own experience.

But much was happening outside. Troop-carrying trucks had reached the edge of Boulder Lake National Park, a very few hours after the workmen from the camp had gotten out of it. They had a story to tell, and if it lacked detail it did not lack imagination. The three missing men had their fate described in various versions, all of which were dramatic and terrifying. The two men who had been paralyzed by some unknown agency described their sensations after their release. Their stories were immediately relayed to all the news media. It now appeared that dozens of men had seen the thing descend from the sky. They had not compared notes, however, and their descriptions varied from a black pear-shaped globe which had hovered for minutes before descending behind the mountains into the lake, to detailed word pictures of a silvery, torpedo-shaped vessel of space with portholes and flaming rockets and an unknown flag displayed from a flagstaff.

Of course, none of those accounts could be right. The velocity of the falling object, as reported from two radar installations, checked against a seismograph record of the time of the impact in the lake and allowed no leeway of time for it to hover in mid-air to be admired.

But there were enough detailed and first-hand accounts of alarming events to make a second statement by the Defense Department necessary. It was an over-correction of the first soothing one. It was intended to be more soothing still.

It said blandly that a bolide—a slow-moving, large meteoric object—had been observed by radar to be descending to earth. It had been tracked throughout its descent. It had landed in Boulder Lake. Air photos taken since its landing showed that an enormous disturbance of the water of the lake had taken place. It had seemed wise to remove workmen from the neighborhood of the meteoric fall, and the whole occurrence had been made the occasion of a full-scale practice emergency response by air and other defense forces. Investigation of the possible bolide itself was under way.

The writer of the bulletin was obviously sitting on Vale's report and that of the workmen so as to tell as little as possible and that slanted to prevent alarm. The bulletin went on to say that there was no justification for the alarming reports now spreading through the country. This happening was not—repeat, was not—in any way associated with the cold war of such long standing. It was simply a very large meteor arriving from space and very fortunately falling in a national park area, and even more fortunately into a deep crater lake so that there was no damage even to the forests of the park.

The bulletin had no effect, of course. It was too late. It was released at just about the time the temperature in the metal prison—which seemed likely to become a metal coffin—had begun to fall. The moving sun had gone behind a mountain and the compost pit shell was in shadow once more.

Again the cover of that giant box was opened. A porcupine was dropped inside. The cover went on again. This was, at a guess, about five o'clock in the afternoon. The chunky man said drearily, "If this is supposed to be the way they'll feed us, they coulda picked something easier to eat than a porcupine!"

The box now held four men, three rabbits—panting in terror in one corner—half a dozen game birds and the just-arrived porcupine. All the wild creatures shrank away from the men. At any sudden movement the birds tended to fly hysterically about in the dimness, dashing themselves against the metal wall.

"I'd say," observed Lockley, "that his guess," he nodded at the tall man, "is the most likely one. Rabbits and birds and porcupines would be considered specimens of the local living creatures. We could be considered specimens too. Maybe we are. Maybe we're simply being held caged until there's time for a scientific examination of us. Let's hope they don't happen to drop a bear down here to wait with us!"

The tall man said, "Or rattlers! I wonder what time it is. I'll feel better when dark comes. They're not so likely to find rattlers in the dark."

Lockley said nothing. But if Boulder Lake had been chosen for a landing place on the basis of previously acquired information, it wasn't likely that either bears or rattlesnakes would be put in confinement with the men. The men would have been killed immediately, unless there was a practical use to be made of them. He began to make guesses. He could make a great many, but none of them added up exactly right.

Only one seemed promising, and that assumed a lot of items Lockley couldn't be sure of. He did know, though, that he'd been lifted up before he was dropped into the round opening of this tank-like metal shell. The top of the box was well above ground. It was not sunk in place as it would eventually be. Evidently it was not yet in its permanent position. The light inside was dim enough, but he could see the other men and the animals and the birds. He could make out the riveted plates which formed the box's sides and top.

Inconspicuously, he worked his hand down through the sand bottom of the prison. Four inches down the sand ended and there was earth. He felt around. He found grass stems. The box, then, rested on top of the ground, which was perfectly natural for a compost pit shell not yet placed where it would finally belong. The sand... He explored further.

He waited. The other three stayed quiet. The faint brightness around the cover hole faded away. The interior of the tank-like box became abysmally black.

"Can anybody guess the time?" he asked, after aeons seemed to have passed.

"It feels like next Thursday," said the voice of the moustached man, "but it's probably ten or eleven o'clock. Looks like we're just going to be left here till they get around to us."

"I think we'd better not wait," said Lockley. "We've been pretty quiet. They probably think we're well-behaved specimens of this planet's wild life. They won't expect us to try anything this late. Suppose we get out."

"How?" demanded the chunky man.

Lockley said carefully, "This box is resting on top of the ground. I've dug down through the sand and found the bottom edge of the metal sidewall. If it's resting only on dirt, not stone, we ought to be able to dig out with our hands. I'll start now. You listen."

He began to dig with his hands, first clearing away the sand for a reasonable space. He felt a certain sardonic interest in what might happen. He strongly suspected that nothing undesirable would take place.

It was at least quaint that aliens from outer space should accept a bottomless metal shell as a suitable prison for animals. It was quaint that they'd put in a sandy floor. How would they know that such a thing meant a cage, on earth?

Of course the whole event might have been a test of animal intelligence. Almost any animal would have tried to burrow out.

Lockley dug. The earth was hard, and its upper part was filled with tenacious grass roots. Lockley pulled them away. Once he'd gotten under them, the digging went faster. Presently he was under the metal side wall. He dug upward. His hand reached open air.

"One of you can spell me now," he reported in a low tone. "It looks like we'll get away. But we've got to make our plans first. We don't want to be talking outside the tank, or even when the hole's fair-sized. For instance, will we want to keep together when we get outside?"

"Nix!" said the chunky man. "We wanna tell everybody about these characters. We scatter. If they catch one they don't catch any more. We couldn't fight any better for bein' together. We better scatter. I call that settled. I'm scatterin'!"

He crawled to Lockley in the darkness.

"Where you diggin'? OK. I got it. Move aside an' give me room."

"Everybody agrees on that?" asked Lockley.

They did. Lockley was relieved. The chunky man dug busily. There was only the sound of breathing, and the occasional fall of thrown-out earth against the metal of the thing that confined them. The chunky man said briskly, "This dirt digs all right. We just got to make the hole bigger."

In a little while the chunky man stopped, panting. The tall man said, "I'll take a shot at it."

There was a breakthrough to the air outside. The atmosphere in the tank improved. The smell of fresh-dug dirt and cool night air was refreshing. The moustached man took his turn at digging. Lockley went at it again. Soon he whispered, "I think it's OK. I'll go ahead. No talking outside!"

He shook hands all around, whispered "Good luck!" and squirmed through the opening to the night. Innumerable stars glittered in the sky. They were reflected on the water of the lake, here very close. Lockley moved silently. In the blackness just behind him, his eyes had become adjusted to almost complete darkness. He headed away from the shining water. He got brushwood between himself and his former companions. He stood very, very still.

He heard them murmuring together. They were outside. But they had proposed entirely separate efforts at escape. He went on, relieved. It happened that the next time he'd see them, circumstances would be entirely different. But he believed they were competent men.

Guided by the Big Dipper, he moved directly toward the place where Jill should be waiting for him. By the angle of the Dipper's handle he knew that it was almost midnight. Jill would surely have known that nearly the worst had happened. He'd have to find her…

It was two o'clock when he reached the place where Jill had intended to wait. He showed himself openly. He called quietly. There was no answer. He called again, and again.

He saw something white. It was a scrap of paper speared on a brushwood branch which had been stripped of leaves to make the paper show clearly. Lockley retrieved it and saw markings on it which the starlight could not help him to read. He went deep into the woods, found a hollow, and bent low, risking the light of his cigarette lighter for a swift look at the message.

"I saw creatures moving around in the camp. They weren't men. I was afraid they might be hunting me. I've gone to wait by the car if I can find it."

She'd written in English, in full confidence that creatures from space would not be able to read it. Lockley was not so sure, but the message hadn't been removed. If it had been read, there'd have been an ambush waiting for him when he found it. So it appeared.

He headed through the night toward the ditched small car.

It seemed a very long way, though he did stop and drink his fill from a little mountain stream over which a highway bridge had almost been completed. In the night, though, and with hard going, it was not easy to estimate how far he'd gone. In fact, he

124

was anxiously debating if he mightn't have passed the abandoned bulldozer when he came upon the place where blasting had been going on. Still, it was a very long way to be negotiated over still-remaining tree stumps and the unfilled holes from which others had been pulled.

He reached the bulldozer and turned south, and at long last reached the highway. His car should be no more than a quarter-mile away. He moved toward it, close to the road's edge. He heard music. It was faint, but vivid because it was the last sound that anybody would expect to hear in the hours before dawn in a wilderness deserted by mankind. He scraped his foot on the roadway. The music stopped instantly. He said, "Jill?"

He heard her gasp.

"I found where Vale had been," he said steadily. "There was no blood there. There's no sign that he's been killed. Then I was caught myself. I was put with three other men who were believed killed but who are still alive. We escaped. It is within reason to hope that Vale is unharmed and that he may escape or somehow be rescued."

What he said was partly to make her sure that it was he who appeared in the darkness. But it was technically true, too. It was within reason to hope for Vale's ultimate safety. One can always hope, whatever the odds against the thing hoped for. But Lockley thought that the odds against Vale's living through the events now in progress were very great indeed.

Jill stepped out into the starlight.

"I wasn't sure it was you," she said with difficulty. "I saw the things, you know, at a distance. At first I thought they were men. So when I first saw you—dimly—I was afraid."

"I'm sorry I haven't better news," said Lockley.

"It's good news! It's very good news," she insisted as he drew near. "If they've captured him, he'll make them understand that he's a man, and that men are intelligent and not just animals, and that they should be our friends and we theirs."

The girl's voice was resolute. Lockley could imagine that all the time she'd been waiting, she'd been preparing to deny that

125

even the worst news was final, until she looked on Vale's dead body itself.

"Do you want to tell me exactly what you found out?" she asked.

"I'll tell you while I work on the car," said Lockley. "We want to get moving away from here before daybreak."

He went down to the little car, wedged in the saplings it had splintered and broken. He began to clear it so he could lever it back on to the highway. He used a broken sapling, and as he worked he told what had happened, including the three men in the compost pit shell and the dumping of assorted small wild life specimens into it with them.

"But they didn't kill you," said Jill insistently, "and they didn't kill those three, and there were the two others you say got over the paralysis and went back to the camp. Counting you, that's six men they had at their mercy that we know weren't harmed. So why should they have harmed a seventh man?"

Lockley did not answer at once. None of the spared six, he thought, had put up a fight. Only Vale had exchanged blows with the crew of the spaceship. Nobody else had seen them.

"That's right, about Vale," he said after a moment in which he had been busy. "But this doesn't look good!"

He felt under the car. He squeezed himself beneath its front end. There was a small, fugitive flicker of flame. It went out and he was silent.

Presently he got to his feet and said evenly, "We're in a fix. One of the front wheels is turned almost at a right angle to the other. A king pin is broken. The car couldn't be driven even if I managed to get it up on the road. We've got to walk. There ought to be soldiers on the way up to the lake today. If we meet them we'll be all right. But this is bad luck!"

It happened that he was mistaken on both counts. There were no soldiers moving into the park, and it was not bad luck that his car couldn't be driven. If he'd been able to get it on the road and trundling down the highway, the car would have been wrecked and they could very well have been killed. But this was for the future to disclose.

They took nothing from the car because they could not see beyond the present. They started out doggedly to follow the highway that soldiers would be likely to follow on the way to the lake. It was not the shortest way to the world outside the Park. It was considerably longer than a footpath would have been. But Lockley expected tanks, at least, against which eccentric unearthly weapons would be useless. So they headed down the main highway. Lockley was unarmed. They had no food. He hadn't eaten since the morning before.

When day came—gray and still—and presently the dew upon grass and tree leaves glittered reflections of the sky, he moved aside into the woods and found a broken-off branch, out of which by very great effort he made a club. When he came back, Jill was listening attentively to the little pocket radio. She turned it off.

"I was hoping for news," she explained determinedly. "The government knows that there are creatures in the spaceship, and he—" that would be Vale "—will be trying to make them understand what kind of beings we are. So there could be friendly communication almost any time. But there aren't any news broadcasts on the air. I suppose it's too early."

He agreed, with reservations. They made their way along the dew-wetted surface of the highway. As the light grew stronger, Lockley glanced again and again at Jill's face. She looked very tired. He reflected sadly that she was thinking of Vale. She'd never thought twice about Lockley. Even now, or especially now, all her thoughts were for Vale.

When sunlight appeared on the peaks around them, he said detachedly, "You've had no rest for twenty-four hours and I doubt that you've had anything to eat. Neither have I. If troops come up this highway we'll hear the engines. I think we'd better get off the highway and try to rest. And I may be able to find something for us to eat."

There are few wildernesses so desolate as to offer no food at all for one who knows what to look for. There is usually some sort of berry available. One kind of acorn is not bad to eat. Shoots of bracken are not unlike asparagus. There are some spiny wild plants whose leaves, if plucked young enough, will yield some nourishment and of course there are mushrooms. Even on stone one can find liverish rock-tripe which is edible if one dries it to complete dessication before soaking it again to make a soup or broth.

Before he searched for food, though, Lockley said abruptly, "You said you saw the creatures and they weren't men. What did they look like?"

"They were a long way away," Jill told him. "I didn't see them clearly. They're about the size of men but they just aren't men. Far away as they were, I could tell that!"

Lockley considered. He shrugged and said, "Rest. I'll be back."

He moved away. He was hungry and he kept his eyes in motion, looking for something to take back to Jill. But his mind struggled to form a picture of a creature who'd be the size of a man but would be known not to be a man even at a distance; whose difference from mankind couldn't be described because seen at such great distance. Presently he shook his head impatiently and gave all his attention to the search for food.

He found a patch of berries on a hillside where there was enough earth for berry bushes, but not for trees. Bears had been at them, but there were many left.

He filled his hat with them and made his way back to Jill. She had the pocket radio on again, but at the lowest possible volume. He put the berry-filled hat down beside her. She held up a warning hand. Speckles of sunshine trickled down through the foliage and the tree trunks were spotted with yellow light. They ate the berries as they heard the news.

A new official news release was out. And now, twelve hours after the last, wholly reassuring bulletin, there was no longer any pretense that the thing in Boulder Lake was merely a meteorite.

OPERATION TERROR

The pretext that it was a natural object, said the news broadcaster, resuming, had been abandoned. But reassurance continued. Photographic planes had been attempting to get a picture of the alien ship as it floated in the lake. So far no satisfactory image had been secured, but pictures of wreckage caused by an enormous wave generated in the lake by the alien spaceship's arrival were sharp and clear. Troops have been posted in a cordon about the Boulder Lake Park area to prevent unauthorized persons from swarming in to see earth's visitors from space. Details of its landing continue to be learned. Workmen from the construction camp have been questioned, and the two men who were paralyzed and then released have told their story. So far four human beings are known to have been seized by the occupants of the spaceship. One is Vale, an eye-witness to the ship's descent and landing. The three others went to investigate the gigantic explosion accompanying the landing in the lake. They have not been seen since. This, however, does not imply that they are dead. Quite possibly the invaders—aliens—guests—who have landed on American soil are trying to learn how to communicate with the American people who are their hosts.

Lockley watched Jill's face. As she heard the references to Vale, she went white, but she saw Lockley looking at her and said fiercely, "They don't know that the visitors didn't kill you and let you and the other three men escape. Someone ought to tell these broadcasters…"

Lockley did not answer. In his own mind, though, there was the fact that of the two workmen who'd been paralyzed and released, the three men in the compost pit shell, and himself, none had seen their captors. But Vale had.

The broadcaster went on with a fine air of confidence, reporting that yesterday afternoon a helicopter had flown into the mountains to examine the landing site in detail since it could not be examined from a high-flying plane.

Lockley remembered the droning he and the others had heard through the metal plates of their prison.

The helicopter had suddenly ceased to communicate. It is believed to have had engine trouble. However, later on a fast jet had attempted a flight below the extreme altitude of the photographic planes. Its pilot reported that at fifteen thousand feet he'd suddenly smelled an appalling odor. Then he was blinded, deafened, and his muscles knotted in spasms. He was paralyzed. The experience lasted for seconds only. It was as if he'd flown into a searchlight beam which produced those sensations and then had flown out of it. He'd instinctively used evasive maneuvers and got away, but twice before he passed the horizon there were instantaneous flashes of the paralysis and the pain. Scientists determined that the report of the men who'd been paralyzed and released agreed with the report of the pilot. It was assumed that whatever or whoever had landed in Boulder Lake possessed a beam—it might as well be called a terror beam because of the effects it had—of some sort of radiation which produced the paralysis and the agony. Unless the three men missing from the construction camp had died of it, however, it was not to be considered a death ray.

The news went on with every appearance of frankness and confidence. It was natural for strangers on a strange planet to take precautions against possibly hostile inhabitants of the newly-found world. But every effort would be exerted to make friendly contact and establish peaceful communications with the beings from space. Their weapon appeared to be of limited range and so far not lethal to human beings. Occasional flashes of its effects had been noted by the troops now forming a cordon about the Park, but it only produced discomfort, not paralysis. Nevertheless the troops in question have been moved back. Meanwhile rocket missiles are being moved to areas where they can deliver atom bombs on the alien ship if it should prove necessary. But the government is extremely anxious to make this contact with extra-terrestrials a friendly one, because contact with a race more advanced than ourselves could be of inestimable value to us. Therefore atom bombs will be used only as a last resort. An atom bomb would destroy aliens and their ship together—and we want the ship. The public is urged to be calm. If the ship should appear dangerous, it can and will be smashed.

The news broadcast ended.

Jill said, obviously speaking of Vale, "He'll make them realize that men aren't like porcupines and rabbits! When they realize that we humans are intelligent people, everything will be all right!"

Lockley said reluctantly, "There's one thing to remember, though, Jill. They didn't blindfold the rabbits or the porcupine. They only blindfolded men."

She stared at him.

"One of the men in the pit with me," said Lockley, "thought they didn't want us to see them because they were monsters. That's not likely." He paused. "Maybe they blindfolded us to keep us from finding out they aren't."

CHAPTER FOUR

"The evidence," said Lockley as Jill looked at him ashen-faced, "the evidence is all for monsters. But there was something in that broadcast that calls for courage, and I want to summon it. We're going to need it."

"If they aren't monsters," said Jill in a stricken voice, "Then—then they're men. And we have a cold war with only one country, and they're the only ones who'd play a deadly trick like this. So if they aren't monsters, in the ship, they must be men, and they'd kill anybody who found it out."

"But again," insisted Lockley, "the evidence is still all for monsters. You've been very loyal and very confident about Vale. But we're in a fix. Vale would want you in a safe place, and there's something in that broadcast that doesn't look good."

"What was in the broadcast?"

Lockley said wryly, "Two things. One was there and one wasn't. There wasn't anything about soldiers marching up to Boulder Lake to welcome visitors from wherever they come from, and to say politely to them that as visitors they are our guests and we'd rather they didn't shoot terror beams or paralysis beams about the landscape. We were more or less counting on that, you and I. We were expecting soldiers to come up the highway headed for the lake. But they aren't coming."

Jill, still pale, wrinkled her forehead in thought.

"That's what wasn't in the broadcast," Lockley told her. "This is what was. The troops have formed a cordon about the Park. They've run into the terror beam. The broadcast said it was weakened by distance and only made the soldiers uncomfortable. But they've moved back. You see the point? They've moved back!"

Jill stared, suddenly understanding.

"But that means—"

"It means," said Lockley, "that the terror beam is pretty much of a weapon. It has a range up in the miles or tens of miles. We don't know how to handle it yet. Whoever or whatever arrived in the thing Vale saw, it or they has or have a weapon our Army can't buck, yet. The point is that we can't wait to be rescued. We've got to get out of here on our own feet. Literally. So we forget about highways. From here on we sneak to safety as best we can. And we've got to put our whole minds on it."

Jill shook her head as if to drive certain thoughts out of it. Then she said, "I guess you're right. He would want me to be safe. And if I can't do anything to help him, at least I can not make him worry. All right! What does sneaking to safety mean?"

Lockley led her down the highway running from Boulder Lake to the outside world. They came to a blasted-out cut for the highway to run through. The road's concrete surface extended to the solid rock on either side. There was no bare earth to take or hold footprints, and there was a climbable slope.

"We go up here and take to the woods," said Lockley, "because we're not as easy to spot in woodland as we'd be on a road. The characters at the lake will know what roads are. If we figure out how to handle their terror beam, they'll expect the attack to come by road. So they'll set up a system to watch the roads. They ought to do it as soon as possible. So we'll avoid notice by not using the roads. It's lucky you've got good walking shoes on. That could be the deciding factor in our staying alive."

He led the way, helping her climb. There would be no sign that they'd abandoned the highway. In fact, there'd be no sign of their existence except the small smashed car. Lockley's existence was known, but not his and Jill's together.

Lockley did not feel comfortable about having deliberately shocked Jill into paying some attention to her own situation instead of staying absorbed in the possible or probable fate of Vale. But for them to get clear was going to call for more than sentimentality on Jill's part. Lockley couldn't carry the load alone.

There was an invasion in process. It could be, apparently, an invasion from space, in which case the terror produced would be terror of the unknown. But Lockley had conceived of the possibility that it might be an invasion only from the other side of the world. Such an invasion was thought of by every American at least once every twenty-four hours. The fears it would arouse would be fears of the all too thoroughly known.

The whole earth had the jitters because of the apparently inevitable trial of strength between its two most gigantic powers. Their rivalry seemed irreconcilable. Most of humanity dreaded their conflict with appalled resignation because there seemed no way to avoid it. Yet it was admittedly possible that an all-out war between them might end with all the world dead, even plants and microbes in the deepest seas. It was ironic that the most reasonable hope that anybody could have was that one or the other nation would come upon some weapon so new and irresistible that it could demand and receive the surrender of the other without atomic war.

Atom bombs could have done the trick, had only one nation owned them. But both were now armed so that by treacherous attack either could almost wipe out the other. There was no way to guard against desperate and terrible retaliation by survivors of the first attacked country. It was the certainty of retaliation which kept the actual war a cold one—a war of provocation and trickery and counter-espionage, but not of mutual extermination.

But Lockley had suggested—because it was the worst of possibilities—that America's rival had developed a new weapon which could win so long as it was not attributed to its user. If the United States believed itself attacked from space, it would not launch missiles against men. It would ask help, and help would be given even by its rival if the invasion were from another planet. Men would always combine against not-men. But if this were a ship from no farther than the other side of the earth, and only pretended to be from an alien world... America could be conquered because it believed it was fighting monsters instead of other men.

This was not likely, but it was believable. There was no proof, but in the nature of things proof would be avoided. And if his idea should happen to be true, the disaster could be enormously worse than an invasion from another star. This first landing could be only a test to make sure that the new weapon was unknown to America and could not be countered by Americans. The crew of this ship would expect to be successful or be killed. In a way, if an atom bomb had to be used to destroy them, they would have succeeded. Because other ships could land in American cities where they could not be bombed without killing millions; where they could demand surrender under pain of death. And get it.

Lockley looked at the sun. He glanced at his watch.

"That would be south," he indicated. "It's the shortest way for us to get to where you'll be reasonably safe and I can tell what I know to someone who may use it."

Jill followed obediently. They disappeared into the woods. They could not be seen from the highway. They could not even be detected from aloft. When they had gone a mile, Jill made her one and final protest.

"But it can't be that they aren't monsters! They must be!"

"Whatever they are," said Lockley, "I don't want them to lay hands on you."

They went on. Once, from the edge of a thicket of trees, they saw the highway below them and to their left. It was empty. It curved out of sight, swinging to the left again. They moved uphill and down. Now the going was easy, through woods with very little underbrush and a carpet of fallen leaves. Again it was a sunlit slope with prickly bushes to be avoided. And yet again it was boulder-strewn terrain that might be nearly level but much more often was a hillside.

Lockley suddenly stopped short. He felt himself go white. He grasped Jill's hand and whirled. He practically dragged her back to the patch of woods they'd just left.

"What's the matter?" The sight of his face made her whisper.

He motioned to her for silence. He'd smelled something. It was faint but utterly revolting. It was the smell of jungle and of foulness. There was the musky reek of reptiles in it. It was a collection of all the smells that could be imagined. It was horrible. It was infinitely worse than the smell of skunk.

Silence. Stillness. Birds sang in the distance. But nothing happened. Absolutely nothing. After a long time Lockley said suddenly, "I've got an idea. It fits into that broadcast. I have to take a chance to find out. If anything happens to me, don't try to help me!"

He'd smelled the foul odor at least fifteen minutes before, and had dragged Jill back, and there had been no other sign of monsters or not-monsters upon the earth. Now he crouched down and crawled among the bushes. He came to the place where he'd smelled the ghastly smell before. He smelled it again. He drew back. It became fainter, though it remained disgusting. He moved forward, stopped, moved back. He went sideways, very, very carefully, extending his hand before him.

He stopped abruptly. He came back, his face angry.

"We were lucky we couldn't use the car," he said when he was near Jill again. "We'd have been killed or worse."

She waited, her eyes frightened.

"The thing that paralyzes men and animals," he told her, "is a projected beam of some sort. We almost ran into it. It's probably akin to radar. I thought they'd put watchers on the highways. They did better. They project this beam. When it blocks a highway, anybody who comes along that highway runs into it. His eyes become blinded by fantastic colored lights, and he hears unbearable noises and feels anguish and they smell what we smelled just now. And he's paralyzed. Such a beam was turned on me yesterday and I was captured. A beam like that on the highway at the lake paralyzed three men who were carried away, and later two others whose car ditched and who stayed paralyzed until the beam was turned off."

"But we only smelled something horrible!" protested Jill.

"You did. I rushed you away. I'd smelled it before. But I went back. And I smelled it, and I crawled forward a little way and I began to see flashes of light and to hear noises and my skin tingled. I pushed my hand ahead of me—and it became paralyzed. Until I pulled it back." Then he said, "Come on."

"What will we do?"

"We change our line of march. If we drove into it or walked into it we'd be paralyzed. It's a tight beam, but there's just a little scatter. Just a little. You might say it leaks at its edges. We'll try to follow alongside until it thins out to nothing or we get where we want to go. Unless," he added, "they've got another beam that crosses it. Then we'll be trapped."

He led the way onward.

They covered four miles of very bad going before Jill showed signs of distress and Lockley halted beside a small, rushing stream. He saw fish in the clear water and tried to improvise a way to catch them. He failed. He said gloomily, "It wouldn't do to catch fish here anyhow. A fire to cook them would show smoke by day and might be seen at night. And whatever's at the Lake might send a terror beam. We'll leave here when you're rested."

He examined the stream. He went up and down its bank. He disappeared around a curve of the stream. Jill waited, at first uneasily, then anxiously.

He came back with his hands full of bracken shoots, their ends tightly curled and their root ends fading almost to white.

"I'm afraid," he observed, "that this is our supper. It'll taste a lot like raw asparagus, which tastes a lot like raw peanuts, and a one-dish meal of it won't stick to your ribs. That's the trouble with eating wild stuff. It's mostly on the order of spinach."

"I'll carry them," said Jill.

She actually looked at him for the first time. Until she found herself anxious because he was out of sight for a long time, she hadn't really regarded him as an individual. He'd been only a person who was helping her because Vale wasn't available. Now she assured herself that Vale would be very grateful to him for aiding her. "I'm rested now," she added.

He nodded and led the way once more. He watched the sun for direction. Two or three miles from their first halt he said abruptly, "I think the terror beam should be over yonder." He waved an arm. "I've got an idea about it. I'll see."

"Be careful!" said Jill uneasily.

He nodded and swung away, moving with a peculiar tentativeness. She knew that he was testing for the smell which was the first symptom of approach to the alien weapon.

He halted half a mile from where Jill watched, resting again while she gazed after him. He moved backward and forward. He marked a place with a stone. He came well back from it and seemed to remove his wrist watch. He laid it on a boulder and stamped on it. He stamped again and again, shifting it between stampings. Then he pounded it with a small rock. He stood up and came back, trailing something which glittered golden for an instant.

He halted before he reached the rock he'd placed as a marker. He did cryptic things, facing away from Jill. From time to time there was a golden glitter in the air near him.

He came back. As he came, he wound something into a little coil. It was the silicon bronze mainspring of his non-magnetic watch. He held it for her to see and put it in his pocket.

"I know what the terror beam is—for what good it'll do!" he said bitterly. "It's a beam of radiation on the order of radar, and for that matter X-rays and everything else. Only an aerial does pick it up and this watchspring makes a good one. I could barely detect the smell at a certain place, but when I touched the laid out spring, it picked up more than my body did and it became horrible! Then I moved in to where my skin began to tingle and I saw lights and heard noises. The spring made all the difference in the world. I even found the direction of the beam."

Jill looked frightened.

"It comes from Boulder Lake," he told her. "It's the terror beam, all right! You can walk into it without knowing it. And I suspect that if it were strong enough it would be a death ray, too!"

Jill seemed to flinch a little.

"They're not using it at killing strength," said Lockley coldly. "They're softening us up. Letting us find out we're frustrated and helpless, and then letting us think it over. I'll bet they intended the four of us to escape from that compost pit thing so we could tell about it! But we'll know, now, if we find dead men in rows in a wiped-out town, we'll know what killed them, and when they ask us politely to become their slaves, we'll know we'll have to do it or die!"

Jill waited. When he seemed to have finished, she said, "If they're monsters, do you think they want to enslave us?"

He hesitated, and then said with a grimace, "I've a habit, Jill, of looking forward to the future and expecting unpleasant things to happen. Maybe it's so I'll be pleasantly surprised when they don't."

"Suppose," said Jill, "that they aren't monsters. What then?"

"Then," said Lockley, "it's a cold war device, to find out if the other side in the cold war can take us over without our suspecting they're the ones doing it. Naturally those in this ship will blow themselves up rather than be found out."

"Which," said Jill steadily, "doesn't offer much hope for…"

She didn't say Vale's name. She couldn't. Lockley grimaced again.

"It's not certain, Jill. The evidence is on the side of the monsters. But in either case the thing for us to do is get to the Army with what I've found out. I've had a stationary beam to test, however crudely. The cordon must have been pushed back by a moving or an intermittent beam. It wouldn't be easy to experiment with one of those. Come on."

She stood up. She followed when he went on. They climbed steep hillsides and went down into winding valleys. The sun began to sink in the west. The going was rough. For Lockley, accustomed to wilderness travel, it was fatiguing. For Jill it was much worse.

They came to a sere, bare hillside on which neither trees nor brushwood grew. It amounted to a natural clearing, acres in extent. Lockley swept his eyes around. There were many thick-foliaged small trees attempting to advance into the clear space. He grunted in satisfaction.

"Sit down and rest," he commanded. "I'll send a message."

He broke off branches from dark green conifers. He went out into the clearing and began to lay them out in a pattern. He came back and broke off more, and still more. Very slowly, because the lines had to be large and thick, the letters S.O.S. appeared in dark green on the clayey open space. The letters were thirty feet high, and the lines were five feet wide. They should show distinctly from the air.

"I think," said Lockley with satisfaction, "that we might get something out of this! If it's sighted, a 'copter might risk coming in after us." He looked at her appraisingly. "I think you'd enjoy a good meal."

139

"I want to say something," said Jill carefully. "I think you've been trying to cheer me up, after saying something to arouse me—which I needed. If the creatures aren't monsters, they'll never actually let anybody loose who's seen that they aren't. Isn't that true? And if it is—"

"We know of six men who were captured," insisted Lockley, "and I was one of them. All six escaped. Vale may have escaped. They're not good at keeping prisoners. We don't know and can't know unless it's mentioned on a news broadcast that he's out and away. So there's absolutely no reason to assume that Vale is dead."

"But if he saw them, when he was fighting them—"

"The evidence," insisted Lockley again, "is that he saw monsters. The only reason to doubt it is that they blindfolded four of us."

Jill seemed to think very hard. Presently she said resolutely, "I'm going to keep on hoping anyhow!"

"Good girl!" said Lockley.

They waited. He was impatient, both with fate and with himself. He felt that he'd made Jill face reality when—if this S.O.S. signal brought help—it wasn't necessary. And there was enough of grimness in the present situation to make it cruelty.

After a very long time they heard a faint droning in the air. There might have been others when they were trudging over bad terrain, and they might not have noticed because they were not listening for such sounds. There were planes aloft all around the lake area. They'd been sent up originally in response to a radar warning of something coming in from space. Now they flew in vast circles around the landing place of that reported object. They flew high, so high that only contrails would have pointed them out. But atmospheric conditions today were such that contrails did not form. The planes were invisible from the ground.

But the pilots could see. When one patrol group was relieved by another, it carried high-magnification photographs of all the park, to be developed and examined with magnifying glasses for any signs of activity by the crew of the object from space.

A second lieutenant spotted the S.O.S. within half an hour of the films' return. There was an immediate and intense conference. The lengths of shadows were measured. The size and slope and probable condition of the clearing's surface were estimated.

A very light plane, intended for artillery-spotting, took off from the nearest airfield to Boulder Lake.

And Lockley and Jill heard it long before it came in sight. It flew low, threading its way among valleys and past mountain-flanks to avoid being spotted against the sky. The two beside the clearing heard it first as a faint mutter. The sound increased, diminished, then increased again.

It shot over a minor mountain-flank and surveyed the bare space with the huge letters on it. Lockley and Jill raced out into view, waving frantically. The plane circled and circled, estimating the landing conditions. It swung away to arrive at a satisfactory approach path.

It wavered. It made a half-wingover, and it side-slipped crazily, and came up and stalled and flipped on its back and dived...

And it came out of its insane antics barely twenty feet above the ground. It raced away as close as possible to touching its wheels to earth. It went away behind the mountains. The sound of its going dwindled and dwindled and was gone. It appeared to have escaped from a deliberately set trap.

Lockley stared after it. Then he went white.

"Idiot!" he cried fiercely. "Come on! Run!"

He seized Jill's hand. They fled together. Evidently, something had played upon the pilot of the light plane. He'd been deafened and blinded and all his senses were a shrieking tumult while his muscles knotted and his hands froze on the controls of his ship. He hadn't flown out of the beam that made him helpless. He'd fallen out of it. And then he raced for the horizon. He got away. And it would appear to those to whom he reported that he'd arrived too late at the distress-signal. If fugitives had made it, they'd been overtaken and captured by the creatures of Boulder Lake, and there'd been an ambush set up for the plane. It was a reasonable decision.

But it puzzled the pilot's superior officers that he hadn't been allowed to land the plane before the beam was turned on him. He could have been paralyzed while on the ground, and he and his plane could have yielded considerable information to creatures from another world. It was puzzling.

Lockley and Jill raced for the woodland at the clearing's edge. Lockley clamped his lips tight shut to waste no breath in speech. The arrival and the circling of the plane had been a public notice that there were fugitives here. If the beam could paralyze a pilot in mid-air, it could be aimed at fugitives on the ground... There could be no faintest hope...

Wholly desperate, Lockley helped Jill down a hillside and into a valley leading still farther down.

He smelled jungle, and muskiness, and decay, and flowers, and every conceivable discordant odor. Flashes of insane colorings formed themselves in his eyes. He heard the chaotic uproar which meant that his auditory nerves, like the nerves in his eyes and nostrils and skin, were stimulated to violent activity, reporting every kind of message they could possibly report all at once.

He groaned. He tried to find a hiding-place for Jill so that if or when the invaders searched for her, they would not find her. But he expected his muscles to knot in spasm and cramp before he could accomplish anything.

They didn't. The smell lessened gradually. The meaningless flashings of preposterous color grew faint. The horrible uproar his auditory nerves reported, ceased. He and Jill had been at the mercy of the unseen operator of the terror beam. Perhaps the beam had grazed them, by accident. Or it could have been weakened...

It was very puzzling.

CHAPTER FIVE

When darkness fell, Lockley and Jill were many miles away from the clearing where he had made the S.O.S. They were under a dense screen of leaves from a monster tree whose roots rose above ground at the foot of its enormous trunk. They formed a shelter of sorts against observation from a distance. Lockley had spotted a fallen tree far gone with wood-rot. He broke pieces of the punky stuff with his fingers. Then he realized that without a pot the bracken shoots he'd gathered could not be cooked. They had to be boiled or not cooked at all.

"We'll call it a salad," he told Jill, "minus vinegar and oil and garlic, and eat what we can."

She'd been pale with exhaustion before the sun sank, but he hadn't dared let her rest more than was absolutely necessary. Once he'd offered to carry her for a while, but she'd refused. Now she sat drearily in the shelter of the roots, resting.

"We might try for news," he suggested.

She made an exhausted gesture of assent. He turned on the tiny radio and tuned it in. There was no scarcity of news, now. A few days past, news went on the air on schedule, mostly limited to five-minute periods in which to cover all the noteworthy events of the world. Part of that five minutes, too, was taken up by advertising matter from a sponsor. Now music was rare. There were occasional melodies, but most were interrupted for new interpretations of the threat to earth at Boulder Lake. Every sort of prominent person was invited to air his views about the thing from the sky and the creatures it brought. Most had no views but only an urge to talk to a large audience. Something, though, had to be put on the air between commercials.

The actual news was specific. Small towns around the fringe of the Park area were being evacuated of all their inhabitants. Foreign scientists had been flown to the United States and were at the temporary area command post not far from Boulder Lake.

Rocket missiles were aimed and ready to blast the lake and the mountains around it should the need arise. A drone plane had been flown to the lake with a television camera transmitting back everything its lens saw. It arrived at the lake and its camera relayed back exactly nothing that had not been photographed and recorded before. But suddenly there was a crash of static and the drone went out of control and crashed. Its camera faithfully transmitted the landscape spinning around until its destruction. Military transmitters were beaming signals on every conceivable frequency to what was now universally called the alien spaceship. They had received no replies. The foreign scientists had agreed that the terror beam—paralysis beam— death beam—was electronic in nature.

Lockley had thought Jill asleep from pure weariness, but her voice came out of the darkness beside the big tree trunk.

"You found that out!" she said. "About its being electronic!"

"I had a sample stationary beam to check on," said Lockley. "They haven't. Which may be a bad thing. Nobody's going to make useful observations of something that makes him blind and deaf and paralyzed while he's in the act. There are some things that puzzle me about that. Why haven't they killed anybody yet? They've got the public about as scared as it can get without some killing. And why didn't we get the full force of the beam after the plane had been driven away? They could have given us the full treatment if they'd wanted to. Why didn't they?"

"If people run away from the towns," said Jill's voice, very tired and sleepy, "maybe they think that's enough. They can take the towns..."

Lockley did not answer, and Jill said no more. Her breathing became deep and regular. She was so weary that even hunger could not keep her awake.

Lockley tried to think. There was the matter of food. Bracken shoots were common enough but unsubstantial. It would need more careful observation to note all the likely spots for mushrooms. Perhaps they were far enough from the lake to take more time hunting food. They were almost exactly in the situation of Australian bushmen who live exclusively by foraging, with some not-too-efficient hunting. But Australian savages were not as finicky as Jill and himself. They ate grubs and insects. For this sort of situation, prejudices were a handicap.

He considered the idea with sardonic appreciation. Two days of inadequate food and such ideas came! But he and Jill wouldn't be the only ones to think such things if matters continued as they were going. The towns around Boulder Lake were being evacuated. The cordon about it had been made to retreat. There was panic not only in America, but everywhere. In Europe there were wild rumors of other landings of other ships of space. The stock markets would undoubtedly close tomorrow, if they hadn't closed today. There'd be the beginning of a mass exodus from the larger cities, starting quietly but building up to frenzy as those who tried to leave jammed all the routes by which they could get away. If the creatures of the spaceship wanted more than the flight of all humans from about their landing place, there would be genuine trouble. Let them move aggressively and there would be panic and disorder and pure catastrophe, with self-exiled city dwellers desperate from hunger because they were away from market centers. It looked as if a dozen or two monsters could wreck a civilization without the need to kill one single human being directly.

He heard a sound. He turned off the radio, gripping the clumsy club which was probably useless against anything really threatening.

The sound continued. There were rustlings of leaves, and then faint rattling, almost clicking noises. Whatever the creature was, it was not large. It seemed to amble tranquilly through the forest and the night, neither alarmed nor considering itself alarming.

The clickings again. And suddenly Lockley knew what it was. Of course! He'd heard it in the compost pit shell, when he was a prisoner of the invaders from space. He rose and moved toward the noise. The creature did not run away. It went about its own affairs with the same peaceful indifference as before. Lockley ran into a tree. He stumbled over a fallen branch on the ground. He came to the place where the creature should be. There was silence. He flicked the flint of his pocket lighter and in the flash of brightness he saw his prey. It had heard his approach. It was a porcupine, prudently curled up into a spiky ball and placidly defying all carnivores, including men. A porcupine is normally the one wild creature without an enemy. Even men customarily spare it because so often it has saved the lives of lost hunters and half-starved travelers. It accomplishes this by its bland refusal to run away from anybody.

Lockley classed himself as a half-starved traveler. He struck with the club after a second spark from his lighter-flint.

Presently he had a small, barely smouldering fire of rotted wood. He cooked over it, and the smell of cooking roused Jill from her exhausted slumber.

"What—"

"We're having a late supper," said Lockley gravely. "A midnight snack. Take this stick. There's a loin of porcupine on it. Be careful! It's hot!"

Jill said, "Oh-h-h-h!" Then, "Is there more for you?"

"Plenty!" he assured her. "I hunted it down with my trusty club, and only got stuck a half-dozen times while I was skinning and cleaning it."

She ate avidly, and when she'd finished he offered more, which she refused until he'd had a share.

They did not quite finish the whole porcupine, but it was an odd and companionable meal, there in the darkness with the barely-glowing coals well-hidden from sight. Lockley said, "I'm sort of a news addict. Shall we see what the wild radio waves are saying?"

"Of course," said Jill. She added awkwardly: "Maybe it's the sudden food, but—I hope you'll remain my friend after this is all over. I don't know anyone else I'd say that to."

"Consider," said Lockley, "that I've made an eloquent and grateful reply."

But his expression in the darkness was not happy. He'd fallen in love with Jill after meeting her only twice, and both times she had been with Vale. She intended to marry Vale. But on the evidence at hand Vale was either dead or a prisoner of the invaders; if the last, his chances of living to marry Jill did not look good, and if the first, this was surely no time to revive his memory.

He found a news broadcast. He suspected that most radio stations would stay on the air all night, now that it was officially admitted that the object in Boulder Lake was a spaceship bringing invaders to earth. The government releases spoke of them as "visitors," in a belated use of the term, but the public was suspicious of reassurances now. At the beginning the landing had seemed like another exaggerated horror tale of the kind that kept up newspaper circulations. Now the public was beginning to believe it, and people might stop going to their offices and the trains might cease to ran on time. When that happened, disaster would be at hand.

The news came in a resonant voice which revealed these facts:

Four more small towns had been ordered evacuated because of their proximity to Boulder Lake. The radiation weapon of the aliens had pushed back the military cordon by as much as five miles. But the big news was that the aliens had broken radio silence. Apparently they'd examined and repaired the short wave communicator from the helicopter they'd knocked down.

Shortly after sundown, said the news report, a call had come through on a military short wave frequency. It was a human voice, first muttering bewilderedly and then speaking with confusion and uneasiness. The message had been taped and now was released to the public.

"What the hell's this...? Oh... What do you characters want me to do? This feels like the short wave set from the 'copter... Hmm... You got

it turned on… What'll I do with it, Broadcast? I don't know whether you want me to talk to you or to back home, wherever that is… Maybe you want me to say I'm havin' a fine time an' wish you was here… I'm not. I wish I was there… If this is goin' on the air I'm Joe Blake, radio man on the 'copter two 'leven. We were headin' in to Boulder Lake when I smelled a stink. Next second there were lights in my eyes. They blinded me. Then I heard a racket like all hell was loose. Then I felt like I had hold of a power transmission line. I couldn't wiggle a finger. I stayed that way till the 'copter crashed. When I come to, I was blindfolded like I am now. I don't know what happened to the other guys. I haven't seen 'em. I haven't seen anything! But they just put me in front of what I think is the 'copter's short wave set an' squeaked at me—"

The recorded voice ended abruptly. The news announcer's voice came back. He said that the member of the 'copter crew had given some other information before he was arbitrarily cut off.

"I'll bet," said Lockley when the newscast ended, "I'll bet the other information was that the invaders have managed to tell him that earth must surrender to them!"

"Why?"

"What else would they want to say? To come and play patty-cake, when they can push the Army around at will and have managed to keep planes from flying anywhere near them? They may not know we've got atom bombs, but I'll bet they do! Part of that extra information could have been a warning not to try to use them. It would be logical to bluff even on that, though they couldn't make good."

Jill said very carefully, "You hinted once that they might be men, pretending to be monsters. But that would mean that somebody I care about would probably be killed because he'd seen them and knew they weren't creatures from beyond the stars."

"I think you can forget that idea," said Lockley. "They don't act like men. Chasing away the plane that was going to land for us, and not using the beam on the fugitives it was plainly going to land for—that's not like men preparing to take over a continent! And nudging the Army back to make the cordoned space larger—that's not like our most likely human enemy, either. They'd wipe out the cordon by stepping up the terror beam to death ray intensity."

"Suppose they couldn't?"

"They wouldn't have landed with a weapon that couldn't kill anybody," said Lockley. "It's much more likely that they're monsters. But they don't act like monsters, either."

Jill was silent for a moment.

"Not even monsters who wanted to make friends?"

"They," said Lockley drily, "would hardly make a surprise landing. They'd have parked on the moon and squeaked at us until we got curious, and then they'd arrange to land, or to meet men in orbit, or something. But they didn't. They made a surprise landing, and cleared a big space of humans, keeping themselves to themselves. But if they do think we're animals, like rabbits, they'd kill people instead of stinging them up a bit, or paralyzing them for a while and then letting them go. That's not like any monster I can imagine!"

"Then—"

"You'd better go to sleep," said Lockley. "We've got a long day's hike before us tomorrow."

"Yes-s-s," agreed Jill reluctantly. "Good-night."

"'Night," said Lockley curtly.

He stayed awake. It was amusing that he was uneasy about wild animals. There were predators in the Park, and he had only an improvised club for a weapon. But he knew well enough that most animals avoid man because of a bewildering sudden development of instinct.

Grizzly bears, before the white man came, were so scornful of man that they could be considered the dominant species in North America. They'd been known to raid a camp of Indians to carry away a man for food. Indian spears and arrows were simply ineffective against them. When Stonewall Jackson was a lieutenant in the United States Army, stationed in the West to protect the white settlers, he and a detachment of mounted troopers were attacked without provocation by a grizzly who was wholly contemptuous of them. The then Lieutenant Jackson rode a horse which was blind in one eye, and he maneuvered to get the bear on the horse's blind side so he could charge it. With his cavalry sabre he split the grizzly's skull down to its chin. It was the only time in history that a grizzly bear was ever killed by a man with a sword. But no grizzly nowadays would attack a man unless cornered. Even cubs with no possible experience of humankind are terrified by the scent of men.

All that was true enough. In addition, preparations for the Park included much activity by the Wild Life Control unit, which persuaded bears to congregate in one area by putting out food for them, and took various other measures for deer and other animals. It had seeded trout streams with fingerlings and the lake itself with baby big-mouthed bass. The huge trailer truck of Wild Life Control was familiar enough. Lockley had seen it headed up to the lake the day before the landing. Now he found himself wondering sardonically to what degree the Wild Life Control men determined where mountain lions should hunt.

He'd slept in the open innumerable times without thinking of mountain lions. With Jill to look after, though, he worried. But he was horribly weary, and he knew somehow that in the back of his mind there was something unpleasant that was trying to move into his conscious thoughts. It was a sort of hunch. Wearily and half asleep, he tried to put his mind on it. He failed.

He awoke suddenly. There were rustlings among the trees. Something moved slowly and intermittently toward him. It could be anything, even a creature from Boulder Lake. He heard other sounds. Another creature. The first drew near, not moving in a straight line. The second creature followed it, drawing closer to the first.

Lockley's scalp crawled. Creatures from space might have some of the highly-developed senses which men had lost while growing civilized—full keenness of scent, for example.

Such a creature might be able to find Lockley and Jill in the darkness after trailing them for miles. And so primitive a talent, in a creature farther advanced than men, was somehow more horrifying than anything else Lockley had thought of about them. He gripped his club desperately, wholly aware that a star creature should be able to paralyze him with the terror beam...

There were whistling, squealing noises. They were very much like the squeaks his captors had directed at each other and at him when he was blindfolded and being led downhill to imprisonment in the compost pit shell. Very much like, but not identical. Nevertheless, Lockley's hair seemed to stand up on end and he raised his club in desperation.

The whistling squeals grew shriller. Then there was an indescribable sound and one of the two creatures rushed frantically away. It traveled in great leaps through the blackness under the trees.

And then there was a sudden whiff of a long-familiar odor, smelled a hundred times before. It was the reek of a skunk, stalked by a carnivore and defending itself as skunks do. But a skunk was nothing like a terror beam. Its effluvium offended only one sense, affected only one set of sensation nerves. The terror beam...

Lockley opened his mouth to laugh, but did not. The thing at the back of his mind had come forward. He was appalled.

Jill said shakily, "What's the matter? What's happened? That smell—"

"It's only a skunk," said Lockley evenly. "He just told me some very bad news. I know how the terror beam works now. And there's not a thing that can be done about it. Not a thing. It can't be!"

He raged suddenly, there in the darkness, because he saw the utter hopelessness of combatting the creatures who'd taken over Boulder Lake. There was nothing to keep them from taking over the whole earth, no matter what sort of monsters or not-monsters they might be.

CHAPTER SIX

It was nine o'clock at night when Lockley killed the porcupine, and ten by the time Jill had gone back to sleep huddled between the projecting roots of a giant tree. Shortly after midnight Lockley had been awakened when a skunk defeated a hungry predator within a hundred yards of their bivouac. But some time in between, there was another happening of much greater importance elsewhere.

Something came out of Boulder Lake National Park. All humans had supposedly fled from it. It was abandoned to the creatures of the thing from the sky. But something came out of it.

Nobody saw the thing, of course. Nobody could approach it, which was the point immediately demonstrated. No human being could endure being within seven miles of whatever it was. It was evidently a vehicle of some sort, however, because it swung terror beams before it, and terror beams on either side, and when it was clear of the Park it played terror beams behind it, too. Men who suffered the lightest touch of those sweeping beams of terror and anguish moved frantically to avoid having the experience again. So when something moved out of the Park and sent wavering terror beams before it, men moved to one side or the other and gave it room.

On a large-scale map in the military area command post, its progress could be watched as it was reported. The reports described a development of unbearable beam strength which showed up as a bulge in the cordon's roughly circular line. That bulge, which was the cordon itself moving back, moved outward and became a half-circle some miles across. It continued to move outward, and on the map it appeared like a pseudopod extruded by an enormous amoeba. It was the area of effectiveness of a weapon previously unknown on earth—the area where humans could not stay.

Deliberately, the unseen moving thing severed itself from the similar and larger weapon field which was its birthplace and its home. It moved with great deliberation toward the small town of Maplewood, twenty miles from the border of the Park.

Jeeps and motorcycles scurried ahead of it, just out of reach of its beams. They made sure that houses and farms and all inhabited places were emptied of people before the moving terror beams could engulf them. They went into the town of Maplewood itself and frantically made sure that nothing alive remained in it. They went on to clear the countryside beyond.

The unseen thing from the Park moved onward. High overhead there was a dull muttering like faraway thunder, but it was planes with filled bomb racks circling above the starlit land. There were men in those planes who ached to dive down and destroy this separated fraction of an invasion. But there were firm orders from the Pentagon. So long as the invaders killed nobody, they were not to be attacked. There was reason for the order in the desire of the government to be on friendly terms with a race which could travel between the stars. But there was an even more urgent reason. The aliens had not yet begun to murder, but it was suspected that they had a horrifying power to kill. So it was firmly commanded that no bomb or missile or bullet was to be used unless the invaders invited hostilities by killing humans. Their captives—the crew of a helicopter— might be freed if aliens and men achieved friendship. So for now—no provocation!

The thing which nobody saw moved comfortably over the ground between the park and Maplewood. In the center of the weapon field there was a something which generated the terror beam and probably carried passengers. Whatever it was, it moved onward and into Maplewood and for seven miles in every direction troops watched for it to move out again. Artillerymen had guns ready to fire upon it if they ever got firing coordinates and permission to go into action. Planes were ready to drop bombs if they ever got leave to do so. And a few miles away there were rockets ready to prove their accuracy and devastating capacity if only given a launching command. But nothing happened. Not even a flare was permitted to be dropped by the planes far up in the sky. A flare might be taken for hostility.

The thing from the Park stayed in Maplewood for two hours. At the end of that time it moved deliberately back toward the Park. It left the town untouched save for certain curious burglaries of hardware stores and radio shops and a garage or two. It looked as if intensely curious not-human beings had moved from their redoubt—Boulder Lake—to find out what civilization human beings had attained. They could guess at it by the buildings and the homes, but most notably in the technical shops of the inhabitants.

It went slowly and deliberately back into the Park. Humans moved cautiously back into the area that had been emptied. Not many, but enough to be sure that the thing had really returned to the place from which it had come. Soldiers were tentatively entering the again-abandoned town of Maplewood when the unseen thing changed the range of its weapon bearing on that little city. It was then presumably not less than seven miles on its way back to Boulder Lake. The military had congratulated themselves on what they'd learned. The beam projectors at the lake had a range of much more than seven miles, but this movable, unidentifiable thing carried a lesser armament. From it, men and animals seven miles away were safe. This was notable news.

Then the unseen object did something. The terror beam that flicked back and forth doubled in intensity. The soldiers just reentering Maplewood smelled foulness and saw bright lights. Bellowings deafened them. They fell with every muscle rigid in spasm. Beyond them other men were paralyzed. For five minutes the invaders' mobile weapon paralyzed all living things for a distance of fifteen miles. Then for thirty seconds it paralyzed living things for a distance of thirty miles. For a bare instant it convulsed men and animals for a greater distance yet. And all these victims of the terror beam knew, thereafter, an invincible horror of the beam.

The thing from the Park which nobody had seen went back into the Park. And then men were permitted to return to exactly the same places they'd been allowed to occupy before the thing began its excursion.

It seemed that nothing was changed, but everything was changed. If there were mobile carriers of the invasion weapon, then victory could not be had by a single atom bomb fired into Boulder Lake. There might be a dozen separate mobile terror beam generators scattered through the Park. Any atomic attack would need to be multiplied in its violence to be certain of results. Instead of one bomb there might be a need for fifty. They would have to destroy the Park utterly, even its mountains. And the fallout from so many atom bombs simply could not be risked. The invaders were effectively invulnerable.

While this undesirable situation was being demonstrated, Jill slept heavily between two roots of a very large tree, and Lockley dozed against a nearby tree trunk. He believed that he guarded Jill most vigilantly.

He awoke at dawn with the din of bird song in his ears. Jill opened her eyes at almost the same instant. She smiled at him and tried to get up. She was stiff and sore from the hardness of the ground on which she'd slept. But it was a new day, and there was breakfast. It was porcupine cooked the night before.

"Somehow," said Jill as she nibbled at a bone, "somehow I feel more cheerful than I did."

"That's a mistake," Lockley told her. "Start out with a few premonitions and the day improves as they turn out wrong. But if you start out hoping, the day ends miserably with most of your hopes denied."

"You've got premonitions?" she asked.

"Definitely," he said.

It was true. As yet he knew nothing of last night's temporary occupation of a human town, but he believed he knew how the terror beam worked even if he couldn't figure out a way to generate it. He could imagine no defense against it. But if Jill had awakened feeling cheerful, there was no reason to depress her. She'd have reason enough to be dejected later, beginning with proof of Vale's death and going on from there.

"We might listen to the news," she suggested. "A premonition or two might be ruled out right away!"

Silently, he turned on the little radio. Automatically, he set it for the lowest volume they could hear distinctly.

The main item in the news was a baldly factual but toned-down report of the thing from the lake which had left the park and examined a small human town in detail and then had returned to the Park. There were reports of peculiar hoofprints found where the invaders had been. They were not the hoofprints of any earthly animal. There was an optimistic report from the scientists at work on the problem of the beam. Someone had come up with an idea and some calculations which seemed to promise that the beam would presently be duplicated. Once it was duplicated, of course a way to neutralize it could be found.

Lockley grunted. The broadcast was enthusiastic in its comments on the scientists. It talked gobbledegook which sounded as if it meant something but was actually nonsense. It barely touched on the fact that human beings were now ordered out of a much larger space than had been evacuated before. There was a statement from an important official that panic buying of food was both unnecessary and unwise. Lockley grunted again when the newscast ended.

"The idea that anything that can be duplicated can be canceled," he announced gloomily, "is unfortunately rot. We can duplicate sounds, but there's no way to make them cancel out! Not accurately!"

Jill had eaten a substantial part of the porcupine while the newscast was on. It was not a satisfying breakfast, but it cheered her immensely after two days of near-starvation.

"But," she observed, "maybe that won't apply to this business when you report what you know. It's not likely that anybody else has stood just outside a beam and made tests of what it's like and how it's aimed and so on."

They started off. For journeying in the Park, Lockley had the advantage that as part of the preparation for making a new map, he'd familiarized himself with all mapping done to date. He knew very nearly where he was. He knew within a close margin just where the terror beam stretched. He'd smashed his watch, which during sunshine substituted admirably for a compass, but he could maintain a reasonably straight line toward that part of the Park's border the terror beam would cross.

They moved doggedly over mountain-flanks and up valleys, and once they followed a winding hollow for a long way because it led toward their destination without demanding that they climb. It was in this area that, pushing through brushwood beside a running stream, they came abruptly upon a big brown bear. He was no more than a hundred feet away. He stared at them inquisitively, raising his nose to sniff for their scent.

Lockley bent and picked up a stone. He threw it. It clattered on rocks on the ground. The bear made a whuffing sound and moved aggrievedly away.

"I'd have been afraid to do that," said Jill.

"It was a he-bear," said Lockley. "I wouldn't have tried it on a she-bear with cubs."

They went on and on. At mid-morning Lockley found some mushrooms. They were insipid and only acute hunger would make them edible raw, but he filled his pockets. A little later there were berries, and as they gathered and ate them he lectured learnedly on edible wild plants to be found in the wilderness. Jill listened with apparent interest. When they left the berry patch they swung to the left to avoid a steep climb directly in their way. And suddenly Lockley stopped short. At the same instant Jill caught at his arm. She'd turned white.

They turned and ran.

A hundred yards back, Lockley slackened his speed. They stopped. After a moment he managed to grin mirthlessly.

"A conditioned reflex," he said wryly. "We smell something and we run. But I think it's the old familiar terror beam that crosses highways to stop men from using them. If it were a portable beam projector with somebody aiming it, we wouldn't be talking about it."

Jill panted, partly with relief.

"I've thought of something I want to try," said Lockley. "I should have tried it yesterday when I first smashed my watch."

He retraced his steps to the spot where they'd caught the first whiff of that disgusting reptilian-jungle-decay odor which had bombarded their nostrils. Jill called anxiously, "Be careful!"

He nodded. He got the coiled bronze watchspring out of his pocket. He went very cautiously to the spot where the smell became noticeable. Standing well back from it, he tossed one end of the spring into it. He drew it back. He repeated the operation. He moved to one side. Again he swung the gold-colored ribbon. He dangled it back and forth. Then he drew back yet again and wrapped his left hand and wrists with many turns of the thin bronze spring, carefully spacing the turns. He moved forward once more.

He came back, his expression showing no elation at all.

"No good," he said unhappily. "In a way, it works. The spring acts as an aerial and picks up more of the beam than my hand. But I tried to make a Faraday cage. That will stop most electromagnetic radiation, but not this stuff! It goes right through, like electrons through a radio tube grid."

He put the spring back in his pocket.

"Well," he grimaced. "Let's go on again. I had a little bit of hope, but some smarter men than I am haven't got the right gimmick yet."

They started off once more. And this time they did not choose a path for easier travel, but went up a steep slope that rose for hundreds of feet to arrive at a crest with another steep slope going downhill. At the top Lockley said sourly, "I did discover one thing, if it means anything. The beam leaks at its edges, but it's only leakage. It doesn't diffuse. It's tight. It's more like a searchlight beam than anything else in that way. You can see a light beam at night because dust motes scatter some part of it. But most of the light goes straight on. This stuff does the same. It's hard to imagine a limit to its range."

He trudged on downhill. Jill followed him. Presently, when they'd covered two miles or more with no lightening of his expression, she said, "You said you understand how it works. Radio and radar beams don't have effects like this. How does this have them?"

"It makes high frequency currents on the surface of anything it hits. High frequency doesn't go into flesh or metal. It travels on the surface only. So when this beam hits a man it generates high frequency on his skin. That induces counter currents underneath, and they stimulate all the sensory nerves we've got—of our eyes and ears and noses as well as our skin. Every nerve reports its own kind of sensation. Run current over your tongue, and you taste. Induce a current in your eyes, and you see flashes of light. So the beam makes all our senses report everything they're capable of reporting, true or not, and we're blinded and deafened. Then the nerves to our muscles report to them that they're to contract, and they do. So we're paralyzed."

"And," said Jill, "if there's a way to generate high frequency on a man's skin there's nothing that can be done?"

"Nothing," said Lockley dourly.

"Maybe," said Jill, "you can figure out a way to prevent that high frequency generation."

He shrugged. Jill frowned as she followed him. She hadn't forgotten Vale, but she owed some gratitude to Lockley. Womanlike, she tried to pay part of it by urging him to do something he considered impossible.

"At least," she suggested, "it can't be a death ray!"

Lockley looked at her.

"You're wrong there," he said coldly. "It can."

Jill frowned again. Not because of his statement, but because she hadn't succeeded in diverting his mind from gloomy things. She had reason enough for sadness, herself. If she spoke of it, Lockley would try to encourage her. But he was concerned with more than his own emotions. Without really knowing it, Jill had come to feel a great confidence in Lockley. It had been reassuring that he could find food, and perhaps more reassuring that he could chase away a bear. Such talents were not logical reasons for being confident that he could solve the alien's seemingly invincible weapon, but she was inclined to feel so. And if she could encourage him to cope with the monsters—why—it would be even a form of loyalty to Vale. So she believed.

In the late afternoon Lockley said, "Another four or five miles and we ought to be out of the Park and on another highway we'll hope won't be blocked by a terror beam. Anyhow there should be an occasional farmhouse where we can find some sort of civilized food."

Jill said hungrily, "Scrambled eggs!"

"Probably," he agreed.

They went on and on. Three miles. Four. Five. Five and a half. They descended a minor slope and came to a hard-surfaced road with tire marks on it and a sign sternly urging care in driving. There were ploughed fields in which crops were growing. There was a row of stubby telephone poles with a sagging wire between them.

"We'll head west," said Lockley. "There ought to be a farmhouse somewhere near."

"And people," said Jill. "I look terrible!"

He regarded her with approval.

"No. You look all right. You look fine!"

It was pleasing that he seemed to mean it. But immediately she said, "Maybe we'll be able to find out about…about…"

"Vale," agreed Lockley. "But don't be disappointed if we don't. He could have escaped or been freed without everybody knowing it."

She said in surprise, "Been freed! That's something I didn't think of. He'd set to work to make them understand that we humans are intelligent and they ought to make friends with us. That would be the first thing he'd think of. And they might set him free to arrange it."

Lockley said, "Yes," in a carefully noncommittal tone.

Another mile, this time on the hard road. It seemed strange to walk on so unyielding a surface after so many miles on quite different kinds of footing. It was almost sunset now. There was a farmhouse set well back from the road and barely discernable beyond nearby growing corn. The house seemed dead. It was neat enough and in good repair. There were clackings of chickens from somewhere behind it. But it had the feel of emptiness.

Lockley called. He called again. He went to the door and would have called once more, but the door opened at a touch.

"Evacuated," he said. "Did you notice that there was a telephone line leading here from the road?"

He hunted in the now shadowy rooms. He found the telephone. He lifted the receiver and heard the humming of the line. He tried to call an operator. He heard the muted buzz that said the call was sounding. But there was no answer. He found a telephone book and dialed one number after another. Sheriff. Preacher. Doctor. Garage. Operator again. General store... He could tell that telephones rang dutifully in remote abandoned places. But there was no answer at all.

"I'll look in the chicken coops," said Jill practically.

She came back with eggs. She said briefly, "The chickens were hungry. I fed them and left the chicken yard gate open. I wonder if the beam hurts them too?"

"It does," said Lockley.

He made a light and then a fire and she cooked eggs which belonged to the unknown people who owned this house and who had walked out of it when instructions for immediate evacuation came. They felt queer, making free with this house of a stranger. They felt that he might come in and be indignant with them.

"I ought to wash the dishes," said Jill when they were finished.

"No," said Lockley. "We go on. We need to find some soldiers, or a telephone that works..."

"I'm not a good dishwasher anyhow," said Jill guiltily.

Lockley put a banknote on the kitchen table, with a weight on it to keep it from blowing away. They closed the house door. They'd eaten fully and luxuriously of eggs and partly stale bread and the sensation was admirable. They went out to the highway again.

"West is still our best bet," said Lockley. "They've blocked the highway to eastward with that terror beam."

The sun had set now, but a fading glory remained in the sky. They saw the slenderest, barest crescent of a new moon practically hidden in the sunset glow. They walked upon a civilized road, with a fence on one side of it and above it a single sagging telephone wire that could be made out against the stars.

"I feel," said Jill, "as if we were almost safe, now. All this looks so ordinary and reassuring."

"But we'd better keep our noses alert," Lockley told her. "We know that one beam comes nearly this far and probably— no, certainly crosses this road. There may be more."

"Oh, yes," agreed Jill. Then she said irrelevantly, "I'll bet they do make him a sort of—ambassador to our government to arrange for making friends. He'll be able to convince them!"

Again she referred to Vale. Lockley said nothing.

Night was now fully fallen. There were myriad stars overhead. They saw the telephone wire dipping between poles against the sky's brightness. They passed an open gate where another telephone wire led away, doubtless to another farmhouse. But if there was no one at the other end of a telephone line, there was no point in using a phone.

There came a rumbling noise behind them. They stared at one another in the starlight. The rumbling approached.

"It—can't be!" said Jill, marvelling.

"It's a motor," said Lockley. He could not feel complete relief. "Sounds like a truck. I wonder—"

He felt uneasiness. But it was absurd. Only human beings would use motor trucks.

There was a glow in the distance behind them. It came nearer as the sound of the motor approached. The motor's mutter became a grumble. It was definitely a truck. They could hear those other sounds that trucks always make in addition to their motor noises.

It came up to the curve they'd rounded last. Its headlight beams glared on the cornstalks growing next to the highway. One headlight appeared around the turn. Then the other. An enormous trailer-truck combination came bumbling toward them. Jill held up her hand for it to stop. Its headlights shone brightly upon her.

Airbrakes came on. The giant combination—cab in front, gigantic box body behind—came to a halt. A man leaned out. He said amazedly, "Hey, what are you folks doin' here? Everybody's supposed to be long gone! Ain't you heard about all civilians clearing out from twenty miles outside the Park? There's boogers in there! Characters from Mars or somewhere. They eat people!"

Even in the starlight Lockley saw the familiar Wild Life Control markings on the trailer. He heard Jill, her voice shaking with relief, explaining that she'd been at the construction camp and had been left behind, and that she and Lockley had made their way out.

"We want to get to a telephone," she added. "He has some information he wants to give to the Army. It's very important." Then she swallowed. "And I'd like to ask if you've heard anything about a Mr. Vale. He was taken prisoner by the creatures up there. Have you heard of his being released?"

The driver hesitated. Then he said, "No, ma'm. Not a word about him. But we'll take care of you two! You musta been through plenty! Jud, you go get in the trailer, back yonder. Make room for these two folks up on the front seat." He added explanatorily, "There's cases and stuff in the back, ma'm. You two folks climb right up here alongside of me. You sure musta had a time!"

The door on the near side of the truck cab opened. A small man got out. Silently, he went to the rear of the trailer and swung up out of sight. Jill climbed into the opened door. Lockley followed her. He still felt an irrational uneasiness, but he put it down to habit. The past few days had formed it.

"We've been cartin' stuff for the soldiers," explained the driver as Lockley closed the door behind him. "They keep track of where that terror beam is workin', and they tell us by truck radio, and we dodge it. Ain't had a bit of trouble. Never thought I'd play games with Martians! Did you see any of 'em? What sort of critters are they?"

He slipped the truck into gear and gunned the motor. Truck and trailer, together, began to roll down the highway. Lockley was irritated with himself because he couldn't relax and feel safe, as this development seemed to warrant.

Later, he would wonder why he hadn't used his head in this as in other matters during the few days just past.

He plainly hadn't.

CHAPTER SEVEN

The driver was avidly curious about the area where supposedly no human being could survive. He asked absorbed questions, especially and insistently about the aliens. Jill said that she'd seen a few of them, but only at a distance. They'd been investigating the evacuated construction camp. They were about the size of men. She couldn't describe them, but they weren't human beings. He seemed to find it unthinkable that she hadn't examined them in detail.

Lockley came to her rescue. He observed that he'd been a prisoner of the invaders, and had escaped. Then the driver's curiosity became insatiable. He wanted to know every imaginable detail of that experience. He expressed almost incredulous disappointment that Lockley couldn't give even a partial description of the creatures. When convinced, he launched a detailed recital of the descriptions offered by the workmen from the camp. He pictured the aliens as hoofed like horses, equipped with horns like antelopes, fitted with multiple arms like octopi and huge multi-faceted eyes like insects.

He seemed to contemplate this picture with vast satisfaction as the truck growled and rumbled through the night.

The headlights glared on ahead of the truck. There were dark fields and darker mountains beyond them. From time to time little side roads branched off. They undoubtedly led to houses, but no speck of lamp light appeared anywhere. This part of the world was empty, with the loneliness of a landscape from which every hint of human activity had been removed.

Jill asked a question. The driver grew garrulous. He gave a dramatic picture of terror throughout the world, the suspension of all ordinary antagonisms in the face of this menace to every man and nation on the earth. There was peace even in the world's trouble spots as appalled agitators saw how much worse things could be if the monsters took over the world to rule. But the driver insisted that the United States was calm. Us Americans, he assured Lockley, weren't scared. We were educated and we knew that them scientists would crack this nut somehow. Like only yesterday a broadcast said this Belgian guy had come up with calculations that said this poison beam had to be something like a radar beam or a laser beam or something like that. And the American scientists were right out there in front, along with guys from England and France and Italy and Germany and even Russia. All the big brains of the world were workin' on it! Those Martians were gonna wish they'd come visitin' polite instead of barging in like they owned the world! They'd be lucky if they wound up ownin' Mars!

Lockley pressed for details about the scientists' results. He didn't expect to get them, but the driver cheerfully obliged.

Radio, said the driver largely, worked by making waves like those on a pond. They spread out and reached places where there were instruments to detect them, and that was that. Radar made the same kind of waves, only smaller, which bounced back to where there was an instrument to detect them. These were ripple waves.

Lockley interpreted the term to mean sine waves, rounded at top and trough. It was a perfectly good word to express the meaning intended.

These were natural kindsa waves, pursued the driver. Lightning made them. Static was them, and sparks from running motors and blown fuses. Waves like that were generated whenever an electric circuit was made or broken besides their occurrence from purely natural causes.

"We can't feel 'em," said the driver expansively. "We're used to waves like that. Animals couldn't do anything about 'em and didn't need to before there was men. So when we come along, we couldn't notice 'em any more than we notice air pressure on our skin. We're used to it! But these scientists say there's waves that ain't natural. They ain't like ripples. They're like storm waves with foam on 'em. And that's the kind of waves we can notice. Like storm waves with sharp edges. We can notice them because they do things to us! These Martians make 'em do things. But now we know what kinda waves they are, we're gonna mess them up! And I'm savin' up a special kick for one o' those Martians when they're licked just as soon as I can find out which end of him is which an' suited to that kinda attention!"

Lockley found himself suspicious and was annoyed. Jill was safe now. This driver was well-informed, but probably everybody was well-informed now. They had reason to become so!

The truck trundled through the night. High overhead, a squadron of planes arrived to take its place in the ever-moving patrol around the Park. Another squadron, relieved, went away to the southwest. There was a deep-toned, faraway roaring from the engines aloft. All the sky behind the trailer seemed to mutter continuously. But the roof of stars ahead was silent.

Lockley stayed tense and was weary of his tenseness, Jill was safe. He tried to reason his uneasiness away. The cab of the truck wobbled and swayed. The feel of the vehicle was entirely unlike the feel of a passenger car. It felt tail-heavy. The driver had ceased to talk. He seemed to be musing as he drove. He'd asked about the invaders but seemed almost indifferent to any adventures Jill and Lockley might have had on their way out. He didn't ask what they'd done for food. He was thinking of something else.

Lockley found himself questioning the driver's statements just after they got in. Driving for the Army. The Army kept track of where the terror beams existed, and notified this truck by truck radio, and he dodged all such road barriers. That was what he said. It seemed plausible, but—

"One thing strikes me funny," said the driver, musingly. "Those critters blindfoldin' you and those other guys. What' you think they did it for?"

"To keep us from seeing them," said Lockley, curtly.

"But why'd they want to do that?"

"Because," said Lockley, "they might not have been Martians. They might not have been critters. They might have been men."

On the instant he regretted bitterly that he'd said it. It was a guess, only, with all the evidence against it. The driver visibly jumped. Then he turned his head.

"Where'd you get that idea?" he demanded. "What's the evidence? Why d'you think it?"

"They blindfolded me," said Lockley briefly.

A pause. Then the driver said vexedly, "That's a funny thing to make you think they was men! Hell! Excuse me, ma'm!—they coulda had all kindsa reasons for blindfoldin' you! It coulda been part of their religion!"

"Maybe," said Lockley. He was angry with himself for having said something which was needlessly dramatic.

"Didn't you have any other reason for thinkin' they were men?" demanded the driver curiously. "No other reason at all?"

"No other at all," said Lockley.

"It's a crazy reason, if you ask me!"

"Quite likely," conceded Lockley.

He'd been indiscreet, but no more. He'd said what he thought, perhaps because he was tired of watching all the country round him for a menace to Jill, and then watching every word he spoke to keep her from abandoning hope for Vale.

Jill said, "Where are we headed for? I hope I can get to a telephone. I want to ask about somebody... He wants to tell the soldiers something."

"We're headed for a army supply dump," said the driver comfortably, "to load up with stuff for the guys that're watching all around the Park. We'll be goin' through Serena presently. Funny. Everybody moved out by the Army. A good thing, too. The folks in Maplewood couldn't ha' been got out last night before the Martians got there."

The trailer-truck went on through the night. The driver lounged in his seat, keeping a negligent but capable eye on the road ahead. The headlights showed a place where another road crossed this one and there was a filling station, still and dark, and four or five dwellings nearby with no single sign of life about them. Then the crossroads settlement fell behind. A mile beyond it Jill said startledly, "Lights! There's a town. It's lighted."

"It's Serena," said the driver. "The street lights are on because the electricity comes from far away. With the lights on it's a marker for the planes, too, so they can tell exactly where they are and the Park too. They can't see the ground so good at night, from away up there."

The white street lamps seemed to twinkle as the trailer-truck rumbled on. A single long line of them appeared to welcome the big vehicle. It went on into the town. It reached the business district. There were side streets, utterly empty, and then the main street divided. The truck bore to the right. There were three and four-story buildings. Every window was blank and empty, reflecting only the white street lamps. No living thing anywhere. There had been no destruction, but the town was dead. Its lights shone on streets so empty that it would have seemed better to leave them to the kindly dark.

Jill exclaimed, "Look! That window!"

And ahead, in the dead and lifeless town, a single window glowed from electric light inside it, and it looked lonelier than anything else in the world.

"I'm gonna look into that!" said the driver. "Nobody's supposed to be here."

The truck came to a stop. The driver got out. There was a stirring, behind, and the small man who'd given his place to Jill and Lockley popped out of the trailer body. Lockley saw the name of a local telephone company silhouetted on the lighted windowpane. He opened the door. Jill followed him instantly. The four of them—driver, helper, Lockley and Jill—crowded into the building hallway to investigate the one lighted room in a town where twenty thousand people were supposed to live.

There was a door with a frosted glass top through which light showed. The driver turned the door-knob and marched in. The room had an alcoholic smell. A man with sunken cheeks slept heavily in a chair, his head forward on his chest.

The driver shook him.

"Wake up, guy!" he said sternly. "Orders are for all civilians to clear outa this town. You wanna soldier to come by an' take you for a looter an' bump you off?"

He shook again. The cadaverous man blinked his eyes open. The smell of alcohol was distinct. He was drunk. He gazed ferociously up at the driver of the truck.

"Who the hell are you?" he demanded belligerently.

The driver spoke sternly, repeating what he'd said before. The drunk assumed an air of outraged dignity.

"If I wanna stay here, that's my business! Who th' hell are you anyways, disturbin' a citizen tax-payer on his lawful occasions? Are you Martians? I wouldn't put it pasht you!"

He sat down and went back to sleep.

The driver said fretfully, "He oughtn't to be here! But we ain't got room to carry him. I'm gonna use the truck radio an' ask what to do. Maybe they'll send a Army truck to get him outa here. He could set the whole town on fire!"

He went out. The small man who was his helper followed him. He hadn't spoken a word. Lockley growled. Then Jill said breathlessly, "The switch-board has some long distance lines. I know how to connect them. Shall I try?"

Lockley agreed emphatically. Jill slipped into the operator's chair and donned the headset. She inserted a plug and pressed a switch.

"I did an article once on how—Hello! Serena calling. I have a very important message for the military officer in command of the cordon. Will you route me through, please?"

Her manner was convincingly professional. She looked up and smiled shakily at Lockley. She spoke again into the mouthpiece before her. Then she said, "One moment, please." She covered the mouthpiece with her hand.

"I can't get the general," she said. "His aide will take the message and if it's important enough—"

"It is," said Lockley. "Give me the phone."

She vacated the chair and handed him the operator's instrument with its light weight earphones and a mouthpiece that rested on his chest.

"My name's Lockley," said Lockley evenly. "I was in the Park on a Survey job the morning the thing came down from the sky. I relayed Vale's message describing the landing and the creatures that came out of the—object. I was talking to him by microwave when he was seized by them. I reported that via Sattell of the Survey. You probably know of these reports."

A tinny voice said with formal cordiality that he did, indeed.

"I've just managed to get out of the park," said Lockley. "I've had a chance to experiment with a stationary terror beam. I've information of some importance about detecting those beams before they strike."

The tinny voice said hastily that Lockley should speak to the general himself. There were clickings and a long wait. Lockley shook his head impatiently. When a new voice spoke, he said,

"I'm at Serena. I was brought here by a Wild Life Control trailer-truck which picked us up just outside the Park. I mention that because the driver says he's driving it for the Army, now. The information I have to pass on is…"

Curtly and succinctly, he began to give exact information about the terror beam. Its detection so that one need not enter it. The total lack of effectiveness of a Faraday cage to check it. Its use to block highways and its one use against a low-flying plane. The failure to search him out with that terror beam was to be noted. There was other evidence that the monsters were not monsters at all—

The new voice interrupted sharply. It asked him to wait. His information would be recorded. Lockley waited, biting his lips. The voice returned after an unconscionably long wait. It told him to go ahead.

The driver of the truck was taking a long time to make contact with the military. He'd have done better by telephone instead of short wave.

The new voice repeated sharply for Lockley to go on with his story. And very, very carefully Lockley explained the contradictions in the behavior of the invaders. The blindfolds. The fact that it had been absurdly easy for four human prisoners in a compost pit shell to escape—almost as if it were intended for them to get away and report that their captors regarded men as on a par with game birds and rabbits and porcupines. True aliens would not have bothered to give such an impression. But men cooperating with aliens would contrive every possible trick to insist that only aliens operated at Boulder Lake.

"I'm saying," said Lockley carefully, "that they do not act like aliens making a first landing on earth. Apparently their ship is designed to land in deep water. On a first landing, they should have chosen the sea. But they knew Boulder Lake was deep enough to cushion their descent. How did they know it? They didn't kill us local animals for study, but they dropped in other local animals to convince us that they wouldn't mind. Why try to fill us with horror—and then let us escape?"

The voice at the other end said sharply, *"What do you infer from all this?"*

"They've been briefed," said Lockley. "They know too much about this planet and us humans. Somebody has told them about human psychology and suggested that they conquer us without destroying our cities or our factories or our usefulness as slaves. We'll be much more valuable if captured that way! I'm saying that they've got humans advising and cooperating with them! I'm suggesting that those humans have made a deal to run earth for the aliens, paying them all the tribute they can demand. I'm saying that we're not up against an invasion only by aliens, but by aliens with humans in active cooperation and acting not only as advisers but probably as spies. I'm—"

"Mr. Lockley!" said the voice at the other end of the wire. It was startled and shocked. It became pompous. *"Mr. Lockley, what has been your training?"* The voice did not wait for an answer. *"Where have you become qualified to offer opinions contradicting all the information and all the decisions of scientists and military men alike? Where do you get the authority to make such statements? They are preposterous! You have wasted my time! You—"*

Lockley reached over and flipped back the switch he'd seen Jill flip over. He carefully put down the headset. He stood up.

The driver and the small man came back. They picked up the sleeping drunk and moved toward the door. Something fell out of the drunk's pocket. It was a wallet. They did not notice. They went out, carrying the drunk. Jill stooped and recovered it. She looked at Lockley's face.

"What—"

"I'm trying," said Lockley in a grating voice, "to figure out what to do next. That didn't work."

"I'll be right back," said Jill.

She went out to deliver the wallet to the driver, who had apparently been ordered to put the drunk in the trailer body and deliver him somewhere.

Lockley swore explosively when she was gone. He clenched and unclenched his hands. He paced the length of the room.

Jill came back, her face white.

"They opened the door of the trailer to pass him in," she said in a thin, strained voice. "And there were other men back there. Several of them! And machinery! Not cages for animals but engines—generators—electrical things! I'm frightened!"

"And I," said Lockley, "am a fool. I should have known it! Look here—"

The frosted-glass door opened. The driver came back. He had a revolver in his hand.

"Too bad!" he said calmly. "We should've been more careful. But the lady saw too much. Now—"

The revolver bore on Lockley. Jill flung herself upon it. Lockley swung, with every ounce of his strength. He connected with the driver's jaw. The driver went limp. Lockley had the revolver almost before he reached the floor.

"Quick!" he snapped. "Where was the machinery? Front or back part of the trailer?"

"All of it," panted Jill. "Mostly front. What—"

"The hall again," Lockley snapped. "Hunt for a back door!"

He thrust her out. She fumbled toward the back of the building while he went to the street entrance. The trailer-truck loomed huge. The driver's helper came out of it. Another man followed him. Still another…

Lockley fired from the doorway. One bullet through the front part of the truck. One near the middle. Then a third halfway between the first two. The three men dived to the ground, thinking themselves his targets. But Jill called inarticulately from the back of the dark hall. Lockley raced back to her. He saw starlight. She waited, shivering. They went out and he closed the door softly behind him.

He took her hand and they ran through the night. Overhead there was a luminous mistiness because of the street light, but here were abysmal darknesses between vague areas on which the starlight fell. Lockley said evenly, "We've got to be quiet.

Maybe I hit some of the machinery. Maybe. If I didn't, it's all over!"

The back of a building. An alleyway. They ran down it. There was a street with trees, where the street lights cast utterly black shadows in between intolerable glare. They ran across the street. On the other side were residences—the business district was not large. Lockley found a gate, and opened it quietly and as quietly closed it behind them. They ran into a lane between two dead, dark, dreary structures in which people had lived but from which all life was now gone.

A back yard. A fence. Lockley helped Jill get over it. Another lane. Another street. But this street was not crossed— not here, anyhow—by another which led back to the street of the telephone office. A man could not look from there and see them running under the lights.

The blessed irregularity of the streets continued. They ran and ran until Jill's breath came in pantings. Lockley was drenched in sweat because he expected at any instant to smell the most loathesome of all possible combinations of odors, and then to see flashing lights originating in his own eyes, and sounds which would exist only in the nerves of his ears, and then to feel all his muscles knot in total and horrible paralysis.

They heard the truck motor rumble into life when they were many blocks away. They heard the clumsy vehicle move. It continued to growl, and they knew that it was moving about the streets with its occupants trying to sight fleeing figures under the darknesses which were trees.

"I hit—I hit the generator," panted Lockley. "I must have! Else they'd swing a beam on us!"

He stopped. Here they were in a district where many large homes pooled their lawns in block-long stretches of soft green. The street lights cast arbitrary patches of brightness against the houses, but their windows were blank and dark. This street, like most in this small town, was lined with trees on either side. There were the fragrances of flowers and grass.

"We aren't safe now," said Lockley, "but I just found out there may not be any safety anywhere."

Jill's teeth chattered.

"What will we do? What was that machinery? I felt—frightened because it wasn't what he said was back there. So I told you. But what was it?".

"At a guess," said Lockley, "a terror beam generator. The invaders must have human friends. To us they're spies. They're cooperating with the monsters. Apparently they're even trusted with terror beam projectors."

He stood still, thinking, while in the distance the trailer-truck ground and rumbled about the streets. It was not a very promising method for finding two fugitives. They could hide if it turned onto a street they used. It could not continue the search indefinitely. The most likely final course would be to leave some of the unknown number of men in its trailer to search the town on foot. Even that might not be successful. But it wouldn't be a good idea for Lockley and Jill to remain here, either.

"We look for two-car garages," said Lockley. "It's not a good chance, but it's all we've got. If somebody had two cars, they might have left one behind when they evacuated. I can jump an ignition switch if necessary. Meanwhile we'll be moving out of town, which is a good idea even if we do it on foot!"

They ceased to use the streets with their dramatic contrast of vivid lights with total shadows. They moved behind a row of what would be considered mansions in Serena, Colorado. Sometimes they stumbled over flower beds, and once there was a hose over which Jill tripped, and once Lockley barked his shin on a garden wheelbarrow. Most of the garages were empty or contained only tools and garden equipment.

Then something made Lockley look up. A slender, truss-braced, mastlike tower rose skyward. It began on the lawn of a house with wide porches. There was a two-car garage with one wide door open.

"A radio ham," said Lockley. "I wonder—"

But he looked first in the garage. There was a car. It looked all right. He climbed in and opened the door. The dome light came on. The key was still in the ignition. He turned it and the gauge showed that the gas tank was three-quarters full. This was unbelievable good fortune.

"They probably intended to use this and then changed their minds," said Lockley. "I'll get the door open and attempt a little burglary. Just one burglary with a prayer that he used a storage battery for his power!"

Breaking in was simple. He tried the windows opening on the main wide porch. One window slid up. He went inside, Jill following.

The ham radio outfit was in the cellar. Like most radio hams, this one had battery-powered equipment as a matter of public responsibility. In case of storm or disaster when power lines are down, the ham operators of the United States can function as emergency communication systems, working without outside power. This operator was equipped as membership in the organization required.

Lockley warmed up the tubes. He tuned to a general call frequency. He began to say, "May Day! May Day! May Day!" in a level voice. This emergency call has precedence over all other calls but S.O.S., which has an identical meaning. But "May Day" is more distinct and unmistakable when heard faintly.

There were answers within minutes. Lockley snapped for them to stay tuned while he called for others. He had half a dozen hams waiting curiously when he began to broadcast what he wanted the world to know.

He told it as briefly and as convincingly as he could. Then he said, "Over" and threw the reception switch for questions.

There were no questions. His broadcast had been jammed. Some other station or stations were transmitting pure static with deafening volume, evidently from somewhere nearby. Lockley could not tell when it had begun. It could have been from the instant he began to speak. It was very likely that not one really useful word had been heard anywhere.

But a direction finder could have betrayed his position.

CHAPTER EIGHT

It was a ticklish job getting the car out of the garage and into the street. Lockley was afraid that starting the motor would make a noise which in the silence of the town's absolute abandonment could be heard for a long way. The grinding of the starter, though, lasted only for seconds. It might make men listen, but they could hardly locate it before the motor caught and ran quietly. Also, the trailer-truck was still in motion and making its own noise. Of course it was probably posting watchers and listeners here and there to try to find Lockley and Jill.

So Lockley backed the car into the street as silently as was possible. He did not turn on the lights. He stopped, headed away from the area in which the truck rumbled. He sent the car forward at a crawl. Then an idea occurred to him and cold chills ran down his spine. It is possible to use a short wave receiver to pick up the ignition sparks of a car. Normally such sparkings are grounded so the car's own radio will work. But sometimes a radio is out of order. It was characteristic of Lockley's acquired distrust of luck and chance that he thought of so unlikely a disaster.

He eased the car into motion, straining his ears for any sign that the truck reacted. Then he moved the car slowly away from the business district. It required enormous self-control to go slowly. While among the lighted streets the urge to flee at top speed was strong. But he clenched his teeth. A car makes much less noise when barely in motion. He made it drift as silently as a wraith under the trees and the street lamps.

They got out of town. The last of the street lamps was behind them. There was only starlight ahead, and an unknown road with many turns and curves. Sometimes there were roadsigns, dimly visible as uninformative shapes beside the highway. They warned of curves and other driving hazards, but they could not be read because Lockley drove without lights. He left the car dark because any glare would have been visible to the men of the trailer-truck for a very long way.

Starlight is not good for fast driving, and when a road passes through a wooded space it is nerve-racking. Lockley drove with foreboding, every sense alert and every muscle tense. But just after a painful progress through a series of curves with high trees on either side which he managed by looking up at the sky and staying under the middle of the ribbon of stars he could see, Lockley touched the brake and stopped the car.

"What's the matter?" asked Jill, as he rummaged under the instrument panel.

"I think," said Lockley, "that I must have damaged something in that truck. Otherwise they'd have turned their beam on us just to get even.

"But maybe they'll be able to make a repair. In any case there are other beams. Those are probably stationary and the truck knows where they are and calls by truck radio to have them shut off when it wants to go by. That would work. Using the Wild Life truck was really very clever."

He wrenched at something. It gave. He pulled out a length of wire and started working on one end of it.

"If they guess we got a car," he observed, "they'll expect us to run into a road block beam that would wreck the car and paralyze us. I'm taking a small precaution against that. Here." He put the wire's end into her hand. "It's the lead-in from this car's radio antenna. It ought to warn us of beams across the road as my watch spring did in the hills. Hold it."

"I will," said Jill.

"One more item," he said. He got out of the car and closed the door quickly. He went to the back. There was the sound of breaking glass. He returned, saying, "No brake lights will go on now. I'll try to do something about that dome light." With a sharp blow he shattered it. "Now we could be as hard to trail as that Wild Life truck was the other night."

Jill groped as the car got into motion again.

"You mean it was—Oh!"

"Most likely," agreed Lockley, "it was the thing that went out of the park and occupied Maplewood, flinging terror beams in all directions. Some of the truck's crew would have had footgear to make hoofprints. They committed a token burglary or two. And there was the illusion of aliens studying these queer creatures, men."

They went on at not more than fifteen miles an hour. The car was almost soundless. They heard insects singing in the night. There was a steady, monotonous rumbling high above where Air Force planes patrolled outside the Park. After a time Jill said, "You seemed discouraged when you talked to that general."

"I was," said Lockley. "I am. He played it safe, refused to admit that anybody in authority over him could possibly be mistaken. That's sound policy, and I was contradicting the official opinion of his superiors. I've got to find somebody of much lower rank, or much higher. Maybe—"

Jill said in a strained voice, "Stop!"

He braked. She said unsteadily, "Holding the wire, I smell that horrible smell."

He put his hand on the wire's end. He shared the sensation.

"Terror beam across the highway," he said calmly. "Maybe on our account, maybe not. But there was a side road a little way back."

He backed the car. He'd smashed the backing lights, too. He guided himself by starlight. Presently he swung the wheel and faced the car about. He drove back the way he had come. A mile or so, and there was another hard-surface road branching off. He took it. Half an hour later Jill said quickly, "Brakes!"

The road was blocked once more by an invisible terror beam, into which any car moving at reasonable speed must move before its driver could receive warning.

"This isn't good," he said coldly. "They may have picked some good places to block. We have to go almost at random, just picking roads that head away from the Park. I don't know how thoroughly they can cage us in, though."

There was a flicker of light in the sky. Lockley jerked his head around. It flashed again. Lightning. The sky was clouding up.

"It's getting worse," he said in a strained voice. "I've been taking every turn that ought to lead us away from the Park, but I've had to use the stars for direction. I didn't think that soldiers would keep us from getting away from here. I was almost confident. But what will I do without the stars?"

He drove on. The clouds piled up, blotting out the heavens. Once Lockley saw a faint glow in the sky and clenched his teeth. He turned away from it at the first opportunity. The glow could be Serena, and he could have been forced back toward it by the windings of the highway he'd followed without lights. Twice Jill warned him of beams across the highway. Once, driven by his increasing anxiety, his brakes almost failed to stop him in time. When the car did stop, he was aware of faint tinglings on his skin. There were erratic flashings in his eyes, too, and a discordant composite of sounds which by association with past suffering made him nauseated. Perhaps this extra leakage from the terror beam was through the metal of the car.

When he got out of that terror beam the sky was three-quarters blacked out and before he was well away from the spot there was only a tiny patch of stars well down toward the horizon. There were lightning flickers overhead. After a time he depended on them to show him the road.

Then the rain came. The lightning increased. The road twisted and turned. Twice the car veered off onto the road's shoulders, but each time he righted it. As time passed conditions grew worse. It was urgent that he get as far as possible from Serena, because of the Wild Life truck which could seize Jill and himself if its beam generators were repaired, and whose occupants could murder them if they weren't. But it was most urgent that he get away beyond the military cordon to find men who would listen to his information and see that use was made of it. Yet in driving rain and darkness, without car lights and daring to drive only at a crawl, he might be completely turned around.

"I think," he said at last, "I'll turn in at the next farm gate the lightning shows us. I'll try to get the car into a barn so it won't show up at daybreak. We might be heading straight back into the Park!"

He did turn, the next time a lightning flash showed him a turn-off beside a rural free delivery mailbox. There was a house at the end of a lane. There was a barn. He got out and was soaked instantly, but he explored the open space behind the wide, open doors. He backed the car in.

"So," he explained to Jill, "if we have a chance to move we won't have to back around first."

They sat in the car and looked out at the rain-filled darkness. There was no light anywhere except when lightning glittered on the rain. In such illuminations they made out the farmhouse, dripping floods of water from its eaves. There was a chicken house. There were fences. They could not see to the gate or the highway through the falling water, but there had been solid woodland where they turned off into the lane.

"We'll wait," said Lockley distastefully, "to see if we are in a tight spot in the morning. If we're well away—and I've no real idea where we are—we'll go on. If not, we'll hide till dark and hope for stars to steer by when we go."

Jill said confidently, "We'll make it. But where to?"

"To any place away from Boulder Lake Park, and where I'm a human being instead of a crackpot civilian. To where I can explain some things to people who'll listen, if it isn't too late."

"It's not," said Jill with as much assurance as before.

There was a pause. The rain poured down. Lightning flashed. Thunder roared.

"I didn't know," said Jill tentatively, "that you believed the invaders—the monsters—had people helping them."

"The overall picture isn't a human one," he told her. "But there's a design that shows somebody knows us. For instance, nobody's been killed. At least not publicly. That was arranged by somebody who understood that if there was a massacre, we'd fight to the end of our lives and teach our children to fight after us."

She thought it over. "You'd be that way," she said presently. "But not everybody. Some people will do anything to stay alive. But you wouldn't."

The rain made drumming sounds on the barn roof. Lockley said, "But what's happened isn't altogether what humans would devise. Humans who planned a conquest would know they couldn't make us surrender to them. If this was a sort of Pearl Harbor attack by human enemies—and you can guess who it might be—they might as well start killing us on the largest possible scale at the beginning. If monsters with no information about us landed, they might perpetrate some massacres with the entirely foolish idea of cowing us. But there haven't been any massacres. So it's neither a cold war trick nor an unadvised landing of monsters. There's another angle in it somewhere. Monster-human cooperation is only a guess. I'm not satisfied, but it's the best answer so far."

Jill was silent for a long time. Then she said irrelevantly, "You must have been a good friend of...of..."

"Vale?" Lockley said. "No. I knew him, but that's all. He only joined the Survey a few months ago. I don't suppose I've talked to him a dozen times, and four of those times he was with you. Why'd you think we were close friends?"

"What you've done for me," she said in the darkness.

He waited for a lightning flash to show him her expression. She was looking at him.

"I didn't do it for Vale," said Lockley.

"Then why?"

"I'd have done it for anyone," said Lockley ungraciously.

In a way it was true, of course. But he wouldn't have gone up to the construction camp to make sure that anyone hadn't been left behind. The idea wouldn't have occurred to him.

"I don't think that's true," said Jill.

He did not answer. If Vale was alive, Jill was engaged to him; although if matters worked out, Lockley would not be such a fool as to play the gentleman and let her marry Vale by default. On the other hand, if Vale was dead, he wouldn't be the kind of fool who'd try to win her for himself before she'd faced and recovered from Vale's death. A girl could forgive herself for breaking her engagement to a living man, but not for disloyalty to a dead one.

"I think," said Lockley deliberately, "that we should change the subject. I will talk about why I went to the Lake after you when everything has settled down. I had reasons. I still have them. I will express them, eventually, whether Vale likes it or not. But not now."

There was a long silence, while rain fell with heavy drumming noises and the world was only a deep curtain of lightning-lighted droplets of falling water.

"Thanks," said Jill very quietly. "I'm glad."

And then they sat in silence while the long hours went by. Eventually they dozed. Lockley was awakened by the ending of the rain. It was then just the beginning of gray dawn. The sky was still filled with clouds. The ground was soaked. There were puddles here and there in the barnyard, and water dripped from the barn's eaves, and from the now vaguely visible house, and from the two or three trees beside it.

Lockley opened the car door and got out quietly. Jill did not waken. He visited the chicken house, and horrendous squawkings came out of it. He found eggs. He went to the house, stepping gingerly from grass patch to grass patch, avoiding the puddles between them. He found bread, jars of preserves and cans of food. He inspected the lane. The car's tracks had been washed out. He nodded to himself.

He went back to the barn. There was still only dusky half-light. He pulled the doors almost shut behind him, leaving only a four-inch gap to see through. Now the car was safely out of sight and there was no sign that any living being was near.

"You closed the doors," said Jill. "Why?"

He said reluctantly, "I'm afraid we're as badly off as we were at the beginning. Unless I'm mistaken, we got turned around in that rainstorm on those twisty roads, and the Park begins nearby. This isn't the highway I drove up on to find you, the one where my car's wrecked. This is another one. I don't think we're more than twenty miles from the Lake, here. And that's something I didn't intend!"

He began to unload his pockets.

"I got something for us to eat. We'll just have to lie low until night and fumble our way out toward the cordon, with the stars to guide us."

There was silence, save for the lessened dripping of water. Lockley was filled with a sort of baffled impatience with himself. He felt that he'd acted like an idiot in trying to escape the evacuated area by car. But there'd been nothing else to do. Before that he'd stupidly been unsuspicious when the Wild Life truck came down a highway that he'd known was blocked by a terror beam. And perhaps he'd been a fool to refuse to discuss why he'd gone up to the construction camp to see to her safety when by all the rules of reason it was none of his business.

The gray light paled a little. Through the gap between the barn doors, he could see past the house. Then he could see the length of the lane and the trees on the far side of the highway.

He was laying out the food when suddenly he froze, listening. The stillness of just-before-dawn was broken by the distant rumble of an internal-combustion engine. It was a familiar kind of rumbling. It drew nearer. Except for the singularly distinct impacts of drippings from leaves and roof to the ground below, it was the only sound in all the world.

It became louder. Jill clenched her hands unconsciously.

"I don't think there are any car tracks at the turn-off where we came in," said Lockley in a level voice. "The rain should have washed them out. It's not likely they're looking for us here anyhow. But I've only got three bullets left in the pistol. Maybe you'd better go off and hide in the cornfield. Then if things go wrong they'll believe I left you somewhere."

"No," said Jill composedly, "I'd leave tracks in the ploughed ground. They'd find me."

Lockley ground his teeth. He got out the pistol he'd taken from the truck driver in the lighted room in Serena. He looked at it grimly. It would be useless, but...

Jill came and stood beside him, watching his face.

The rumbling of the truck was still nearer and louder. It diminished for a moment where a curve in the road took the vehicle behind some trees that deadened its noise. But then the sound increased suddenly. It was very loud and frighteningly near.

Lockley watched through the gap between the barn doors. He stayed well back lest his face be seen.

The trailer-truck with the Wild Life Control markings on it rumbled past. It growled and roared. The noise seemed thunderous. Its wheels splashed as they went through a puddle close by the gate.

It went away into the distance. Jill took a deep breath of relief. Lockley made a warning gesture.

He listened. The noise went on steadily for what he guessed to be a mile or more. Then they heard it stop. Only by straining his ears could Lockley pick up the sound of an idling motor. Maybe that was imagination. Certainly at any other less silent time he could not possibly have heard it. Jill whispered, "Do you think—"

He gestured for silence again. The distant heavy engine continued to idle. One minute. Two. Three. Then the grinding of gears and the roar of the engine once more. The truck went on. Its sound diminished. It faded away altogether.

"They got to a place where the road's blocked with a terror beam," said Lockley evenly. "They stopped and called by short wave and the beam was cut off, then they went past the block-point and undoubtedly the beam was turned on again."

He debated a decision.

"We'll have breakfast," he said shortly. "We'll have to eat the eggs raw, but we need to eat. Then we'll figure things out. It may be that we'd be sensible to forget about cars and try to get to the cordon on foot, robbing farmhouses of food on the way. There can't be too many...collaborators. And we could keep out of sight."

He opened a jar of preserves.

"But it would be better for you to be travelling by car, if tonight's clear and there's starlight to drive by."

Jill said practically, "There might be some news..."

Her hands shook as she put the pocket radio on the hood of the car. Lockley noticed it. He felt, himself, the strain of their long march through the wilderness with danger in every breath they drew. And he was shaken in a different way by the proof that humans were cooperating fully with the invading monsters. It was unthinkable that anybody could be a traitor not only to his own country but to all the human race. He felt incredulous. It couldn't be true! But it obviously was.

The radio made noises. Lockley turned it in another direction. There was music. Jill's face worked. She struggled not to show how she felt.

The radio said, "*Special news bulletin! Special news bulletin! The Pentagon announces that for the first time there has been practically complete success in duplicating the terror beam used by the space invaders at Boulder Lake! Working around the clock, teams of foreign and American scientists have built a projector of what is an entirely new type of electronic radiation which produces every one of the physiological effects of the alien terror beam! It is low-power, so far, and has not produced complete paralysis in experimental animals. Volunteers have submitted themselves to it, however, and report that it produces the sensations experienced by members of the military cordon around Boulder Lake. A crash program for the*

186

development of the projector is already under way. At the same time a crash program to develop a counter to it is already showing promising results. The authorities are entirely confident that a complete defense against the no longer mysterious weapon will be found. There is no longer any reason to fear that earth will be unable to defend itself against the invaders now present on earth, or any reinforcements they may receive!"

The newscast stopped and a commercial called the attention of listeners to the virtues of an anti-allergy pill. Jill watched Lockley's face. He did not relax.

The broadcast resumed. With this full and certain hope of a defense against the invasion weapon, said the announcer, it remained important not to destroy the alien ship if it could be captured for study. The use of atom bombs was, therefore, again postponed. But they would be used if necessary. Meanwhile, against such an emergency, the areas of evacuation would be enlarged. People would be removed from additional territory so if bombs were used there would be no humans near to be harmed.

Another commercial. Lockley turned off the radio.

"What do you think?" asked Jill.

"I wish they hadn't made that broadcast," said Lockley. "If there were only monsters involved and they didn't understand English, it would be all right. But with humans helping them, it sets a deadline. If we're going to counter their weapon, they have to use it before we finish the job."

After a moment he said bitterly, "There was a time, right after the last big war, when we had the bomb and nobody else did. There couldn't be a cold war then! There were years when we could destroy others and they couldn't have fought back. Now somebody else is in that position. They can destroy us and we can't do a thing. It'll be that way for a week, or maybe two, or even three. It'll be strange if they don't take advantage of their opportunity."

Jill tried to eat the food Lockley had laid out. She couldn't. She began to cry quietly. Lockley swore at himself for telling her the worst, which it was always his instinct to see. He said urgently, "Hold it! That's the worst that could happen. But it's not the most likely!"

She tried to control her tears.

"We're in a fix, yes!" he said insistently. "It does look like there may be a flock of other space ship landings within days. But the monsters don't want to kill people. They want a world with people working for them, not dead. They've proved it. They'll avoid massacres. They won't let the humans who're their allies destroy the people they want alive and useful."

Jill clenched her fists. "But it would be better to be dead than like that!"

"But wait!" protested Lockley. "We've duplicated the terror beam. Do you think they'll leave it at that? The men who know how to do it will be scattered to a dozen or a hundred places, so they can't possibly all be found, and they'll keep on secretly working until they've made the beams and a protection against them and then something more deadly still! We humans can't be conquered! We'll fight to the end of time!"

"But you yourself," said Jill desperately, "you said there couldn't be a defense against the beam! You said it!"

"I was discouraged," he protested. "I wasn't thinking straight. Look! With no equipment at all, I found out how to detect the stuff before it was strong enough to paralyze us. You know that. The scientists will have equipment and instruments, and now that they've got the beam they'll be able to try things. They'll do better than I did. They can try heterodyning the beam. They can try for interference effects. They may find something to reflect it, or they can try refraction."

He paused anxiously. She sobbed, once. "But other weapons—"

"There may not be any. And there's bound to be some trick of refraction that'll help. It thins out at the edges now. That's how we get warning of it. It's refracted by ions in the air. That's why it isn't a completely tight beam. Ions in the air act like drops of mist; they refract sunshine and make rainbows after rain. And we got the smell-effect first. That proves there's refraction."

He watched her face. She swallowed. What he'd said was largely without meaning. Actually, it wasn't even right. The evidence so far was that the nerves of smell were more sensitive than the optic nerves or the auditory ones, while nerves to bundles of muscle were less sensitive still. But Lockley wasn't concerned with accuracy just now. He wanted to reassure Jill.

Then his eyes widened suddenly and he stared past her. He'd been speaking feverishly out of emotion, while a part of his mind stood aside and listened. And that detached part of his mind had heard him say something worth noting.

He stood stock-still for seconds, staring blankly. Then he said very quietly, "You made me think, then. I don't know why I didn't, before. The terror beam does scatter a little, like a searchlight beam in thin mist. It's scattered by ions, like light by mist-droplets. That's right!"

He stopped, thinking ahead. Jill said challengingly, "Go on!" Again what he'd said had little meaning to her, but she could see that he believed it important.

"Why, a searchlight beam is stopped by a cloud, which is many mist-droplets in one place. It's scattered until it simply doesn't penetrate!" Lockley suddenly seemed indignant at his own failure to see something that had been so obvious all along. "If we could make a cloud of ions, it should stop the terror beam as clouds stop light! We could—"

Again he stopped short, and Jill's expression changed. She looked confident again. She even looked proud as she watched Lockley wrestling with his problem, unconsciously snapping his fingers.

"Vale and I," he said jerkily, "had electronic base-measuring instruments. Some of their elements had to be buried in plastic because otherwise they ionized the air and leaked current like a short. If I had that instrument now—No. I'd have to take the plastic away and it couldn't be done without smashing things."

"What would happen," asked Jill, "if you made what you're thinking about?"

"I might," said Lockley. "I just possibly might make a gadget that would create a cloud of ions around the person who carried it. And it might reflect some of the terror beam and refract the rest so none got through to the man!"

Jill said hopefully, "Then tonight we go into a deserted town and steal the things you need…"

Lockley interrupted in a relieved voice, "No-o-o-o. What I need, I think, is a cheese grater and the pocket radio. And there should be a cheese grater in the house."

He listened at the barn door gap, and then went out. Presently he was back. He had not only a cheese grater but also a nutmeg grater. Both were made of thin sheet metal in which many tiny holes had been punched, so that sharp bits of torn metal stood out to make the grating surface. Lockley knew that sharp points, when charged electrically, make tiny jets of ionized air which will deflect a candle flame. Here there were thousands of such points.

He set to work on the car seat, pushing the pistol with its three remaining bullets out of the way. The pistol was reserved for Jill in case of untoward events, when it would be of little or no practical value.

He operated on the tiny radio with his pocket-knife to establish a circuit which should oscillate when the battery was turned on. There was induction, to raise the voltage at the peaks and troughs of the oscillations. A transistor acted as a valve to make the oscillations repeated surges of current of one sign in the innumerable sharp points of the graters. And there was an effect he did not anticipate. The ion-forming points were of minutely different lengths and patterns, so the radiation inevitably accompanying the ion clouds was of minutely varying wave lengths. The consequence of using the two graters was, of course, that rather astonishing peaks of energy manifested themselves in ultra-microscopic packages for a considerable distance from the device. But Lockley did not plan that. It happened because of the materials he had to use in lieu of something better.

When it was finished he told Jill, "I can only check ion production here. If it works, it ought to make a lighter-flame flicker when near the points. If it does that, I'll go up the road to where the trailer-truck stopped. I've a pretty good idea that the road's blocked by a terror beam there."

Absorbed, he threw the switch. And instantly there was a racking, deafening explosion. The pistol on the car seat blew itself to bits, smashing the windshield and ripping the cushion open. The three cartridges in its cylinder had exploded simultaneously.

Lockley seized a pitchfork. He stood savagely, ready for anything. Powder smoke drifted through the barn. Nothing else happened.

After long, tense moments, Lockley said slowly, "That could be another weapon the monsters have turned on. It's been imagined. They could be using a broadcast or a beam we haven't suspected to disarm the troops of the cordon. They could have a detonator beam that sets off explosives at a distance. It's possible. And if that's what they're turning on they only have to sweep the sky and the bombers aloft will be wiped out."

But there were no sounds other than the slowly diminishing drip of water from the barn roof, and the house eaves, and the few trees in the barnyard.

"Anyhow they've ruined our only weapon," said Lockley coldly. "It would be a detonation beam setting off the cartridges. That would be a perfect protection against atomic bombs, if the chemical explosive that makes them go off could be triggered from a distance. Clever people, these monsters!"

Then he said abruptly, "Come on! It's ten times more necessary for us to get to where somebody can make use of our information!"

"Go where?" asked Jill, shaken once more.

"We take to the woods until dark," said Lockley, "and meanwhile I'll check this supposedly promising gadget—though it looks pretty feeble if the monsters have a detonating beam— against the road blocking beam up yonder. Come on!"

He stuffed his pockets with food. He led the way.

The morning had now arrived. The sun was visible, red at the eastern horizon.

"Walk on the grass!" commanded Lockley.

There was no point in leaving footprints, though there was no reason to believe the explosion on the car seat had been heard. Lockley, indeed, considered that if the aliens had just used a previously undisclosed weapon, there would be explosions of greater or lesser violence all over the evacuated territory and all other areas within its range. There wouldn't be many farmhouses without a shotgun put away somewhere. There would be shotgun shells, too. If the aliens had a detonator beam as well as one that produced the terror beam's effects, then all hope of resistance was probably gone.

They crossed to the house and moved alongside it. They went with instinctive furtiveness out of the lane and quickly into the woodland on the farther side. They were soaked almost immediately. Fallen leaves clung to their shoes. Drooping branches smeared them with wetness. Lockley went barely out of sight of the highway and then trudged doggedly in the direction the Wild Life Control trailer-truck had taken. He handed Jill the ribbon of bronze that had been the mainspring of his watch.

"We might pick up the beam from the wetness underfoot," he said, "but we'll play it safe and use this too."

They went on for a long way. Lockley fumed, "I don't like this! We ought to be there—"

"I think," said Jill, "I smell it."

"I'll try it," said Lockley.

He detected the jungle smell and its concomitant revolting odors. He led Jill back.

"Wait here, by this big tree stump. I'll be able to find you and you're safe enough from the beam."

He turned away. Jill said pleadingly, "Please be careful!"

"A little while ago," he told her gloomily, "I felt that I had too much useful information to take any chances with my life, let alone yours. I'm not so sure of my importance now. But I think you still need somebody else around."

"I do!" said Jill. "And you know it! I'd much rather—"

"I'll be back," he repeated.

He went away, trailing the watch spring.

He was extra cautious now. The smell recurred and grew stronger. He began to feel the first faint flashes of light in his eyes. It was the symptom which followed the smell when approaching a terror beam. Then a faint, discordant murmur, originating in his own ears. He turned on the device made of two graters and the elements of a pocket radio. The smell ceased. The faint flashes of light stopped. There was no longer a raucous sound.

He turned off the ion producing device. The symptoms returned. He turned it on and off. He took a step forward. He tested again. The cloud of ions from the innumerable jagged points was invisible, but somehow it refracted or reflected—in any case, neutralized—the weapon of the beings at Boulder Lake. He went on and presently he felt the very faintest possible tingling of his skin and heard the barest whisper of a sound, and smelled the jungle reek as something so diluted that he was hardly sure he smelled it.

He went on, and those faint sensations ceased. Presently, impatient of his own timorousness, he turned the device off again. He had walked through the terror beam.

He started back with the device turned on once more and at the point where he'd felt the beam's manifestations faintly, he stopped to savor his now seemingly useless triumph. If the monsters had a detonating beam this meant nothing. Yet it could have meant everything. He paid close attention and distinctly but weakly experienced the effect of the terror beam.

Then he didn't. Not at all. The sensations were cut off.

He heard Jill cry out shrilly. He plunged toward the place where he had left her. He raced. He leaped. Once he fell, and frantically swore at the wet stuff that had caused him to slip. He reached the tree stump and Jill was not there. He saw the saucer-sized tracks her feet had made on the saturated fallen leaves. They led toward the road.

He heard a car door slam and a motor roar. He plunged onward more desperately than before.

The motor raced away. And Lockley got out on the highway only in time to see the rear of a brown-painted, military-marked car some three hundred yards away. It swept around a curve of the highway and was gone. It was going through the space where the road was blocked by a terror beam, headed obviously for Boulder Lake.

What had happened was self-evident. From her place beside the huge stump she'd seen a military car approaching. And she and Lockley had been trying to reach the cordon of troops around Boulder Lake. There was no reason to distrust men in uniform or in a military car. She'd run to flag it down. She had. By a coincidence, it was undoubtedly where a carload of collaborating humans would have stopped to have the road-blocking beam cut off by their monster allies. She'd approached the stopped car. And something frightened her. She screamed.

But she'd been pulled into the car, which went on before the beam could come on again to stop it.

CHAPTER NINE

It was very likely that at that moment Lockley despised himself more bitterly than any other man alive. He blamed himself absolutely for Jill's capture. If there were humans acting with the alien invaders, her fate would unquestionably be more horrible than at the hands of the monsters alone. After all, there was one nation most likely to deal with extra-terrestrial creatures to help them in the conquest of earth, and its troops were not notorious for their kindly behavior to civilians.

And Jill was their captive. He'd been carried past the place where a terror beam blocked the road. The military markings might mean the car was stolen, or that its markings and paint were counterfeit. It seemed certain that Jill had gone up to it in confidence that there could only be American soldiers in such a car, and when near it found out her mistake too late.

These were not things that Lockley thought out in detail at the beginning. He ran after the car like a mad man, unable to feel anything but horror and so terrible a fury that it should have killed its objects by sheer intensity.

Presently he heard hoarse, gasping sounds. He realized that the sounds were the breath going in and out of his own throat, while Jill was carried farther and farther away from him in a car which traveled ten yards to his one. He sobbed then, and suddenly he was strangely and unnaturally calm. He was able to think quite coolly. The only difference between this and normal thinking was that now he could only think about one thing—full and complete and terrible revenge for the crimes committed and to be committed against Jill. She would be taken to Boulder Lake. So he would go to Boulder Lake, and somehow, in some manner, he would destroy utterly all living beings there and every trace of their coming.

Which, of course, was both natural and unreasonable. But reason would have been unnatural at such a time as this.

He moved along the highway in a passion of ultimate resolve. In the rest of the world, time passed without knowledge of his emotional state. The rest of the world was suffering emotional agonies of its own.

The United States had become popular among peoples who disliked all things American except those they were given free, and who continued to dislike the givers. Now though, the United States had been invaded from space by creatures using weapons of unprecedented type and effect. If the United States were conquered, there was no other nation likely to remain free.

So a great deal of anti-Americanism faded under pressure of an ardent desire for America to be successful in its self-defense.

Moreover, anticipating other alien landings which could take place anywhere, the United States offered to share its stock of atom bombs with any nation so invaded. American popularity increased. The fact that the USSR made no such proposal also had its effect. The United States invited scientists of every country to help in solving the menace of the terror beam, and committed itself to share any discoveries for defense against it with all the world. Again there was an improvement in the public image of the United States abroad.

But Lockley knew nothing of this. His pocket radio no longer existed to give him news. It had been rebuilt into something else, whose most conspicuous parts were cheese and nutmeg graters, slung over his shoulder as he marched. But if he had known of changes in the popularity of his country, he wouldn't have been interested. He could fix his mind only on one subject and matters related to it.

He tramped along the highway, possessed by a cold demon of hatred. He was on foot for lack of a car. He was unarmed. At the moment he believed that all the rest of humanity was disarmed, in effect if not in fact. So he had no plans, only an infinite hatred.

But because he would have to pass through terror beams to get at those he meant to destroy, he realized that it was necessary to make sure that he would be able to pass through them, that his equipment for reaching Boulder Lake was in good order. It was still turned on. He turned it off to be economical of its batteries. He went on, thinking of only one subject, examining every possibility for revenge with a passionate patience, undiscouraged because one idea after another was plainly impossible, but continuing obsessively to think of others.

He smelled the foetid odor, which cut through his absorption because of its connotations. He turned on his device and went doggedly ahead. He knew he had entered a terror beam by the faint perceptions which came through the cloud of ions his instrument produced. Then they ceased. He knew that the beam had been cut off. He heard a motor rev up. A car or truck had stopped beyond the road-blocking beam and waited for it to be cut off, as it had been.

Lockley stepped into the woods hating the vehicle bitterly as it approached, but wanting to save destruction for those where Jill had been taken.

He was hidden when the car appeared. It was a perfectly commonplace car with a whip aerial at its rear. It came confidently along the highway. A hundred yards from him, there were explosions. Smoke came out of the open windows. The engine stopped and the car bucked crazily and went into the ditch beside the highway. A man plunged out, slapping at his leg. A revolver in its holster had exploded all its shells. The leather holster had saved him from serious injury, but his clothing was on fire. Other men, two of them, got out hastily. Things had exploded in the back of the car, too. The three men swore agitatedly.

Then one of them said something which stimulated the others to frantic flight down the highway away from the ditched car. The third man limped anxiously after the faster-moving two.

Lockley, watching and hating with undivided attention, knew when the terror beam came on again. He felt it, very faint because of his protection, but quite distinct. The explosions had taken place when the car was in the area now covered again by the terror beam. The men in the car, astonished and scorched, had fled because the beam was due to come back on and they didn't want to be caught in it.

Lockley noted that the human confederates of the monsters had no protection against the beam to match his own. Perhaps the monsters themselves were protected only near the projectors. This was an item affecting his plans of revenge for Jill. He stored it away in his mind. Then he realized that the weapons in the car had exploded just like the pistol on his own seat cushion. The explosion was not associated with the terror beam. There'd been no beam in action when his own pistol blew up. It did not seem reasonable that if the monsters possessed a detonation beam that they'd turn it on their own confederates.

No. Rational beings would do nothing so self-contradictory.

Then Lockley looked down at the cheese grater-pocket radio device of his own manufacture. He considered the fact that his own pistol had exploded the instant he'd turned the gadget on. The weapons in the other car detonated when that car was near him.

He plodded onward thinking very clearly and precisely about the matter. He even remembered to turn off his gadget because he would need it to avenge Jill. But when he tried to think of any subject unconnected with revenge, his mind became confused and agitated.

Two miles along the highway, which had not yet turned to head in toward Boulder Lake, there was a farmhouse. Lockley walked heavily to the abandoned building. He found the door locked. Without conscious thought, he forced it. He searched the closets. He found a shotgun and half a box of shells. He considered them, then left the gun and all the shells but three. He went out. Presently he laid a shotgun shell down on the road. He paced off twenty-five yards and dropped another. He dropped a third twenty-five yards farther on, and then carefully counted off three hundred feet. The car had been just about that far away when the explosions came.

He turned on his device. Two of the three shells exploded smokily. The farthest away did not explode.

He did not rejoice. He went on without elation, but it became a part of his painstaking search for vengeance that he knew he could set off explosives within a hundred and twenty-five yards of himself. There was something about the device he'd constructed which made explosives detonate, up to a distance of a little over one hundred yards. He felt no curiosity about it, though it was simple enough. The heterodyning of extremely saw-toothed waves produced peaks of energy until the saw-teeth began to smooth out. There were infinitesimal spots in which, for infinitesimal lengths of time, energy conditions comparable to sparks existed. This had not been worked out in advance, but the reason was clear.

He came to the place where the main highway to Boulder Lake branched off from the road he was following. He turned into it, walking doggedly.

Three miles toward the lake, an engine sounded from behind him. He got off the highway and turned the switch. A half-ton truck came trundling openly along the road. It came closer and closer.

Small-arm ammunition exploded. The engine stopped and the light truck toppled over onto its side. Lockley did not approach it. Its driver might not be dead, and he would not find it possible to leave any man alive who was associated with Jill's captors. He passed the truck and went on up the highway.

Seven miles up the road a truck came down from Boulder Lake. Lockley placed himself discreetly out of sight. He turned on his instrument. A gun flew to pieces with a thunderous detonation. The truck crashed. It was interesting to Lockley that automobile engines invariably went dead at about the time that explosives went off. The fact was, of course, that ionized air is more or less conductive. In an ion cloud the spark plugs shorted and did not fire in the cylinders.

There were two other vehicles which essayed to pass Lockley as he went on up the long way to the lake. Both came from the interior of the Park. He left them wrecked beside the highway. Between times, he walked with a dogged grimness toward the place where Vale had been the first to report a thing come down from the sky. That had been how many days ago? Three? Four?

Then Lockley had been a quiet and well-conducted citizen inclined to pessimism about future events, but duly considerate of the rights of others. Now he'd changed. He felt only one emotion, which was hatred such as he'd never imagined before.

He had only one motive, which was to take total and annihilating vengeance for what had been done to Jill.

He plodded on and on. He had to make a march of not less than twenty miles from the Park's beginning. He journeyed on foot because there were terror beams to pass and automobile engines did not run when his protective device operated. He could not arm himself from the cars that ditched, because all chemical explosive weapons and their ammunition blew at the same time. He was a minute figure among the mountains, marching alone upon a winding highway, moving resolutely to destroy—alone—the invaders from outer space and the men who worked with them for the conquest of earth. For his purpose he carried the strangest of equipment, a device made of a pocket radio and a cheese grater.

He had food in his pockets, but he could not eat. During the afternoon he became impatient of its weight and threw it away. But he thirsted often. More than once he drank from small streams over which the highway builders had made small concrete bridges.

At three in the afternoon a truck came up from behind. Here he trudged between steep cliffs which made him seem almost a midget. The highway went through a crevice between adjoining mountainsides. There was no place for him to conceal himself. When he heard the engine, he stopped and faced it. The truck had picked up many men from wrecked cars along its route. There were scorched and scratched and wounded men, hurt by the explosion of their firearms. The truck brought them along and overtook Lockley.

He waited very calmly since it did not seem likely that they would realize that one man had caused the crashes. The driver of the truck with the picked-up men did not even think of such a thing. Lockley seemed much more likely the victim of still another wreck.

The overtaking truck slowed down. There would be no strangers in Boulder Lake Park. There would only be the task force aiding the monsters, as Lockley reasoned it out. So the truck slowed, preparatory to taking Lockley aboard.

At a hundred and twenty-five yards from Lockley, weapons in the truck cab blew themselves violently apart. The engine, stopped in gear, acted as a violently applied brake. The truck swerved off the highway. It turned over and was still.

Lockley turned and walked on. He considered coldly that it was perfectly safe for him to go on. There were no weapons left behind him. The men themselves were shaken up. They would attempt to make no trouble beyond a report of their situation and a plea for help. The report could be made by the radio, which was not smashed.

Half an hour later, Lockley felt the tingling which meant that his instrument was protecting him from a terror beam. The tingling lasted only a short time, but fifteen minutes later it came back. Then it returned at odd intervals. Five minutes—eight—ten—three—six—one. Each time the terror beam should have paralyzed him and caused intense suffering. A man with no protective device would have had his nerves shattered by torment coming so violently at unpredictable intervals.

Lockley tried to reason out why this nerve-wracking application of the terror beam hadn't been used before. To an unprotected man it would be worse than continuous pain. No living man could remain able to resist any demand if exposed to such torture.

The beam was evidently swung at random intervals, and the phenomenon lasted for an hour and a half. Anyone but Lockley behind a cloud of ions would have been reduced to shivering hysteria. Then, suddenly, the beamings stopped. But Lockley left his device in operation.

Half an hour later still—close to five o'clock—it appeared that the invaders assumed that any enemy should have been softened up for capture. They sent an expedition to find out what had happened to their trucks and cars.

Lockley saw four cars and a light truck in close formation moving toward him from the Lake. They were close, as if for mutual protection. They moved steadily, as if inviting the fate that had overtaken others. The short wave reports from smashed trucks seemed improbable to them, but the expedition was equipped to investigate even such unlikely happenings.

The four cars in the lead contained five men each. Each man was armed with a rifle containing a single cartridge in its chamber and none in its magazine. The rifles pointed straight up. There was more ammunition in the light truck behind, and it was in clips ready for use, but the truck body was of iron. If that ammunition detonated, it could do no harm. If it did not, it would be available for use against the single man mentioned by the driver of the last truck to be wrecked.

But Lockley saw them coming. They came sedately down a long straight stretch of road. He climbed a rocky wall beside the highway to a little ravine that led away from the road. He posted himself where he was extremely unlikely to be seen. Then he waited.

The cavalcade of cars appeared. It drove briskly toward Lockley at something like thirty miles an hour. Perhaps ten yards separated the lead car from the second. The truck was a trifle closer to the four man-carrying vehicles. They swept along, every man alert. They would pass forty feet below Lockley.

He did nothing. His device was already turned on. He watched in detached calm.

The lead car stopped as if it had run into a brick wall, while rifles inside it blew holes in its top. The second car crashed into it, rifles detonating. The third car. The fourth. The truck piled into the others with a gigantic flare and furious report, each separate brass cartridge case exploding in the same instant. The truck became scrap iron.

Lockley went away along the small ravine. From now on he would avoid the highway. He estimated that he would arrive at Boulder Lake itself about half an hour after dark. It occurred to him that then Jill would have been a prisoner of the invaders for something more than twelve hours, at least ten of them at their headquarters.

Before he began the climb that would take him to the invaders, Lockley stopped at a small stream.

He drank thirstily.

CHAPTER TEN

There was a three-day-old moon in the sky when the last colors faded in the west. When darkness fell it was already low. It gave little light; not much more than the stars alone. It did help Lockley while it lasted however. He knew the terrain about Boulder Lake but not in detail. And it would not be wise for him to move openly to wreak destruction on the enemies of his nation.

He used the moonlight for his approach by the least practical route to the lake. When it dimmed and went behind the mountains, he continued to climb, sliding dangerously, then descend and climb again as the rough going demanded. His mind was absorbed with reflections upon what he meant to do. The wrecks on the highway would have given notice to the invaders that he could do damage. They would take every possible precaution against him.

It was typical of Lockley that he painstakingly imagined every obstacle that might be put in his way. During the last half hour of his scrambling travel, for example, he was tormented by a measure his enemies might have used to make him advertise his presence. If they simply laid rifle cartridges on the ground at intervals of twenty-five or fifty yards, he could not cross that line with his device in operation without blowing up those shells. It was a possible countermeasure that caused him to sweat with worry.

But it wasn't thought of by anyone else. To contrive it, a man would have to know how the detonation field worked and how far it extended. Nobody but Lockley knew. Therefore no one could contrive this defense against him.

He worked his way to Boulder Lake's back door through brushwood and over boulders. Presently he looked down upon his destination. To his right and left rocky masses were silhouetted against the starry sky. He gazed down on the lake and the shoreline where the hotel would be built, and the places where roads came out of the wilderness.

There were changes since the time he'd looked down from Vale's survey post and before the terror beam captured him. He catalogued them mentally, but the sight before him was intolerable. Everything he saw, here where space monsters were believed to hold sway, was in reality the work of men. Rage filled him at the sight. Hatred. Fury...

In the rest of the world an entirely different sort of emotion was felt about the subject of the invaders. The United States had announced to all the world that American and other scientists, working together, had solved the mystery of the alien weapon. They had produced a duplicate of the terror beam. It was no less effective and no less an absolute weapon than the invaders'. And a defense had been found which was complete. It was being rushed into production. The experimental counter beam generators would be moved into position to frustrate and defeat the monsters who had landed upon earth. Military detachments, protected by the counter generators, would move upon Boulder Lake at dawn. By sunset tomorrow the aliens would be dead or captive, and their ship would undoubtedly be in the hands of scientists for study.

Moreover, the United States would provide counter weapons for other nations. In no more than months every continent and nation on earth would be equipped to defy any alien landing that might take place. The world would be able to defend itself. It would be equipped to do so. And this was the resolve of the United States because the world could not exist half free and half enslaved by creatures from a distant planet. The news poured out from all sources. The alien weapon was understood and now could be defied. Soon all the world would be provided with counter weapons. It was necessary for all the world to be prepared and prepared it would be.

This was the information which made all the world rejoice, though not yet at ease because aliens still occupied a tiny part of the earth. But all the world was eager for confirmation of the news it had just received.

Lockley had no such soothing anticipations. He shook with fury because what he saw before him was so appalling as to be almost unbelievable.

It was not dark in the space he looked down upon. There were bright floodlights placed here and there to drench a large area with light. There were few figures in sight. But what the floodlights showed made Lockley quiver with hatred.

The floodlights were of typically human type. There were vehicles parked on a level grassy space. They were of human manufacture. There was no space ship in the lake, but there was a three-stage rocket set up, ready for firing. It was of the kind used by humans to put artificial satellites into orbit. Lockley even knew its designation, and that it used the new solid fuels for propulsion.

In the lair of the creatures from outer space there was nothing from outer space. There was nothing in view which was alien or unearthly or extra-terrestrial. And Lockley made inarticulate growling sounds because he saw with absolute clarity and certainty that there never had been anything from outer space at this spot.

There were no monsters. There never had been. And the truth was more horribly enraging than the deception had been.

Because this could mean the death of the world. This was an attempt to fight the last war on earth in disguise. Humans had posed as non-human beings so that America would fight against phantoms while its great military rival pretended to help and actually stabbed from behind.

It was completely logical, of course. An admitted attack by terror beams in the form of death rays would involve retaliation by America. Against a human enemy great, roaring missiles could circle earth to plunge down upon that enemy's cities to turn them and their inhabitants into incandescent gas. An attack known to be by humans and upon humans must touch off the world's last war in which every living thing might die. No conceivable success at the beginning could prevent full retaliation. But if the attack were believed to be from space, then American weapons and valor would be spent against creatures which were no more than ghosts.

Lockley moved forward. Only he could know the situation as it presented itself here. Even vengeance for Jill should be put aside, if it called for action irrelevant to this state of things. But it did not. A full and terrible revenge for her required exactly the action the coolest of cold-blooded resolutions would suggest be taken now. And Lockley moved on and downward to take it.

He began to crawl downhill toward the lights, unaware that there were some gaps in his picture of the total scene. For example, these lights could be detected by aircraft overhead. The fact did not occur to Lockley. He was not given pause by the relaxation of the enemy's disguise so far as air observation was concerned. He didn't think of it. He moved on.

He drew near the lighted area. He did not walk, he crawled. He began to listen with fury-sharpened ears. If he could get close to that huge rocket, close enough to detonate its solid fuel stores...

That would be at once revenge and expedience. If the rocket's fuel blew up instead of burning as intended, it would annihilate the camp. It would wipe out every living creature present. But there would be fragments left by the explosion. There would be corpses. There would be wreckage. And that wreckage and those corpses would be unmistakably human. The last war on earth might not be avoided, but at the worst it would be fought against America's actual enemy and not against imaginary monsters.

It was worth dying to accomplish even that. But Jill...

Lockley's progress was infinitely slow, but he needed to take the greatest pains. He listened carefully.

He heard the faint high roaring of the planes overhead. They were far away. There were sounds of insects, and the cries of night birds, and the rustling of leaves and foliage.

There was another sound. A new sound. It was inexplicable. It was a strange and intermittent muttering. There was a certain irregular rhythm to it, a familiar rhythm.

He crawled on.

There was movement suddenly, off to his left. Then it stopped. It could be a man on watch against him simply shifting his position. Lockley froze, and then went on with even greater caution. He felt the ground before him for small twigs that might crack under his weight.

The muttering continued. Presently Lockley realized that it was a human voice. It was resonant and with many overtones, but still too faint for him to distinguish words.

He crossed a slight rise that had much brushwood. The brushwood grew in clumps and he circled them with a patient caution foreign to his feelings.

The muttering changed and went on. Lockley pressed himself to the ground. Men went past him a hundred feet away. He saw them in outline against the illuminated parked cars and trucks and in the space around the huge rocket. They carried no rifles, probably no firearms at all. Lockley's march up the highway had warned them of the uselessness of guns, at least at short range. They were watching for him now. Perhaps these men were relieving other watchers on the hillside.

He saw other men. They seemed to move restlessly around the lighted area.

The muttering was louder now. He could almost catch the words. He made another hundred yards toward the rocket and the voice changed again. Then he was dazed. The voice was speaking to him! Calling him by name!

"Lockley! Lockley! Don't do anything crazy! Everything can be explained! You'll recognize my voice. You talked to me on the telephone from Serena!"

Lockley did recognize the voice. It was that of the general who'd sounded pompous and indignant as he refused to listen to Lockley's statements. Now, coming out of many loudspeakers and echoing hollowly from cliffs, it was the same voice but with an intonation that was persuasive and forthright.

"*You startled me,*" said the voice crisply. "*You'd found out there were humans involved in this business. It was important that the fact be suppressed. I tried to browbeat you, which was a mistake. While I was talking to you your suspicion was reported on short wave by the Wild Life driver. I tried to overawe you. You're the wrong kind of man for that. But everything can be explained. Everything! Here's Vale to prove it!*"

There was only an instant's pause. Then Vale's voice came out of the loudspeakers spread all about.

"*Lockley, this is Vale. The whole thing's faked. There's a good reason for it, but you stumbled on the facts. They had to be kept secret. I didn't even tell Jill. This isn't treason, Lockley. We aren't traitors! Come out and I'll explain everything. Here's Sattell.*"

And Sattell's voice boomed against the hills.

"*Vale's right, Lockley! I didn't know what was up. I was fooled as much as anybody. But it's all right! It's perfectly all right! When you understand you'll realize that you had to be deceived just as I was. Come on out and everything will be explained to your satisfaction. I promise!*"

Lockley grimaced. How did Sattell get up here? And the general in command of the cordon? More than that, why did they call his name instead of simply trying to kill him? Why post watchers on the hillsides if they were anxious to explain and not to murder? How could they hope to deceive him after Jill...

There was a pause, and then what was evidently considered a decisive message came. It was Jill's voice, weary and desperate. It said, "*Please come out and listen! Please come and let them explain everything. They can do it. I understand and I believe them. It's true. It's not treason. I—I beg you to come out and let them tell you why all this has happened...*"

Her voice trailed off. It had trembled. It was tense. It was strained. And Lockley cursed softly, shaking with rage. Then the first voice returned, "*Lockley! Lockley! Don't do anything crazy!*"

Everything can be explained. You'll recognize my voice. You talked to me on the telephone from Serena."

This voice repeated, word for word and intonation for intonation, exactly what it had said before. The other voices followed in the same order. They were taped.

In Lockley's state of mind, the taping took away all authority from the voices. Jill, in particular, sounded as she might have if torture had been used to break her will and force her to say what her captors wished. She could not put any warning into it, because she could have been forced to repeat and repeat the message until her captors were satisfied.

That would all be avenged now. All of it. And Jill would be grateful to Lockley even if they never saw each other again; grateful for the monstrous blast that would wipe this place clean of living creatures.

Lockley suddenly saw a way by which his vengeance could be increased by just a little. It could be made even more satisfying and just. Hiding under brushwood while the voices tirelessly repeated their recorded persuasion, he made a very simple device. It switched onto the instrument he carried. If his hand clenched, it would go on. If his hand relaxed, it would go on. So if he could get within a hundred and twenty-five yards of the rocket he could show himself and let them know what waited for them, and why.

With infinite patience he got to a place almost near the circle of unarmed guards about the rocket. He waited. The guards were tense. They did not like trying to protect something with no weapons. They were jumpy. The endlessly repeated messages booming into the night frayed their nerves. They were plainly on edge.

Their tenseness made the oldest trick in the world serve Lockley's purpose. He threw a stone from an especially dark shadow. It struck and bounced upon another stone, and it created a rustling of brushwood at a place distant from Lockley. And the unarmed guards plunged for that place to seize whatever or whoever had made the disturbance.

They were too eager. They stumbled upon each other.

And Lockley ran, and a voice cried out in terror. And then Lockley stood with his back to the rocket's lower parts, and he waved the cheese grater derisively and shouted.

Then there was stillness. Only the booming voice from the speakers went on. It happened to be Sattell's voice.

"...*all right. It's perfectly all right. When you understand you'll realize that you had to be deceived as I was. It was necessary. Come out and everything*—"

Somebody cut off the recorder. There was a moment of blank indecision, and then a man in uniform with two general's stars on his shoulders came out of somewhere and walked to face Lockley.

"Ah, Lockley!" he said briskly. "That's the thing you smash cars and explode ammunition with, eh? Do you think it will blow the rocket?"

"I'm going to try it!" said Lockley. "Listen." He showed how anything that could be done to him would close the switch one way or the other. "I wanted you to know before I blow it!" he said fiercely. "Where's Jill? Jill Holmes? One of your cars picked her up and brought her here. Where is she?"

"We sent her," said the general, "over to the construction camp, in case you managed to get in the exact situation you're in. In other words, she's safe. She'll be coming shortly, though. She was to be notified the instant you appeared—if the rocket didn't blast as your greeting."

Lockley ground his teeth.

"We'll have this settled before she gets here!"

Vale appeared. He walked forward and stood beside the general.

"We did a job that was several times too good, Lockley," he said ruefully. "I'd rehearsed my song-and-dance until we thought it was perfect. What made you suspicious, Lockley? Did you notice we kept the communicator aimed right so you'd hear through to the end? A fine point, that. We worried about it."

The headlights of a car moved against a mountainside.

"You see," said Vale, "the thing had to be done this way! Sattell swore a blue streak when it was explained to him. He felt he'd been made a fool of. But there are some things that can't be handled forthrightly!"

Lockley felt physically ill. Jill had been—still was—engaged to Vale. She'd been anxious about him. She'd been loyal to him. And he was helping the invaders! He opened his mouth to speak bitterly, when Sattell appeared. He lined up beside the general and Vale.

"They fooled me too, Lockley," he said wryly. "But it's all right. They had to. They thought you were fooled. Those three men in the box with you the other day, they said you were fooled, too. And they're sharp secret service men!"

"You're very convincing, aren't you?" he raged. "But—"

"You believe," said Sattell, "I've joined up with spies and traitors. You believe…"

He outlined, with precision, exactly what Lockley did believe; that phantom monsters were to be credited with waging war against America while another nation actually murdered Americans. It was a remarkably accurate picture of Lockley's state of mind.

"But that's all wrong!" insisted Sattell. "This is a quick trick by our own people for our own safety. For the benefit of all the world. It's a trick to forestall just what I described!"

The far away headlights drew nearer. But no car could have come from the construction camp as quickly as this.

"The fact is," said the general, "that our spies tell us that another very great nation has developed this beam we've been demonstrating to all the world. So did we. And we couldn't use it, but they would! If they didn't use it against us, they'd use it for any sort of emergency dirty trick. So we made up this invasion to persuade every country on earth to arm itself against this particular weapon. Nothing less than monsters in space would justify arming, in the eyes of some politicians! Of course, they'll arm against us as well as—anybody else."

He spoke matter-of-factly. A glance at Lockley's face would have told him that persuasiveness would not work.

"This trick, with the defense we intended to reveal," the general added, "should mean that a very nasty weapon won't ever be used, either to start or end a war. Maybe the war won't occur because we've said there are monsters who fly around in space ships."

Lockley had a confused impression that he was dreaming this. It was not the way things should happen! This was not true! When he squeezed or released the improvised switch in his hand, the rocket behind him would disappear in a monstrous flame, and he and the three men who faced him would, vanish, and there would be an explosion crater here and a shattered mass of wrecked cars—

"It was an interesting job," said Vale. "The Army dumped a hundred tons of high explosive into the lake. The two radars that reported a ship in space were arranged to be operated by two special men, who got their orders directly from the President. We picked a day with full cloud cover; the radar operators inserted their faked tapes and made their reports; and the Army set off the hundred-ton explosion in the lake. From there on, it was just a matter of using the terror beam."

"I mention," said the general mildly, "that not one human being has been killed by anything we've done. Would you expect traitors to be so careful? Or spies?"

Lockley said thickly, "You stand there arguing. You're trying to make me believe you. But there's Jill! What's happened to her? How did you make her record that tape? Where's Jill? She won't tell me it's all right!"

Headlights swept up to the floodlit space. The car stopped.

Jill came into view. She saw Lockley, standing against the rocket's base. She ran.

She stood beside the general and Vale and Sattell. She looked worn and desperately anxious.

"What have they done to you?" demanded Lockley fiercely.

She shook her head.

"N-nothing. I couldn't stay at the camp when I was so sure you'd come to try to help me. So I came here. I don't know what they've told you yet, but it's all right. We were fooled as the world has to be. Believe it! Please believe it!"

"What have they done to you?" he repeated terribly.

"What have they done to the world?" demanded Jill. "They've made every nation look to us as the defender of their freedom. And we are! They've made everybody ready to fight against more monsters if they come, and to fight against men if they try to enslave them with the terror beam or anything else! Would traitors have done that?"

Lockley knew that he had to decide. It was an unbearable responsibility. He was not convinced, even by Jill. But he was no longer certain that he'd been right.

"Why didn't you kill me?" he demanded. "I could have been shot down from a distance. You didn't have to come close to talk to me. If the rocket blew, what would it matter?"

"You've got a protection against the terror beam," said the general matter-of-factly. "So have we. But ours weighs two tons. Yours can be carried without being a burden. And—" his eyes went to the unlikely cheese grater over Lockley's shoulder—"and yours detonates explosives. If we can equip the world with those, Lockley, we'll have peace!"

Lockley thought of a decisive test. He grimaced.

"You want me to risk being a traitor! All right, what's in it for me? What am I offered?"

The general shrugged, his eyes hardening. Vale spread out his hands. Sattell snorted. Jill moistened her lips. Lockley turned upon her.

"You want me to believe," he said harshly. "What do you offer if I turn over the thing to these men you say are honest men and neither spies or traitors. What do you offer?"

She stared at him. Then she said quietly, "Nothing."

Lockley hesitated once more, for a long instant. But that was the right answer. Nobody who'd been bought or bribed or frightened into being a traitor would have thought of it.

"That," said Lockley, "by a strange coincidence happens to be my price."

He ripped away a wire. He flung the queer combination of pocket radio and cheese and nutmeg graters to the general.

"I'll explain later how it works," he said wearily, "—if I haven't made a mistake."

After a suitable time the general came to him. Lockley was convinced, now. The reaction of the men who'd been guards and truck drivers and the like was conclusive. They regarded him with a certain cordial respect which was not the reaction of either traitors or invaders.

"We've been checking that little device, Lockley," said the general happily. "It's perfect for our purposes! So much better than a two-ton generator to interfere with and cancel the terror beams! Marvelous! And do you know what it means? With all the world believing we've been attacked from space, and with our great show of taking back Boulder Lake—"

"How will you manage that?" asked Lockley, without too much interest.

"The rocket," said the general, beaming. "When troops start into the Park, the rocket takes off. It heads for empty space. And we explain that the aliens went away when they found their weapon useless and we started to get rough with them!"

"Oh," said Lockley listlessly.

"But the really beautiful thing," the general told him, "is your gadget! They can be made by millions. Ridiculously cheap, they tell me. Everybody in the world will want one, and we'll pass them out. No government could stop that! Not even Russia! But—d'you see, Lockley?"

Lockley shook his head. He had a tendency to look on the dark side of the future, and it did not look bright to him.

"Don't you see?" demanded the general, chuckling. "They detonate explosives, those little gadgets! There's no harm in that! Where explosives are used in industry you've only to make sure that nobody turns one on too close. In nine-tenths of the world, anyhow, civilians aren't allowed to have guns. But think of the consequences there!"

Lockley was weary. He was dejected. The general grinned from ear to ear.

"Why, when these are distributed, even the secret police can't go armed! What price dictators then? For that matter, what price soldiers? The cold war ends, Lockley, because there couldn't be a conquering army in the modern sense. The tanks wouldn't run. The cars would stall. And the guns— An invasion would have to be made with horse-drawn transport and the troops armed with bows and spears. That amounts to disarmament, Lockley! A consummation devoutly to be wished! I'm going to look forward to a ripe old age now. I never could before!"

Presently Lockley talked to Jill. She was constrained. She seemed uneasy. Lockley felt that there wasn't much to say, now that Vale was alive and well and there was no more danger for her. He offered his hand to say good-bye.

"I think," she said with a little difficulty, "I think I should tell you I'm not—engaged any longer. I—told him I—wouldn't want to be married to someone whose work made him keep secrets from me."

Lockley tensed. He said incredulously, "You're not going to marry Vale?"

She said nervously.

"No-o-o. I've told him."

Lockley swallowed.

"What did he say?"

"He—didn't like it," said Jill. "But he understood. I explained things. He said—he said to congratulate you."

Lockley made an appropriate movement. She wept quietly, held close in his arms.

"I was so afraid you didn't—you wouldn't—"

Lockley took appropriate measures to comfort her and to assure her that he did and he would, forever and ever. A very long time later he asked interestedly, "What did you say to Vale when he asked you to congratulate me?"

"I said," said Jill comfortably, "that I would if things worked out all right. And they have. I congratulate you, darling. Now how about congratulating me?"

The rocket took off and went away into emptiness. This was near dawn, when military announcements of the reoccupation of Boulder Lake were being passed out to the news media. As much of the public as was awake was informed that the monstrous aliens had fled from earth, their intentions frustrated by the work of scientists. It wasn't necessary for a large force to march in. A special detail took over at the lake itself. Curiously enough, it seemed to be already there when the question arose. It would report a regrettable absence of alien artifacts by which the monsters might be kept in mind.

But there would be reminders. Later bulletins would report that the United States was putting into quantity production the small, individual protective devices which defied the terror beam and would supply them to all the world. There could not be greater friendship than that! The United States also proposed a world wide alliance for defense against future attacks by space monsters, with pooled armament and completely cooperative governments.

The world, obviously, would unite against monsters. And people in a posture of defense against enemies from the stars obviously wouldn't fight each other.

And there were some people who were pleased. They knew about the possibilities of the small gadgets, brought down in production to the size of a pack of cigarettes. Knowing what they could do, they waited very interestedly to see what would happen in certain nations when secret police couldn't carry firearms and soldiers could only be armed with spears.

They expected it to be very interesting indeed.

THE END